BREAD, DEAD AND WED

A CHARLOTTE DENVER COZY MYSTERY
BOOK NINE

SHERRI BRYAN

Sherri Bryan

Contents

Dedication..5
Prologue..7
Chapter 1 10
Chapter 2 19
Chapter 3 27
Chapter 4 45
Chapter 5 64
Chapter 6 72
Chapter 7 81
Chapter 8 90
Chapter 9 99
Chapter 10 117
Chapter 11 138
Chapter 12 146
Chapter 13 157
Chapter 14 171
Chapter 15 193
Chapter 16 205
Chapter 17 215
Chapter 18 228
Chapter 19 241
Chapter 20 252
Chapter 21 268
Chapter 22 289
Chapter 23 307
Chapter 24 320
Chapter 25 324
Epilogue 328

Other Books by Sherri Bryan 342
A Selection of Recipes from This Book 343
A Message from Sherri...353
About Sherri Bryan 355
All Rights Reserved 356

Sherri Bryan

DEDICATION
To Mum,
With love.

Sherri Bryan

PROLOGUE

With just the radio and a newspaper for company, the lone figure smoothed out the page and read the article again.

Culinary School on Schedule for February Opening

Following the recent announcement by celebrated Restaurant Critic and TV Star, Roman Haley, that he has acquired a new culinary school in the coastal town of St. Eves, it has been confirmed that the school will be ready to take in students from February of next year.

"I believe a culinary school in that area of the country will be very well patronised, and will make good use of the area's excellent local produce," said Mr. Haley. "There's been a huge surge in the number of people wanting to take their culinary skills to the next level, most likely due—in part—to the popularity of shows such as Easy Peasy Bakey Cakey, which has become Channel Ten's top-rated show since I joined as a member of the judging panel."

When asked what his long-time acquaintance and one-time colleague, Olivia Floyd-Martin, thought of his new acquisition, Mr. Haley's response was simply, "I have no idea. I haven't discussed it with her."

As local woman, Olivia Floyd-Martin, is the Executive Chef at The President Hotel in St. Eves, one does wonder if Mr. Haley's establishment being so close to the hotel will be a distraction for the temperamental chef.

Our reporter, Seema Dupti, attempted to interview Ms. Floyd-Martin yesterday to ask her opinion on the recent announcement, but was abruptly informed that she wasn't taking any questions.

In the wake of this news, it is anticipated that Mr. Haley's culinary school will be inundated with enquiries from people eager to sign up to his courses, while Ms. Floyd-Martin's exclusive rooftop restaurant at The President Hotel will continue to draw in the crowds. It's possible, of course, that business at the hotel will increase, with visitors flocking to St. Eves in the hope of catching a glimpse of Roman Haley.

However, not everyone in the town is happy to learn of the plans. We spoke to several members of the community who wasted no time in making their disapproval known. Here are just a few of their opinions:

*"That bloomin' Haley and Floyd-Martin have always thought they're better than everyone else. Having **one** of them in St. Eves is bad enough, let alone **both** of them."*

"It's about time someone taught them a lesson. They can't keep treating people the way they do and get away with it."

"They don't deserve to have loyal customers. If people only knew what they're really like, they'd spend their money elsewhere, and those two would be ruined."

The swish of the door in its frame signalled the arrival of a companion, who settled into an armchair by the window before accepting a sweet pastry and a cup of coffee, inhaling the aroma-filled steam before adding six spoons of sugar to the potent brew.

The companion touched a fingertip to the flaky pastry to taste a blob of tangy icing. "Hmm, a little more orange essence wouldn't go amiss, but it'll do." Every mouthful of the pastry was savoured, and every crumb licked from sticky fingers, before the plate was set aside. "Anything interesting in the news?"

The figure handed over the newspaper before taking a jacket from the coat stand.

"Have you read this article?" The companion's voice was suddenly sharp. "It says here that some of the St. Eves' locals are of the opinion that if people knew what Roman and Olivia are *really* like, they'd be ruined."

The figure smiled slowly and pulled on the jacket, a hand closing around the small bottle and its precious contents, safe within the inside pocket.

Oh, they'll be ruined, alright… and not a moment too soon. I've waited a long time to get my revenge, and I'm going to enjoy every second.

CHAPTER 1

Ten months later

On a chilly Friday in February, Ava Whittington, Harriett Reeves and Betty Tubbs sat in the audience at the St. Eves' town hall, for what had been billed as 'An Evening of Scintillating Entertainment.'

The event had been organised in aid of the local library which had been in dire need of funds ever since a lightning bolt during a recent storm had struck the weather vane and blown a skylight clean through the roof.

"I cannot believe I paid good money to sit through this drivel," grumbled Ava, tucking under the ends of her short, steel-grey bob with the palm of her hand. "Why on earth the organisers thought we'd be interested in a juggler who drops every other ball, an Origami demonstration, a stamp collector's musings, and a local artist recounting her journey through early menopause, heaven only knows. Where's the music? Where are the dancers? The singers? The magicians? The comedians?"

She blew out a disgruntled sigh and shuffled in her seat. "And as if that wasn't bad enough, these chairs have been chiselled from the hardest material known to mankind. I think I can safely say the entire evening's been about as scintillating as an enema."

"Agreed on all counts," muttered Harriett. "Especially the chairs—my bottom's gone completely numb. You know, I could have gone to my martial arts class with Leo instead of sitting here, bored to tears."

"Oh yes, how's the Teriyaki going?" asked Ava.

Harriett rolled her eyes. "I don't know how many times I've told you, it's *Ju-Jitsu*. And I've only had two lessons, but it seems quite good so far."

Ava sniffed. "Well, whatever it's called, I'm sure it's more exciting than this." She gestured to the stage with an expansive sweep of her hand.

"Actually, I thought the Origami chap was quite good," whispered Betty as she unwrapped a barley sugar and popped it into her mouth. "Although I could hardly see the polar bear he made from here." She frowned. "He really needed *much* bigger paper. The chairs don't bother me, though, because I always bring my haemorrhoid cushion when I know I'm going to be sitting down for a long time. It only takes a minute to blow up, and it's ever so comfortable." She gave each of her friends a benign smile. "You really should get one for yourselves, you know."

Ava's nostrils flared to their very widest. "I'm very happy it works for you, Betty, but if you think I'd be seen dead sitting on one of those things in public, you're grossly mistaken."

Betty shrugged and scratched her head through freshly-permed, snow-white curls. Unlike Ava and Harriett, she put comfort above all else and couldn't give two hoots if her slightly unconventional methods to achieve it were a source of embarrassment or amusement to others. "Suit yourself." She hummed a quiet tune as she sucked on her barley sugar, and flexed her feet to drum the toes of her sensible shoes on the parquet floor.

"Can I have your attention, please, ladies and gentlemen?" Ophelia Smalls, the town's librarian, and host for the evening, tapped on the microphone. "It's time for the next act." She settled her pince-nez halfway down her long aquiline nose and flicked absentmindedly through the programme of events.

"Ah, here we are... now, Shakira and Terence Dibble own a company that holds murder-mystery weekends all over the county, and they're here this evening with a little cryptic entertainment, so please all join me in giving them a big St. Eves' welcome!"

A ripple of applause accompanied Shakira and Terence as they took to the stage, each giving a theatrical bow.

"Good evening, ladies and gentlemen," said Terence in a nasally, monotone voice. He prowled the boards in his crepe-soled shoes, peering out at the audience from between two lanky strands of a greasy fringe, his beady eyes magnified behind the thick lenses of his glasses. "Now, who loves a good murder mystery? Anyone? No one? Ah, yes, I can see a few hands going up. Well, we're going to have a little fun."

"If only," murmured Ava, crossing her legs and tapping an impatient foot in mid-air.

Shakira took over. "We certainly are!" She threw back her head and let out a hee-hawing laugh which showed off two rows of large teeth, rather like one might find behind the lips of a shire horse. "Now listen carefully, because you might not be able to keep up if you don't know what's going on. Terry and I are going to relate a short fictional story to you which centres around the murder of a man named Bertie Kravitz. We've stuck pictures of all the suspects on this board here and all *you* have to do is guess whodunnit, and what killed him."

"£10 says he dropped dead from utter boredom," said Ava, under her breath, as she felt her eyelids droop.

"So, the story begins when Bertie arrives at the country residence of his uncle, Lord Denning." Terence droned on. "He parks his car outside the manor house and walks across the gravel drive, where he sees the gardener, Finbar Dawson, tending to the flowerbeds. He rings the bell and the door is opened presently by a stern-faced butler in a tailcoat. Now…"

Betty shook Ava's arm. "Wake up! They're about to announce the winners of the raffle."

Ava opened her eyes with a start. "What? What about the dynamic duo and their murder mystery?"

"They've just finished. You fell asleep."

"I most certainly did not," said Ava, who prided herself on having the staying power of someone half her age.

Betty nodded. "You most certainly did. You and Harriett have been asleep for almost three-quarters of an hour."

Ava stifled a yawn. "I take it I haven't missed anything interesting?"

"Not really," said Betty. "The butler did it,"

Ophelia took the microphone from the stand again and patted the bun on the back of her head. "I'd like to say a huge thank you to every one of you for

supporting us in our fundraising efforts. We're well on
our way to being able to repair the annexe roof. Now,
as you know, your £20 admission ticket entitled you to
entry into our raffle, and I'd like to call upon local
councillor, Steven Bates, to draw the winners."

Steven bounded onto the stage like a Springer
Spaniel and tossed his floppy fringe out of his eyes. He
treated the audience to his sincere politician's smile and
was rewarded by whoops of approval from a small
army of his constituents who were taking up the entire
first and second rows. He posed for their pictures before
grabbing the microphone.

"Well, to echo Ophelia, I'd like to thank you all
for coming tonight to what I'm sure you'll agree has
been a truly... er... spectacular evening. And special
thanks to those who've been generous enough to donate
our raffle prizes, speaking of which, I'm sure you're all
dying to know if you've won."

He flashed another smile. "So, without further
ado." He dug his hand into the bucket Ophelia was
holding. "The third prize of a month's supply of scones
and teacakes, donated by Lydia Callum from the
Bakehouse Bakery, has been won by..." He turned the
ticket over and read the name on the back. "Sheila
Truss! Are you here, Sheila? Ah, there you are. Here's
your envelope with all the details on how to claim your
prize. Congratulations! Oh, hang on, don't rush off—
we need to get a quick shot for the local rag." He pulled
a reluctant Sheila into a pose for the photographer at the
front of the stage before she scuttled back to her seat.

He rummaged in the bucket again. "Second prize of dinner for two at Porcinis vegetarian restaurant, donated by the Manager, Luigi Di Gavini, goes to… Virginia Tate! Come on up here and get your envelope, Virginia, and take a minute for a quick photo.

"Now, the first prize really is something special. As I'm sure you know, Roman Haley, the renowned restaurant critic and judge on the TV baking show, *Easy Peasy Bakey Cakey*, recently opened his brand new culinary school in the town." Steven paused to let the suspense build. "And he's offering two lucky people a five-day cookery course at the school next week! And, as if that wasn't amazing enough, the winners will receive a certificate signed by Roman, and will have their photograph taken with the man himself. I can't think of any better way to put the icing on such a fantastic prize."

An excited murmur rippled through the audience at the prospect of cookery lessons at the controversial star's school.

Restaurant critic Roman's celebrity status had been catapulted to super-stardom when one of the much-loved judges of an outdated TV baking show had been trampled after falling off his horse two years before, and Roman had taken his place at short notice.

His popularity had sky-rocketed overnight. Not because of his pleasant demeanour—he didn't possess one of those—but because of his scathing comments, which ranged from toe-curlingly cringeworthy to downright libellous.

Viewers couldn't get enough of his acerbic critiques and the show's ratings had soared. To everyone's surprise, Roman had swept in like a whirlwind of fresh air and given the flagging show the CPR it had needed to revive it.

Steven grinned and dug his hand into the bucket again, making a show of digging around before pulling out a ticket. "And the winner of this exclusive prize is…"

A commotion at the door stopped him mid-sentence. Stan Cripps, the town hall caretaker and ticket collector for social events, was grappling with a gatecrasher in an attempt to stop him gaining entry to the hall.

"You can't come in 'ere without a ticket!" said Stan, blocking the doorway, and losing his flat cap in the scuffle.

"I don't need a ticket, you nitwit! I donated the top prize, you stupid little man. Don't you know who I am?"

"Oh, my goodness! What an absolutely fabulous surprise! We're honoured!" simpered Steven, as the gatecrasher made his way down the aisle, followed by a bespectacled weasel-faced brunette in a suit, holding a tape recorder in the air, and running to keep up. "Will everyone please give a big St. Eves' round of applause to Roman Haley!"

Gasps, ooohs, and aaahhs reverberated around the room as Roman climbed onto the stage in his ankle-length fur cloak and snatched the microphone from Steven's hand. He glowered at the audience and twirled the end of his handlebar moustache as he waited for absolute silence before he spoke.

"Before I award this prize, I'd like to make an announcement. As you may know, my old colleague, Olivia Floyd-Martin, is very successful in her own right here in St. Eves, as the Executive Chef at *The President Hotel*." He lowered his eyes and coughed behind his hand. "Not *quite* as successful as me, of course, but successful, nevertheless.

"So, with that in mind, I'd like to extend an invitation to her to attend a tasting session at the school next Monday, as my guest. We haven't seen each other for so long, I'm sure she won't refuse."

He smirked and pointed to the local reporter who was covering the event for publication in his paper's weekend edition. "You! Did you get all that down? I want that invitation to Olivia to be the focal point of your article, do you understand? If you've missed anything, speak to my assistant, Monique, and she can fill you in. She keeps a record of everything I say."

Monique adjusted her glasses and gave the reporter a mean-spirited look of self-importance.

"Right, then. I have a car waiting outside. Can we get this prize awarded so I can get out of here?" Roman handed the microphone back to Steven who stopped gazing at him in awe and pulled himself together.

"Yes, of course. Sorry, we weren't expecting you to be here, you see, so you took us by surprise. A *fabulous* surprise, of course, but a surprise all the same. It's not often we have the pleasure of..."

"If you could just draw the winning ticket?" snapped Roman.

"Ah, yes, the winning ticket! Hah!" Steven put his hand in the bucket again and delved deep. "And the winner of this exclusive prize is... wait for it... Harriett Reeves! Where are you, Harriett?"

The hall went quiet for a moment and Ava nudged Harriett as she gave an extra-loud snore, knocking her elbow off the arm of the chair and waking her up from her doze.

"What? What's happening?" said Harriett, sitting bolt upright and blinking repeatedly. "Was that thunder?"

The crowd began to clap. "You've won first prize!" said Betty. "Go on—go up and get your envelope from Roman Haley!"

"And wipe that dribble off your chin," hissed Ava, as she passed Harriett a tissue.

CHAPTER 2

Charlotte Costello fluttered a blanket across the sand and squinted against the sun at her daughter, Molly. Wrapped up against the elements in a fleece onesie, bobble hat, and pink wellingtons, the seven-year old was ankle-deep in the sea and concentrating on how many times she could bounce a shuttlecock on a racquet as the dogs, Pippin and Panda, chased each other up and down the beach, making figures of eight in the sand.

Charlotte dug a fist into the small of her back and winced as her baby attempted to make itself more comfortable. There was still another two months to go before it was due to make an appearance but until then, it seemed perfectly content to play Twister while it waited

She breathed in a deep gulp of cold fresh air. Saturdays were her favourite day of the week, especially when the weather was good enough to spend them outside. Unless they had other plans, or the rain was falling at a rapid rate, most Saturday mornings, she and Molly would dress accordingly, pack up a picnic basket, something to read, a couple of badminton racquets or the Swingball, and head for the beach. Even if it was only for an hour or so, Charlotte liked to keep up the tradition started by her own mum. It was no hardship, after all, seeing as they lived directly opposite the long stretch of sand.

The only thing missing from their blissful starts to the weekends was her husband, Nathan, but as he was the Detective Chief Inspector, she accepted his frequent absences with good grace.

"Come on, Molly, come and have some lunch. We can play again later."

Pink-cheeked and bright-eyed, her daughter came running, still bouncing the shuttlecock, the dogs at her heels. "Did you bring my book, Mummy?" She pulled off her hat, had a quick wiggle of her loose tooth, flopped onto the blanket, and took a chicken sandwich and a bottle of water from the basket.

"It's in my bag," said Charlotte, filling a bowl with water for the dogs.

"Which one did you bring?"

"*The Case of the Vanishing Cucumbers*. That's the one you're reading, isn't it?"

Molly nodded. "That's good—that's my favourite. I'm glad you didn't bring the one about the bald men with the red eyes and long fingers and noses. That one gave me bad dreams." She shook out her light-brown curls and settled down to read her book as she ate her lunch.

Charlotte lay down on the blanket for thirty seconds, then sat up again as she felt the first twinges of heartburn. She shuffled around until she found a comfortable position and took another deep breath of sea air, relaxing as she let it out slowly to the sounds of the surf gently tumbling the pebbles on the shore.

The weak February sunshine had lured out a few diehard beach lovers, wrapped up against the chill, their deckchairs dotted here and there, but not so many as to disturb the peace and quiet.

"Mummy?" Molly finished her mouthful and looked up from her book, a small furrow at her brow. "You know I'm going to camp on Wednesday?"

"Yes, poppet."

"Does that mean I don't have to go to school?" Her eyes crossed as she stuck out her bottom jaw and tried to see the tooth she was wobbling back and forth with her finger.

Charlotte nodded. "Don't do that with your eyes, please, sweetheart. You won't have to go to school, but you'll still be learning loads of new things. You'll be having so much fun, I bet you won't want to come home."

"And how many days am I going to be away?" Molly took her finger out of her mouth and climbed onto Charlotte's lap.

"Five. Well, four and a half, actually." Charlotte stroked her daughter's hair. Are you still looking forward to it?"

Molly shrugged. "I think I'm going to miss you and Daddy a lot."

"Well, we're going to miss you, too, but the days will fly by. You'll be home before you know it— and think of all the stories you'll have to tell us."

Molly's bottom lip began to quiver and she buried her face in Charlotte's shoulder. "What will happen if the baby comes while I'm not here?"

"I doubt very much that's going to happen but if it does, then you'll see it when you get home."

Molly's head dropped and her shoulders sagged. "But what happens if it comes when I'm not here, and you love it more than you love me?" she said in a tiny voice.

Charlotte pulled her into another hug. Even though she and Nathan had reassured her countless times that they would love her and the baby equally, Molly wore her insecurities in plain sight.

"Look, whenever it arrives, Daddy and I aren't going to love this baby any more than we love you. And, anyway, you'll always, always be our favourite, most special girl."

"D'you promise?" A muffled voice drifted up from the depths of Charlotte's fleece.

"With all my heart."

Molly lifted her head, a lopsided grin immediately replacing the frown. She planted a kiss on Charlotte's cheek and slid off her lap before settling herself cross-legged on the blanket again, running her finger along the lines of text in her book as she silently mouthed the words to herself.

Charlotte chuckled. If Molly only knew how much she and Nathan loved her, she'd never spend another second worrying about it for as long as she lived.

The sudden thunkety-thunk of steps along the seafront prompted Molly to look up from her book, her mouth dropping open and the frown returning to her face.

"Mummy, look! It's that horrid man."

Charlotte's gaze followed Molly's pointing finger to see a tall, instantly-recognisable man dressed in black, apart from the red, fur cloak that billowed out behind him, a red cravat, and a red top-hat. His rotund stomach jiggled under his shirt, but his trademark handlebar moustache and long goatee beard remained perfectly still as he strode along, his cane and the heels of his red cowboy boots tapping out an urgent rhythm, like a distress call in Morse code.

Charlotte and Molly had had the misfortune of experiencing Roman Haley's particular brand of humour three weeks previously, when he'd arrived in town for the grand opening of his culinary school. As the crowd had been waiting for him to cut the ribbon and declare the school open, he'd happened to overhear Molly's remark that he looked like a wizard in his cloak.

He'd spun round on the heel of his boot and fixed her with a sinister stare, pointed at her with his cane, and uttered a stream of gobbledygook which he assured her was a spell for keeping ill-mannered children quiet for the rest of the year.

Molly's tears hadn't lasted long, but Charlotte had been livid. She'd tried to explain that Molly was just seven years old, and that she'd meant no offence, but Roman had completely ignored her and strode off to have his picture taken with the mayor.

As Charlotte watched him now, a couple who were ambling along the seafront stopped in their tracks when they saw him striding towards them.

"Oh my good gawd! You're that chap from the telly, aren't you? The one who's just opened that cooking school? We're here on holiday, and we're huge fans." The woman fumbled in her bag with gloved hands as she and her husband blocked his path.

"Are you really?" replied Roman in a bored voice, his surly face not registering a modicum of gratitude. He lifted his cane and waggled it back and forth between the couple, forcing them to move apart to let him pass. "And you can put that pen away—I don't give autographs. Especially not to people who can't even remember my name."

Leaving the couple open-mouthed, he carried on walking, not stopping until he reached *The President Hotel*, where he disappeared inside.

"We don't like him, do we, Mummy?" said Molly, hiding behind Charlotte.

Charlotte shook her head. "He's not very nice, is he? Never mind, he's nothing to do with us, so you don't have to think about him ever again."

That evening, with dinner over and Molly tucked up in bed, there was nothing more than the promise of a quiet night in looming ahead.

"We'll see you in the morning, okay?" said Charlotte, putting the storybook on the bedside table.

Molly nodded and yawned. "Daddy, will you come to see me off when I go to camp?"

Nathan pulled the duvet up to her chin and blew a raspberry on her forehead.

She giggled, threw her arms around his neck and returned the raspberry before gently patting his cheeks.

"So, will you?"

"Course I will."

"'kay. The mummies like it when you come to the school."

Nathan chuckled at Charlotte's raised eyebrow. "Do they, now?"

"Uh-huh. Esme said..." Molly took a furtive look to the right and left before cupping a hand around her mouth and divulging the playground gossip her best friend had shared with her the day before. "She said they think you're a hottie. She heard her mummy talking about it with Floella Knight's mummy." She giggled behind her hand.

"Er, we've spoken about this before, Molly," said Charlotte. "I don't think Esme should be repeating things like that, and neither should you."

"Don't you?" said Nathan, giving her a mischievous wink. "I think it's very interesting." He gave Molly's nose a gentle flick. "We'll see you tomorrow, okay?"

Charlotte caught the kiss Molly blew. "Night night, sweetheart."

As usual, Pippin and Panda circled and flopped down at the side of the bed, their chins resting on the floor between their paws. They both took a contented sigh, and settled down for the evening.

"We saw Roman Haley again when we were on the beach earlier," said Charlotte, as she loaded the dishwasher. "He was on his way to The President. He's been staying there since before his new school opened—must be costing him a fortune. Mind you, I don't suppose he's short of a few hundred thousand pounds." She jammed the plates into the dishwasher rack with rather more force than she'd intended.

"I take it you're still fuming about the way he spoke to Molly?" Nathan pulled a beer from the fridge, and a sparkling pear juice for Charlotte.

"Actually, yes, I am." She ran a hand through her hair before placing it firmly on her hip. "I was really hoping all that arrogance was just a show for TV, but it obviously isn't. He was so rude to someone who stopped him for an autograph today, so it's not even as though he's just got a dislike of kids—he doesn't seem to be keen on anyone."

"Well, I've got no patience for prima donnas," said Nathan, putting his arms around Charlotte and kissing her neck, "so however long he's here for, I sincerely hope we don't cross paths."

CHAPTER 3

"I'm so relieved that Betty wasn't bothered about the cookery lessons," said Harriett, as she and Ava made their way to Roman Haley's culinary school to make the final arrangements for the following week. "I don't know how I would have chosen between the two of you."

"Well, Bet's never really been one for following instructions, has she?" said Ava. "She's always been more of an experimental cook—you know, chuck it all in the pot and hope for the best."

I hope Roman's in a good mood," said Harriett, changing the subject. "I'm not usually such a scaredy-cat, but I really find him intimidating. When I went up on stage to collect my prize yesterday, I could feel the hostility coming off him in waves. And he's got such a sharp tongue, you never know what he's going to say next."

"Usually something not very nice," said Ava. "But I'm sure we won't see him today—he'll get one of his minions to deal with us. And I very much doubt we'll see him next week, either, apart from at that tasting session thingy, because *he* won't be teaching us, will he? He's not a tutor, he just owns the school."

They arrived outside the small, understated white-walled building on the edge of the market square. Its bottle-green door was flanked by two bay trees, and a smart green and white sign, which simply said *Haley's Culinary School*, told them they were in the right place.

Ava peered through the window. "Well, I can't see anyone because the blinds are closed, but those instructions in your prize envelope said there'd be someone here until seven o'clock, Monday to Saturday, and it's only half-past six. Come on, we can't stand out here on the doorstep all evening."

"Just a minute," said Harriet, putting a hand on Ava's arm. She strained to hear through the door. "Can you hear someone shouting? Perhaps we should wait? We don't want to walk in on someone's argument."

Ava elbowed her out of the way and put an ear flat against the gloss painted wood. "Here, let me try. You can hear much better this way. The trick is not to get caught." She gave the side of her nose a sly tap, before shrieking and stumbling forward as the door was flung open, and she was saved from falling flat on her face due only to her bouncing off Roman Haley's large stomach.

"You can hear a lot better on *this* side of the door, you know," he said, a droll expression on his angry red face. He looked down his nose at Ava and Harriett as though they were bacteria, before stroking his beard, putting on his top hat, and pushing past them, his cane swinging and his cloak flying out behind him as he marched up the road.

"How very *rude*!" blustered Ava. "Why he's so popular, heaven only knows. If I was twenty years younger, I'd put him over my knee and give him a jolly good spanking." She poked her head around the open front door and called after him. "I say! Did you hear that, Mr. Haley? You're never too old for a spanking, you know!"

The man and woman Roman had been yelling at each stifled a grin.

Ava composed herself and flashed a smile. "Have we called at a bad time?" she asked, sweetly. "We've come to register for the course on Monday. My friend won it in the library roof fundraiser raffle."

The man rolled his eyes, barely disguising his contempt.

Ava opened her mouth to object, but the short blonde woman took the wind out of her sails with a huge grin.

"No, it's not a bad time at all," she said, in a jolly voice. "We'll be closing soon, so you got here just in time. And take no notice of Roman. We've known him for ages and he's always been the same."

"What? Obnoxious, you mean?" said Ava.

The woman chuckled as she went behind the reception desk and pulled out a large leather-bound book. A mass of blonde curls pulled into a ponytail swung from the top of her head as she turned the pages. "Do you have your certificate, please?"

Harriett handed her the envelope. "Everything I was given is in there. By the way, will we need to bring anything with us? You know, aprons, hairnets, stuff like that."

The man snorted.

Ava gave him a withering glare and reached up and poked him on the shoulder. "What exactly is so funny, young man? When *we* were young, hairnets were compulsory in lots of working kitchens. Harriett and I both had jobs in the school canteen, and we weren't allowed through the door unless we were wearing our hairnets. My friend has asked a perfectly reasonable question, so the least you can do is afford her the courtesy of not laughing in her face. Quite frankly, I've had enough of rude men, eye rolling and sheer insolence today."

The man's eyebrows met in a frown. His shiny black hair was slicked back off his face, showing off his sculpted jawline and deep-set blue eyes. He crossed his arms and his muscles looked like they might burst through the seams of his chef's jacket.

"My apologies," he said curtly, a pulse jumping in his neck.

"Hmpf, I should think so." Ava turned her attention back to the woman behind the desk. "I think it's about time someone taught some people some manners." She jerked her head towards muscle-man.

The woman avoided looking at her colleague and stuck out her hand over the desk. "Well, speaking of manners, I'm sure I don't know where mine have gone. I haven't even introduced myself. I'm Larissa Reece—very nice to meet you. And that's Gavin Doyle. Altogether, there are six tutors at the school, specialising in different techniques, but we'll be taking you for your course next week. And we'll provide the aprons. No hairnets required," she said, with a smile. "Just dress so you'll feel relaxed, and wear some comfortable shoes."

She handed two glossy leaflets to Harriett. "I noticed you don't have these. They go out to every student who takes a course with us, but they were obviously missed out from your envelope. They're itineraries, with details of what we'll be covering, and what we'll be baking each day. There are only four booked on the course you're taking, so it'll be nice and cosy. It's all very informal."

"Ooh, look, Ava! We're going to be making bread on the first day," said Harriett. "Mini raisin loaves, a cottage loaf, and granary baguettes. You know I've never been able to make bread—this is going to be a real treat."

Larissa nodded. "We do an entire week-long course, just on artisan bread making, and it's proving to be one of our most popular. Bread's just one of the things you'll be tackling during your week, though." She closed the bookings diary. "There, all done. You're booked in for Monday. And if you could be sure to arrive on time, please, because we have a lot to cram into each day."

"Oh, we will," said Harriett. "We're never late."

The ladies smiled at Larissa and gave Gavin a brief nod before going on their way.

"Well, she seems very nice, but he's a bit grim," said Harriett when they were well out of earshot of the school.

"He's probably Roman's henchman, what d'you expect?" said Ava, winding her scarf around her neck and pulling on her gloves.

Harriett stopped and opened her handbag. "Oh, bother. I've left those leaflets behind." She looked at her watch. "It's just coming up to five to seven—I hope they haven't locked the door yet. I'll just pop back—I won't be a tick."

She rushed back up the road and gave a sigh of relief when she pushed the door and it opened.

"Oh, my goodness! I'm so sorry!" she said, covering her eyes as she walked in to find Larissa and Gavin in a very passionate embrace across the reception desk.

They jumped apart, their faces blazing red.

"Larissa's a bit, er, upset. I was just, er, comforting her," said Gavin, adjusting his chef's whites.

"Yes. Yes, that's right, he was." Larissa rubbed the back of her hand across her forehead and looked at the floor.

"Oh, well, no explanation necessary," said Harriett. "I just came back for my leaflets—I left them here. Sorry to barge in like that, but I wanted to get back before you closed."

Larissa nodded. "Of course."

Gavin strode over to the door and held it open, and Harriett took her cue to leave.

"Well, I'd better be off. See you both on Monday. I hope you'll be feeling much better by then."

As she walked back down the road, Larissa caught her up.

"Look, this is a bit awkward, but we'd really appreciate it if you didn't say anything to Roman about this. He can be funny about his employees getting too friendly, if you know what I mean."

"Say anything about what?" said Harriett with a wink. "Whatever your secret is, he won't find out about it from me."

Larissa sighed with relief. "Thanks. That's good of you. Gavin and I would both be looking for new jobs if Roman knew we were 'fraternising' with each other, as he calls it."

"Don't even give it another thought," said Harriett. "See you on Monday."

"What was all that about?" said Ava, when Harriett caught her up.

"You'll never believe it! I walked back in and found them snogging! They were all over each other. I didn't know where to look."

"Good grief, what's wrong with them? Can't they wait until they get home?" Ava tutted and shook her head. "Young people these days have no sense of decorum—I blame E-additives and energy drinks for all those urges of theirs. We never behaved like that in our day when we used to eat proper food, and drinks in every colour of the rainbow didn't exist. I hope they'll be able to restrain themselves next week and we won't have to keep stopping so they can go off and have a quickie."

"Don't be ridiculous!" said Harriett. "I only caught them at it because they weren't expecting anyone to walk in. Anyway, they don't want Roman to know, so you mustn't say anything about it in front of him, okay? They'd be in trouble if he found out."

"Don't worry, I won't say a word," said Ava with a sniff. "It's nothing to do with me. If Roman Haley wants to employ staff who behave like rabbits on heat, that's his business." She linked her arm through Harriett's. "Anyway, I don't know about you, but I fancy a coffee to warm me up. Come on, let's go to that new place on the seafront and get one of those lovely frothy chia-latte-hazelnut thingies on the way home."

———————

Sundays at Charlotte's café were always guaranteed to be barnstormers but this Sunday was busier than ever, mainly due to all the customers, and other bar, café and restaurant owners on the marina, who'd made a point of popping in to wish her luck.

It was her last shift before going on maternity leave, after which her godmother, Laura, would take over in the kitchen, with her best friend, Jess, running the bar and terrace as she always did.

Charlotte knew all would be well. The two of them had run things without a hitch after Molly was born, but she couldn't help but feel a little sad at the thought of not being around for a while. The café and its customers—many of whom had become good friends—were such a huge part of her life.

"You should pop outside and see Harriett. She's had a bit of good luck," said Jess, as she brought in a pile of empty plates from the terrace at the end of a busy lunch service. "There are no more food orders, except a few desserts and Betty's second helping of peach pie, but I can see to those."

Bread, Dead and Wed

Charlotte looked at the pile of washing up. "Okay. I think that can wait for a bit."

Jess nodded. "Go on, Harriett's dying to speak to you. I'll keep an eye on everything while you have a sit down for five minutes."

"Afternoon, all," said Charlotte, pulling up a chair at the table with her old friends. She turned to Harriett. "Jess said you've had some good news."

Harriett nodded and reached into her handbag. "Here, look at this. I won first prize at the library roof fundraiser."

"Wow! You lucky thing!" Charlotte pointed to the course itinerary, her eyes popping. "You're going to be making bread! I'm so jealous. What I wouldn't give for a professional to teach me how to make bread. And it says here there'll be a tasting session at the end of every day, so you can all try each other's baking. That sounds like fun. You'll have to remember everything they teach you and let me know."

"We will," said Harriett, as she spooned up her last mouthful of peach pie and custard. "Unfortunately, though, not only is Roman Haley going to be at Monday's tasting session, but he's invited Olivia Floyd-Martin along, too. Talk about cooking under pressure."

"I'm sure it'll be fine once you get started," said Charlotte, "just wait and see."

Harriett nodded. "You're probably right. I'm looking forward to it. We both are, aren't we, Ava? I'm just a bit nervous, that's all. Although I have to say, we're a little disappointed that the man himself is such a complete pillock. Not that we'll see much of him, probably."

Harriett's husband, Leo, raised an eyebrow. "I could have told you he was a pillock the first time I saw him on TV. Acting like he owns the place and looking down his nose at everyone. I don't know why people think he's so great. Here, listen to this." He picked up his newspaper. *"'Diabolical, hideous and appalling are just some of Roman Haley's favourite put-downs as he dismisses hours of hard work by the contestants of Easy Peasy Bakey Cakey with a single stroke of his acerbic tongue.*

"Let's hope none of those adjectives are necessary next Monday, which is when he's invited Olivia Floyd-Martin to join him for a joint tasting session at his new culinary school. Two of the most highly-respected experts in their field in the same room, at the same time. Students beware!'"

"That's from the article in *The St. Eves' Herald*," said Leo, as he neatly folded the newspaper. "The bloke sounds like a complete moron."

His friend, Harry Jenkins, harrumphed noisily. He was always wary of newcomers to the town, especially ones who thought they were better than everyone else. "Well, if you ask me," he said, refilling his glass with red wine, "that school has no place in St. Eves. Haley only opened it here to spite Olivia, so I heard from the boys at the bowling club. I told you what they said, didn't I, Leo?"

"Well you didn't tell us," said Ava. "What *did* they say?" She drew closer to hear the gossip.

"And what's it got to do with Olivia?" said Harriett.

Olivia Floyd-Martin was the Executive Chef at The President; St. Eves' only five-star hotel. She'd started out as a pot washer and potato peeler, but her ambition had seen her rise quickly through the ranks, leaving the hotel behind when she made the decision to become the best.

Since then, she'd worked under the guidance of some of the most highly-respected chefs in the world, attaining a standard of culinary excellence that others in her field could only dream of.

However, in earning the accolade of world-class chef, she'd also earned a reputation for being disagreeable at best, and a downright liability at worst. Many were the unsuspecting diners, or members of kitchen staff, who'd made the mistake of giving the daunting chef the smallest critique, only to feel the full force of her fury in response.

The hotel's management, though, had long turned a blind eye to her bad temperament, ever since luring her back to The President years before, on an astronomical wage. Left to work her culinary magic, Olivia had transformed the hotel's rooftop restaurant into a destination eatery that people flocked to in their droves from far beyond the boundaries of the town. Since casting her uncompromising eye over the kitchen staff and the menu, the restaurant had become the go-to venue in every good-food guide in the country.

"Well, come on, Harry," said Ava. "Spill the beans."

Sherri Bryan

Harry pulled his chair closer to the table. "These two brothers I play bowls with know Olivia's parents. Apparently, years ago, at the start of their careers, Roman and Olivia used to work together in the same restaurant. Back then, they were as thick as thieves."

"I didn't know he used to work in a restaurant," said Betty, her face lighting up as Jess put down a second helping of peach pie in front of her.

Harry nodded and took a sip of wine. "Anyway, word has it that after Olivia left the restaurant, Roman stayed on, but when it looked like her career was taking off, he couldn't bear the thought of being overshadowed by her, so *he* left to further *his* career. He decided he didn't want to cook food for a living any more, though, he wanted to write about it, so he took a job as a restaurant critic for a local newspaper.

"After a while, his restaurant review feature was spotted by the editor of a national newspaper, and he was invited to write a column for the Sunday edition, which is when his own career really started to go places, and he and Olivia lost touch completely. They only saw or spoke to each other if it couldn't be avoided, you know, at culinary events or award ceremonies, things like that."

"Why didn't they keep in touch?" asked Betty.

"Because they became jealous of each other's success, and this stupid rivalry started up between them," said Harry. "Apparently, when Roman was offered that TV judging role, Olivia went ballistic. Let's face it, she's never been one for sharing the limelight, has she?"

Page 38

"I still have no idea why Roman was such a big name before he became a judge on *Easy Peasy Bakey Cakey*," said Ava, blotting the corners of her mouth on a serviette. "I mean, he was just a restaurant critic with a newspaper column."

"He may have been "just" a restaurant critic to you, Ava, but in the food world, he was like a god—one of his reviews could make or break a restaurant," said Harry. "That's how powerful he was. If he gave a place a good write-up, you could bet its custom would go through the roof, but if he didn't, it could plummet. As I understand, his negative reviews have contributed to countless restaurants going out of business."

"That's terrible!" said Ava. "He sounds even more awful than I'd already decided he was. What a way to make a living."

"Ironically, it was one of his negative reviews that pushed him into the elite bracket," said Harry. "It was for a meal he had at a world-famous restaurant owned by a chef who was considered food royalty by his peers. The chef in question was so revered, no other critic or fellow restaurateur had ever dared to give him an unfavourable critique.

"Roman didn't care about that, though. His review was so scathing, the poor chef had to have time off to recover. It caused such a scandal, the offers to appear on TV chat shows came flooding in, along with the offers to do magazine interviews, and guest on cookery shows. All of a sudden, everyone wanted him. It must have been very difficult for Olivia to see him becoming so in-demand, just because of that one review, when she'd had to work so hard to get to where she was."

"But why *was* there so much rivalry between them?" said Harriett. "They weren't even in the same line of work, so I don't see why either of them would be jealous of the other."

Harry shrugged. "Competition, I suppose. People who've been friends for years often end up at each other's throats, and it can be the smallest thing that escalates something trivial into a full-blown conflict. With Olivia and Roman, their rivalry came to a head when he became a TV star. She had a hard time coping with his fast-track to fame, although the final straw was him buying the culinary school. She was absolutely livid about it. It had always been an ambition of hers to open a school in St. Eves, but then he comes along and does exactly that, right under her nose. And in her own hometown."

"And her parents think he did it deliberately? Just to get under her skin?" said Charlotte.

Harry nodded. "That's what Olivia thinks, too. Her dad said she and Roman used to talk about their ambitions all the time when they worked together. Back then, opening a culinary school was hers, and it's never changed. I can't see any other reason why Haley would want to have a business here, other than to spite her. He has no other connection to St. Eves, does he?"

"I told Harriett I reckon the only reason he invited Olivia to the school next week was to put her on the spot," said Leo. "I don't imagine she'll be keen to set foot in there but now he's invited her so publicly, she's going to look like a sore loser if she turns him down."

"Well, I'm glad he's not one of the tutors on the cookery course," said Ava. "I've got a good mind to punch him on the nose."

"Why are you suddenly sticking up for Olivia?" said Betty, her eyebrows shooting right up to the fringe of her bubble perm. "You don't even like her."

"It's not that I don't like her, Betty," said Ava, picking her teeth, "it's just that she's not really my cup of tea. She's a bit rough around the edges, if you know what I mean, but she's a local girl, so unless she's done something really awful, I'll always take her side over an idiot like Roman Haley, celebrity or not."

"But Olivia *has* done some really awful things in her time, hasn't she?" said Leo.

Harry pulled a face. "You can say that again." He began counting on his fingers. "Let's see… she's made goodness knows how many kitchen staff and customers cry. She took a couple's dinner away on their wedding anniversary because one of them said the paté needed a little more seasoning. Some poor chap was yanked away from the dinner table by his collar when he complained his steak wasn't cooked properly. She threatened a prop-forward from the local rugby team with bodily harm when he asked for tomato ketchup with his lobster thermidor. And we already know she had an aversion towards restaurant critics long before Roman Haley came along, because she threw one through a window when he found fault with a sauce."

"Hmm, that's true," said Ava, "although the incidents with the anniversary couple and the restaurant critic were years ago, not recently."

"Whenever they were," said Harry. "They're all proof that she *had* a volatile temperament, and she's probably *still* got one."

"But everyone deserves a second chance, don't they?" said Ava. "And she's been having treatment for years. All that relaxation therapy and anger management counselling, and whatnot."

"I'm not so sure the therapy's doing much good," said Leo. "She's hardly the best-humoured woman in town, is she? And she still blows up every now and then."

"She's got a very stressful job," said Betty, running a finger around the rim of her dessert bowl to get the last traces of custard. "Running a kitchen like the one at The President can't be easy, especially when you've got such high standards to maintain."

"I heard she's been in a foul mood ever since she found out what Roman Haley's plans were," said Jess, as she came back to clear the table. "Mind you, I've known her since we were at school and it didn't take a lot to put her in a bad mood then. Seems like nothing's changed."

"Well, I'm sticking up for her," said Charlotte. "She was amazing when Nathan and I got married—she couldn't do enough for us to make sure the day went without a hitch. And I agree with you, Betty. Running a kitchen *is* stressful. Not that this one is anything like the one at The President, but I know how stressed I can get when it's busy and I want to be sure everything's nice for people. If you multiply that by about a million percent, you're probably close to the stress Olivia's under every day. I mean, this place just does home cooking, but she does fine dining. Not that I'm excusing her bad behaviour, I'm just saying it's a lot of pressure."

Ava folded her serviette and sighed. "Well, whatever Olivia's argument is with Roman, I'm sure it won't affect us, will it, Harriett? I wasn't sure if I was keen on cookery lessons when you first won the prize, but I'm really looking forward to it now. And it couldn't have come at a better time, because Derek and I are going to be like passing ships for the next few weeks. He's going to be at rehearsals every day for the next month, and then away at competitions."

"Didn't you say the dance company's performing in Windsor soon?" said Charlotte.

Ava nodded. "And at a festival in Horsham after that. And we're both taking part in a couples' competition in Tonbridge in September, although we won't be dancing together *all* the time because they're going to split us up on the second night and pair us with other people." She took a powder compact from her bag and examined her teeth for stray food particles. "Sort of like wife swapping, I suppose," she said, thoughtfully.

Charlotte chuckled. "I don't think it'll be *quite* the same." She pushed herself up from the chair and groaned. "Oof, that's the trouble with being on your feet all day—when you sit down, you don't want to get up again. Right, I'll see you again before you leave, but right now, there's a pile of washing up with my name on it."

CHAPTER 4

"For heaven's sake! How much longer are we going to have to wait?"

Outside the culinary school, Ava stepped from one foot to the other and puffed out an impatient breath. "We've been standing here for ages."

"Only because you insisted on getting here so early," said Harriett. "There was no need to, you know—Larissa just asked us to arrive on time, not at the crack of dawn."

"Yes, I know, but I wanted us to be first so we could get good seats at the front," said Ava.

Harriett clicked her tongue. "It's a cookery course, not a Michael Bublé concert. And there's only going to be four of us, so I doubt we'll get caught in the crush. In any case, we're going to be standing up—we can't cook sitting down, can we?"

"Here, look." Ava gave her a nudge and nodded to an approaching couple. "They could be the other two."

A scruffy-looking giant of a man with his hair in a short ponytail, slightly stooped shoulders, and munching on a Danish pastry, and a slim woman with her ginger hair styled in an urchin cut, stopped and sat on the edge of the nearby fountain in the market square.

"Or maybe not," said Harriett.

The faraway purr of an engine turned to a roar as a motorbike appeared from around the corner, carrying a rider and a passenger. The rider parked in the small driveway at the side of the school and revved the engine before switching it off.

Ava spluttered and covered her mouth with a handkerchief. "Is that really necessary?" she protested, clutching her throat. "If I have a funny turn halfway through the morning from breathing in your fumes, I'll be giving the police your registration number. And I'm very good friends with the Detective Chief Inspector, so don't think I'm bluffing."

The rider walked towards her, menacing in his bike leathers and black crash helmet.

"Stay away from me, you thug!" Ava stepped back and grabbed Harriett's arm. "My friend knows Shih Tzu, so you'd better not mess with us or she'll karate chop you in the goolies."

"It's *Ju-Jitsu*!" Harriett squeaked. "And I'm just a beginner," she said, shaking Ava's hand from her arm and casting a nervous smile at the leather-clad figure, "so don't worry, I won't be karate chopping anyone anywhere."

The bike rider took off his helmet and fixed Ava with a frosty glare.

"Oh, it's you," she said, heaving a sigh of relief.

"We're not getting off on the right foot at all, are we? We're going to have to try much harder." Gavin Doyle's big biker boots drowned out his sarcasm as they thudded against the pavement, the buckles jangling like a villainous cowboy's spurs.

"Sorry about that," said Larissa, as she pulled off her helmet and shook out her curls. "It wasn't intentional." She put a hand on Ava's arm and gave her an apologetic smile.

"It's not your fault," said Ava, slightly pacified, her courage returning once she realised she wasn't about to be set upon by a leather-clad homicidal maniac. "It's his." She jabbed a finger in Gavin's direction. "He'd better hope I don't start feeling odd—I must have gulped down at least a lungful of those fumes."

"Can we please just go inside?" said Harriett. "I don't know why, Ava, but everything always turns into a commotion whenever you're involved. You're like a drama magnet."

Ava was about to answer when someone behind her stifled a cough. She turned and looked up to see the man and woman who'd been sitting by the fountain. "Oh, so you *are* taking part in the course?"

The man finished his Danish pastry and licked the tips of his fingers. "Roy Tanner," he said, his dark eyes darting from Harriett to Ava. "Pardon me for not shaking hands, but they're a bit sticky, see? I'll just go and see if I can find the bathroom before we get started. 'Scuse me."

"And I'm Izzy Davenport," said the woman, smiling shyly, her huge cornflower blue eyes dancing in a face covered with russet freckles.

"Are you a couple?" said Ava. "How lovely that you're doing this together."

"Together? Me and Roy? Oh, good grief, no!" Izzy laughed and shook her head. "We're just friends." She made sure Roy was out of earshot before lowering her voice. "Don't tell him I told you, but his wife gave him the elbow last year, and he's been a bit lost since the divorce. He booked this course as a surprise for her, but as she won't be taking it now, he's come along himself. He's been a bit down in the dumps recently."

"Well, I hope he's not banking on Roman Haley to cheer him up," said Harriett. "He's hardly what you'd call a ray of sunshine."

"I don't think Roy's banking on *anyone* to cheer him up," said Izzy. "He said he'll get over it in his own time. A cookery class isn't the kind of thing he'd ever get involved in usually, but he thought doing something new would help take his mind off Becky."

"And what about you, dear?" said Ava. "Are you a Roman Haley fan?"

Izzy grinned. "Only a huge one. And I get a bit star struck if I see a celeb, so if I faint when he walks in, pick me up, will you?"

"Honestly, it's beyond me why so many women think he's such a heartthrob." said Ava. "I can't see the attraction, myself. He's excessively hairy and he hardly oozes charm, does he? Mind you, I suppose it wouldn't do it we all liked the same thing, would it?"

They walked past the reception desk and through a frosted glass door, into a large bright room with windows on either side, and bright worktops in primary colours; the only splash of colour against the stark white walls, floors, and furniture.

"Okay, everyone, Gavin and I are just going to get changed, so hang up your jackets, put your things in a locker, and choose a workbench," said Larissa. "We'll be back in a sec, and then we can get started."

———————

Gavin was halfway through the rules of the kitchen.

"Now, I'm sure it won't surprise you to know that cleanliness is key. Wash your hands, and wash them often. A kitchen is an ideal breeding ground for bacteria and we wouldn't want anything that's prepared in this kitchen to make anyone ill, would we?"

"I don't think anyone's going to get food poisoning from anything that's prepared in here," said Harriett, wiping a finger across a worktop. "This place is so clean, it's positively clinical."

Gavin nodded. "All the same, you'll all be tasting your own, and each other's bread when it's baked, and don't forget Roman will be dropping in later. He doesn't get involved in the lessons but if he's around, he does like to sample everyone's efforts at the end of the day." He patted his stomach and smirked at Larissa. "And Olivia Floyd-Martin might be here for the tasting session, too."

"I don't know about anyone else, but the thought of cooking for Roman Haley makes me feel a bit queasy," said Harriett, a look of unease spreading across her face. "He's not the most complimentary critic, is he?"

"Don't worry," said Larissa, cheerfully, "Gavin and I will be here to check everything throughout the day, and if something isn't up to standard, it won't make it past his lips. In any case, he won't know who's cooked what—we'll just present him with a selection of everyone's baking."

The room dimmed slightly as the light streaming in through the frosted glass door was obscured, seconds before it was flung open and Roman marched in, the weasel-faced brunette scurrying along behind him.

There was a crash as the stainless-steel flour caddy Izzy had been inspecting slipped from her fingers and bounced off the worktop. "Oh my good grief! It's Roman Haley," she spluttered, fanning her hand through a white cloud.

He cut her dead with a glare. "How very observant of you." He stared around the room before making himself comfortable in an armchair at the front of the kitchen. "I trust you'll all be leaving excellent reviews of the school, and your experience here, at the end of the course?" He didn't wait for anyone to answer before turning to Gavin and Larissa. "Everything going according to plan?"

As Roman spoke, Monique made sure the tape recorder got every word.

Gavin and Larissa stood up a little straighter. "Everything's going very smoothly," said Gavin, a steely edge to his voice. "We were just explaining to the students that you like to sample their efforts at the end of the day."

"Good. That'll keep them on their toes," said Roman, completely ignoring everyone else in the room. "I'll be back at half-past four, on the dot, and I'll send

Monique in later to let you know whether or not Ms. Floyd-Martin's decided to grace us with her presence." He pounded a fist on the arm of the chair. "I'm furious that she hasn't bothered to get back to me yet."

As he turned and flounced out of the room without another word, Monique raced to keep up and Gavin shot him a look of pure contempt.

"Oh, blimey," said Izzy, dusting flour off herself. "That could have gone better."

"Who's that woman with him?" said Roy.

The smile left Larissa's face for a split second. "Monique Hathaway—she's Roman's assistant. Just so you know, she records all Roman's conversations. He's had so many people threaten to sue him over the years for things he's said, he asked Monique to start keeping a record so he can check back to see whether or not he actually did say what he's being accused of."

"And he usually did," said Gavin, with a dark look.

Larissa clapped her hands. "Right, well, I think a change of mood is in order. "She threw Gavin a glare. "We'd better get on, or we won't be ready for Roman when he comes back, and that'll never do."

The next hour was spent going through kitchen etiquette, and all the equipment. "Okay," said Larissa. "As you'll have seen from your itineraries, we're going to be making bread today; mini raisin loaves, a cottage loaf, and granary baguettes. As with all the lessons, this will be a watch and learn format. Gavin and I will take turns with the practical demonstrations while the other will be on hand to help should you need to call on us.

And don't worry if you feel you're being left behind—
this isn't a race, so we'll wait until you've caught up.
Everyone ready to start?"

"Ready and waiting," said Ava, tying her apron
strings behind her back. "This could get messy. I
always remember my mother telling me that dough
should be as wet as possible for the best bread. 'The
wetter, the better', she used to say." She flashed a
knowing smile at the rest of the class.

The students followed along with Gavin as he
measured ingredients and demonstrated how to knead
the dough by hand until it was smooth and elastic.

"My wrists are killing me," grumbled Roy. "Is
this the workout version of the course? I thought we'd
be using electricity."

Larissa grinned. "Kneading by hand is hard
work, especially if you've never done it before, but the
results are so worth it. Take a rest if you need to but,
believe me, there aren't many things as satisfying as
seeing bread come out of the oven that you've made
yourself, completely from scratch, and completely by
hand. We could use machines but this way's much
better." She reached up and patted Roy on the shoulder.
"Trust me, you won't be sorry."

"She's right," puffed Ava, as she punched and
pummelled her dough into submission. "Unlike making
a cake, where a light touch is essential, making bread
requires completely the opposite." She blew her fringe
out of one eye. "The more you bash the dough around,
the better… unless you're working with a no-knead
dough, of course, when vigorous kneading isn't

necessary, but an extra-long proving time is essential. I remember when..."

"*Ava!*" said Harriett, her cheeks bright pink and covered in flour. "We could do without the running commentary, if you don't mind. It's like sharing a bench with Mrs. Beeton."

Ava's eyebrows lifted in surprise, and she gave a disgruntled tut. "Well, I'm sorry I spoke. I was only trying to share my extensive knowledge of bread making. I used to bake every day when Derek and I first got married, remember? But if you're not interested, I won't say another word." She zipped a floury finger across her pursed lips and Harriett shook her head in exasperation.

"Okay, everyone," said Gavin, "when you've finished kneading your doughs, and they're nice and smooth and stretchy, put each batch into one of the large bowls on your bench. Don't forget to oil the bowl lightly first, then cover it with cling-film. We're going to leave them for a couple of hours to prove, and then we'll carry on after lunch. If you'd like to..."

He was interrupted by the door flying open again, and Monique scuttling in, tape recorder in hand.

"Just to let you know that I called Olivia Floyd-Martin to ask if she was coming to the tasting session this afternoon, and she's confirmed she is, so make sure that everything's perfect for her, won't you?" She twitched and cleared her throat.

"Everything *will* be perfect," said Gavin, coolly. "Just as it's been every day since we opened, and will continue to be. As I've told Roman countless times, we always do our best to maintain high standards, but you already know that, don't you, Sneak? You must have recorded it on that little machine of yours a hundred times.

"I'm warning you, Gavin," said Monique, her eyes flashing with anger. "Stop calling me that!" She switched on the tape machine, thrusting it in front of his face. "I swear, if you say it again, I'll…"

"You'll what? You'll run and tell tales to Roman, like you always do?" said Gavin, speaking defiantly into the machine with a stony-faced expression. "Is it any wonder we call you Monique the Sneak?"

Monique put her face closer to his, her lips curled in a sneer, and lowered her voice to a murmur. "If Roman hears what you just said, he won't be very happy—you know how protective of me he can be. If I was you, I wouldn't want to do anything that made him any more annoyed with you than he already is. Such a shame he found out about your extra-curricular activity." She jerked her head towards Larissa. "How you thought you'd get away with it, I don't know, especially as you know how he feels about that kind of after-work pastime.

"And we all know how much you both need these jobs, what with your personal circumstances being as they are. Shame your name's been removed from the shortlist of people who are in the frame to become the manager of this place." She smirked. "Your days are numbered, Doyle. Roman's on the lookout for replacements for you and Goldilocks over there, and I hear *The President Hotel* has some very good staff. I suggest you both start looking for other jobs, pronto." She threw him a spiteful smile before twirling on her heel and leaving the room.

Ava and Harriett exchanged a look of amazement. Being at the front of the room, with their scandal-seeking ears on stalks, they'd heard every whispered word Monique had said.

"Did you hear that?" said Harriett to Ava out of the corner of her mouth. "She said Gavin's days are numbered because Roman found out about his relationship with Larissa. The poor things—they must feel awful."

"And what about Olivia coming to the tasting session?" muttered Ava, her sulk of moments before forgotten. "If what Harry told us yesterday is true, why on earth would she have agreed to set foot in this school?"

Harriett shrugged. "We'll find out soon enough, won't we?"

As Gavin glowered, Larissa pointed to the far side of the kitchen, her face flushed. "Er, sorry about that. Lunch has been set out for you in the staff dining room, just through that door. Help yourself to as much as you like, but please be back by two o'clock. We'll see you all later."

———————

"Well, it's pretty obvious there's no love lost between Gavin and Monique," said Roy, loading his plate with sandwiches, "I was trying to hear what she was saying, but I couldn't make it out." He gave Ava and Harriett a pointed look. "You didn't happen to hear, did you?"

"No. No, we didn't," said Harriett, jumping in before Ava said anything, and accidentally gave the game away about Gavin and Larissa's relationship. "Whatever the problem is, though, I expect it'll blow over soon."

"I don't know about you, but I'm going to be shaking in my shoes when Olivia Floyd-Martin walks in," said Izzy, as she scattered croutons over a bowl of pea and ham soup. "It was bad enough when Roman turned up, but Olivia's the real deal as far as I'm concerned. The way she's got to the top of her field through sheer hard work is amazing. *And* she hasn't needed any TV show to help her get there. They've both got massive egos, though, haven't they? I'll be interested to see how they are in each other's company."

"Actually," said Ava, who couldn't bear to let the opportunity to name-drop pass her by, "Harriett and I know Olivia quite well. Of course, you don't live in St. Eves, do you, but we've lived here all our lives."

"What, you mean you actually *know* her?" said Izzy, wide-eyed as she buttered a bread roll.

"Oh, yes," said Ava. "And as we're talking about her..." She took a furtive look around the dining room. "I shouldn't really tell you this, but..."

"Then don't," said Harriett, giving her a warning look. "You just can't help yourself, can you?

You see a chance to gossip to someone, and you're off."

"Oh, piffle," said Ava, waving away Harriett's concern. "It's perfectly harmless information." She turned back to Izzy. "Anyway, years ago, when Olivia was just starting out, she worked at a restaurant out in the sticks called *The Old Barn*."

"Didn't she start her career at The President, then?" said Roy.

Ava shook her head. "That's what most people think, but we know the *real* story."

Izzy gave her a quizzical look. "What story?"

"Well, she was working at *The Old Barn* as a commis chef when the sous chef and the head chef both went down with flu. She had to step in at short notice, and that's when she got a real taste for running a kitchen. It went so well, she stood in regularly after that but one night, a restaurant critic for the local newspaper came in and complained about one of her sauces. From what we can gather, he was perfectly polite about it, but Olivia went bonkers. She's a bit like a mother bear protecting her cubs when people criticise her kitchen, you see. Anyway, the next time he came in, she threw him out."

"Oh. Well, I can understand she didn't like the criticism, but that's what restaurant critics do, isn't it? They critique," said Izzy. "It was a bit petty to throw him out."

Ava shook her head. "No, dear, you don't understand. When I say, "she threw him out", I mean that quite literally. She threw him out of the restaurant through a plate-glass window. Apparently, he recovered from his injuries, but one of the conditions of him not pressing charges against her was that she had to promise to see a professional about her anger issues."

"Wow!" Izzy's jaw dropped. "You're kidding?"

"I'm not surprised," said Roy, stuffing a sandwich into his mouth. "I got caught short this morning when I went out for a walk, and had to stop at The President to use the loo. There's a full-size framed photo of her hanging in the lobby, and she looks mean."

"Well, she wouldn't look quite so mean if she made a little effort to look less like a street-thug, and more like a lady," said Ava. "She's a prime candidate for a makeover, that one."

Roy shrugged and wiped a blob of mustard from his chin. "I dunno about that, but I wouldn't cross her, that's for sure, and I'm six-foot six. So what happened after she threw the bloke through the window?"

"She came back to St. Eves, started having therapy, and ended up at *The President Hotel* with her tail between her legs," said Ava, spreading paté onto a cracker.

"Did she tell them why she'd had to leave the other restaurant?" asked Roy.

"Yes, she told them everything, apparently," said Ava. "It was only because she'd started having therapy that they took her on, but they didn't stand for any nonsense—she had to start at the bottom and work her way up. She had to earn her cooking stripes all over again, but that's when her career really took off, because that's when she realised she wanted to be a world-class chef. After a year, she left The President, went all over the world, and ended up back here in St. Eves fifteen years ago."

Roy nodded as he tucked into his lunch like he hadn't eaten for a month. He reached for a flaky apple pastry and dunked it into a mug of coffee. "Well, not that I'm condoning what she did to that guy, but what's done is done, and she's obviously doing alright now, so good for her."

"Yeah, good for her," repeated Izzy, punching the air. "Girl Power!"

"I'm just popping to the bathroom," said Harriett. "Then I expect we'd better get back to the kitchen. I won't be long."

The dining room had two doors; one which led back into the kitchen, and the other which led into a small corridor where the bathrooms and a cloakroom could be found. As she pushed open the door to the ladies' room, she heard raised voices coming from the kitchen, and went back to listen.

"Monique must be bluffing, don't you think?" said Larissa's shaky voice. "How could Roman have found out about us?"

There was a pause before Gavin's voice broke the silence. "She's not bluffing. He found out because when we went out for your birthday, he and Monique were in the Italian restaurant on the marina. You and I rolled out of the pub and walked right past them on our way home. If you recall, we weren't exactly behaving like platonic friends, were we?"

"But how do you *know* he saw us?" asked Larissa.

"Because he told me the next day. We were talking about the financial forecast for next year and he suddenly asked me how long you and I been seeing each other. It caught me completely off-guard."

"Oh, Gavin! You didn't tell him, did you?"

"Well, that wasn't the intention, but he put me on the spot. I tried to deny it but you know what Roman's like. He can see through a lie at ten paces. And why is there never enough damn sugar for my coffee in this place?! It's a kitchen, for God's sake!"

"Oh, stop shouting!" said Larissa. "There's some more sugar in the cupboard next to the fridge. And don't change the subject. Why didn't you tell me he's known about us for so long?"

"Because I didn't want to worry you."

"Well I'm worried now, so that plan didn't work out, did it?" Larissa's voice rose an octave. "What did he say? Did he say he was going to fire us? Did he say anything about me?"

"No, he just said he was very disappointed," said Gavin, "and that he'd have to think about what he was going to do about it. He gave me a long lecture about how he'd thought I was the right guy to manage this place, but now he's not so sure. I reckon he was just trying to make me sweat, though. Considering I thought I was going to get the sack, I think I got off pretty lucky."

"Maybe he's getting soft in his old age?" said Larissa, her voice hopeful.

Gavin laughed. "Not likely. If anything, the more successful he gets, the more ruthless he gets. But he didn't fire me on the spot, so maybe he's having second thoughts about his ridiculous rule that staff shouldn't 'fraternise' with each other outside of work."

"I can't believe it," said Larissa. "We've been so careful for so long, and the one time we let our guard slip, that grumpy git was there to see it."

"We weren't careful the other day, were we?" said Gavin. "When that bloody woman walked in on us. Look, stop worrying so much. If Roman was going to do anything about it, he'd have done it by now."

"But neither of us can afford to lose these jobs," whined Larissa. "What if he *does* decide to get rid of us? And what about your shares in the school? He can't take them away, can he?"

Gavin swore loudly. "Look, I told you not to worry. If Roman even thinks about taking away our jobs or my shares, I won't be responsible for my actions. You know I can't afford to lose this salary, so if he's planning to get rid of me, he'd better think again. Anyway, I don't know how, but I'll take care of it, okay? Right, I need a pee before the afternoon session gets started."

As Harriett heard the sound of Gavin's footsteps approaching the door, she slipped away into the ladies' room.

———————

At precisely four-thirty, the door to the kitchen opened and Roman burst in, followed by Monique with her tape recorder, and Olivia, the expression on her face completely unreadable.

"I'm sure no introductions are necessary, but in case they are, this is Olivia Floyd-Martin," said Roman, settling himself at the head of the long table and rubbing his hands together. "Sit down, Olivia. You're in for a treat. You wouldn't know, of course, but the most satisfying thing about having a culinary school is seeing first-hand how much the students have learned." He gave her a sly sidewards look, knowing how deep his words would cut.

Olivia sucked in a deep breath and pulled out a chair. "Yes, I'm sure it's very rewarding," she said, through gritted teeth, throwing a scowl at her nemesis.

"Right, what do we have here?" Roman beckoned Gavin with a flick of his index finger.

"There's a white cottage loaf, granary baguettes, and mini raisin loaves, which will go very nicely with the sharp cheddar cheese that's on the board."

Roman licked his lips. "Come on, Olivia," he said, munching on a raisin loaf and pushing the breadboard towards her. "Get stuck in."

Olivia stared at the board before picking up a slice of bread. She turned it over and over in her hands before tossing it to one side and pushing her chair away from the table, sending it toppling to the floor with a crash. "This was a mistake. I should never have come." With a face like thunder, she stomped out of the room, leaving only the sound of Roman stuffing his face behind her.

He looked after her, a triumphant smile on his lips. "Oh dear, looks like poor Olivia can't handle a little competition. Probably a little too close to home for her, I expect," he said, pulling the breadboard towards him. "Never mind, all the more for me."

He chuckled to himself as he slathered another raisin loaf with butter before shoving the whole thing into his mouth.

During the exchange of words, every pair of eyes in the room had flitted between Roman and Olivia.

Every pair of eyes except one.

From the moment Olivia had entered the room to the moment she left, one person's intense gaze had been trained only on her.

When she left, the person smiled and half-listened to the chatter in the room.

CHAPTER 5

"Now, I'm sure you've all eaten pastry before,
but you may not have made it yourself."

Larissa smiled out at the class during Tuesday's
lesson. "Although the shop bought varieties are
perfectly acceptable, and they certainly save time, today
we're going to show you how to make your own, and
it's really not as daunting as you might think. We're
going to start with a basic shortcrust pastry which we're
going to use later to make custard tarts. And then we're
going to…"

The door burst open and Monique rushed in.
Her usually neatly styled hair was dishevelled, her
flawless make-up absent. Dark circles under her eyes
only highlighted the fact that her face was blotchy and
tear-streaked.

Gavin opened his mouth to make a snide remark
but shut it again when he realised something was amiss.

"Can I s-speak to both of you outside, please?"
said Monique, clutching at the front of her jacket, the
buttons of which were all in the wrong buttonholes.

"What on earth can be going on?" said Ava, as
Gavin and Larissa left the room. "She looked ever so
distressed, didn't she?"

"Maybe she dropped her tape recorder down the
toilet," said Roy.

"Don't be mean," said Izzy. "Even major divas
have their off days. We don't know what's wrong, so
you shouldn't be so quick to judge."

"Maybe she's had a disagreement with Roman?" said Harriett. "Perhaps he's fired her?"

Izzy shrugged. "Maybe. Although that wouldn't be such a bad thing, based on his behaviour yesterday. He was so rude, don't you think?"

"I don't know why you're so surprised," said Roy. "He's *always* rude. That's why he's so popular, although I've no idea why."

"Because rude seems to be the in-thing," said Izzy. "Look at all the TV chefs and talent show judges who've made a fortune by behaving badly. Roman's just jumping on the bandwagon."

Roy nodded. "That's probably why he's so mega-rich. He must have been right at the back of the queue when manners were handed out."

"I have to admit," said Izzy, "seeing him behave that way isn't quite so entertaining when you experience it in person, as it is when you see it on TV."

The door opened and Gavin and Larissa walked back in with sombre expressions on their pale faces.

"I'm sorry, but we're going to have to cancel today's lesson." Gavin scratched the back of his neck awkwardly. "Possibly the rest of the course."

"Why?" asked Harriett. "What's happened?"

"Roman was taken ill yesterday evening. The doctors aren't sure what's wrong with him but he's in a critical condition. Monique's come straight from the hospital."

"Oh my goodness!" said Ava, her hands flying to her mouth. "How dreadful! I wonder what on earth could have happened?"

Gavin shrugged. "No idea. Monique just said he had really bad stomach pains, and he seemed to be paralysed."

"He's staying at The President, isn't he?" said Harriett. "I know he and Olivia have had their differences but, even so, this will be terribly upsetting for her."

"It's things like this that resolve feuds between friends, you know," said Ava. "It'll probably make Olivia realise that their stupid rivalry is just petty."

"Well, let's hope it was nothing Roman ate in her restaurant that made him bad," Roy piped up. "It won't do her reputation any good if it's her food that's given him gut ache."

Everyone exchanged glances amid an uneasy silence.

"I'm sure it wasn't," said Gavin hastily. "And I'm sure we'll find out more sooner or later but, under the circumstances, I think it'd be better if we called it a day. I'm sorry, but it wouldn't be right to carry on with the course until Roman's at least off the critical list. If it suits you all, we can pick up again then."

Everyone began to pack up their things in silence, then Roy said, "But after this week, you've got bookings all the way to Christmas, haven't you? When are you going to fit us in? Look, I know this probably isn't the best time to ask, but if the course *doesn't* restart, will we get a refund? It cost a fortune, and we've only done a day."

"Roy! How could you ask something like that at a time like this?" said Izzy, shaking her head. "Talk about inappropriate."

Roy shrugged. "Well, as we might not be coming back here, when was I *supposed* to ask? I'm not expecting anyone to whip out their wallet and refund me on the spot, but if someone could arrange for us to get at least *some* of our money back if we don't make up the time, that'd be good. Don't tell me the same thought wasn't going through your mind, Izzy." He pulled out the linings of his empty pockets. "I don't know about you, but I'm fresh out of money trees."

Larissa held up a hand. "Look, can you leave it with us for the time being? This news has knocked us sideways—I hope you understand. If all goes well, we could be back here in a day or two, but we just can't say at the moment. We've got all your details on file, so we'll be in touch as soon as we know what's happening."

Roy nodded. "No problem. I'm booked in at *The St. Eves' Tavern* for the rest of the week so I'll be around until Saturday. It's not like I've got anyone to get back to, so I'm in no rush to leave. I might as well be here as anywhere else."

"Same here," said Izzy. "I'm not expected back at work until next Tuesday."

They gathered their things and congregated outside on the pavement.

"I don't know what your plans are," said Ava to Izzy and Roy, "but we're going to lunch tomorrow at a lovely little café we know. It's called Charlotte's Plaice, and it's at the end of the marina. No pressure, of course, but you're both very welcome to come along if you'd like to. We can introduce you to some of our friends."

"Izzy nodded. "Thanks, that's super kind of you. I feel a bit odd after that news, so it'd be nice not to be wandering around on my own."

Ava smiled and hung her handbag over her arm. "Well, there's no point in mooching around with miserable faces, is there? Shall we meet you at the café tomorrow? Say, around one o'clock?"

"Suits me," said Izzy. "You fancy coming along, Roy?"

He shrugged a broad shoulder. "Might as well."

"And our main news this morning, which we'll be updating you on throughout the day, is that TV star and restaurant critic, Roman Haley, was taken ill yesterday evening at The President Hotel in St. Eves, and rushed to St. Eves' General Hospital where he remains in critical condition. Doctors are said to be extremely concerned for Mr. Haley's health and have indicated that the prognosis is not good. Early reports suggest that Mr. Haley may have been suffering from some kind of gastric issue. We're going live now to our reporter, Andrew Somerfield, who's outside the hospital. Andrew, what can you tell us?"

"Well, Patricia, all we know so far is that a call was made to the emergency services yesterday evening at around ten-forty-five by the hotel Manager, Simon Clancy, after he was informed that Mr. Haley had been

found in his bedroom, in a semi-conscious state. We understand that earlier in the evening, he'd been suffering from excruciating stomach pains and had been vomiting.

"An ambulance arrived soon after it was called, and Mr. Haley received medical attention en route to the hospital, where he was put on a ventilator. At the moment, we don't have any clear information as to the exact cause of his condition, but as soon as we do, you'll be the first to know. At the request of Mr. Haley's assistant, Monique Hathaway, the hotel and hospital staff have been doing their best to keep the situation under wraps but, during the night, a hospital porter confirmed that Mr. Haley had been admitted.

"Who alerted the hotel Manager to Mr. Haley's condition, Andrew? Do you know?"

"We think it might have been Miss. Hathaway, although that has yet to be confirmed. Since news of Mr. Haley's admission to hospital was announced during the early hours of this morning, fans have been making their way here to leave get well cards and bouquets of flowers outside the hospital entrance. I have a feeling the next time we speak, Patricia, that crowd will have grown considerably. For the moment, back to you in the studio."

"See, what did we tell you?" said Ava, as she sat at Charlotte's kitchen table, pouring tea from a giant teapot.

"You should have seen Roman's assistant," said Harriett. "She looked absolutely dreadful when she came to the school to break the news. She was as white as a sheet and she looked like she hadn't had a wink of sleep. Poor thing."

"I bet Olivia's feeling awful, too," said Charlotte, folding a basket of clean laundry. "I know they'd had their differences, but he was still an old friend, wasn't he?"

"That's what *I* said, but you wouldn't have thought so if you'd seen them yesterday," said Ava. "She came to the tasting session after Roman invited her, but she stormed out without eating a thing. It was all she could do to look at him—she obviously didn't want to be there at all."

"Well, it must have been difficult for her, mustn't it?" said Charlotte. "Seeing as she was the one who always wanted to open a culinary school in St. Eves. I'm sure she was upset yesterday, but I bet she'll be thinking how petty it all is today. "

"Hmm, I expect you're right." Ava stirred her tea and looked at Charlotte's stomach. "D'you still think you're going to go full-term?"

"I reckon so." Charlotte sat down and put her feet on a footstool. "Unlike Molly, I have a feeling this one's staying put until the last minute."

"I'm counting the days," said Ava. "I just can't wait to meet the little one. Actually, talking of meeting people, we met a lovely couple at the school. They're staying at *The St. Eves' Tavern*, but they'll be at a loose end until the course gets going again—*if* it gets going— so I invited them to join us for lunch at the café tomorrow. If you're not busy, you could come along and meet them if you'd like to? They're awfully nice."

Charlotte nodded. "Okay, I will. And Molly's going to camp tomorrow, so I'll be able to come and have lunch without having to rush off to pick her up from school."

"Wonderful," said Ava. "Tomorrow it is, then."

CHAPTER 6

At the school gates, Nathan and Charlotte were doing their best to comfort Molly, who was sobbing against Nathan's shoulder.

"You'll be fine, Mol." Nathan hugged her as she clung to him like a Velcro monkey.

"I don't want to go," she wailed, and tightened her grip around his neck.

Charlotte chewed on her lip, fighting against the instinct to bundle Molly into the car and drive back home where they could snuggle under a blanket on the couch and read books all day in their pyjamas.

From the moment she'd received the email from the school about the trip, Charlotte had ignored the niggling doubt that Molly might not be ready to spend a week away from home. Sleepovers with friends were one thing, but a whole week away from her family was an entirely different scenario.

"It'll be great for her to experience stuff like this," Nathan had said. "I went to camp twice when I was at school and I loved every minute."

Mrs. Willetts, Molly's teacher, approached.

"Hi, Mr. and Mrs. Costello. Hi, Molly." She gave Charlotte and Nathan a wink and looked up at the grey sky. "Shame we haven't got a bit of sun to see us off, isn't it? You know, Molly, if you want to come to camp, we'll have to leave soon if we're going to get to the farm in time to feed the animals this afternoon."

Molly's wailing turned to a whimper. "What animals?" she said, in a muffled voice.

"The animals at the farm. There are chickens and goats and cows and rabbits and sheep. And I think there are some lambs and puppies, too. Oh, and four rescue donkeys."

The whimpering stopped. "I didn't know about the animals." Molly sniffed as she peered at Mrs. Willetts through tear-drenched lashes. "Are you *sure* there'll be animals?" she asked, quirking a sceptical brow, a mannerism she'd inherited from Nathan.

Mrs. Willetts chuckled. "Yes, I'm positive."

"That sounds alright, doesn't it, Mol?" said Nathan.

She nodded, and released her grip on his neck. "When are we leaving?" she said, as she wriggled to get down from his arms and pulled a sleeve across her eyes. "I have to go and tell Esme and Erin!" she called over her shoulder to Charlotte and Nathan, throwing them a smile as she went in search of her friends.

As she ran off, in a decidedly happier mood, Charlotte breathed a sigh of relief.

———————

Roy settled himself at a table on the café's terrace and stretched out his long legs. "Charlotte's *Plaice?* Is that a spelling mistake?"

"No, it's a play on words," said Ava. "When Charlotte bought the café, the first thing she cooked was plaice, hence the name."

Izzy joined them at the table after admiring the boats in the marina. "What a fabulous spot," she said, pulling off her hat and gloves. "What I wouldn't give for a place like this of my own." She pointed to Jess, who was serving a nearby table. "Is that Charlotte?"

"Oh no," said Harriett. "She's on maternity leave. That's Jess. They're very close friends. Charlotte should be here any minute, though. And this is Betty. She's a friend of mine and Ava's."

Betty looked up from her magazine and reached out a hand. "I wondered when someone was going to introduce me," she said, with a welcoming smile. "Nice to meet you both."

"I don't suppose Charlotte's looking for anyone to help out, is she?" asked Roy. "I could just see myself behind a bar, serving drinks and being front of house."

"I shouldn't think so," said Ava. "When Charlotte's not here, her godmother, Laura, and Jess, run the place very well on their own, so I think you'd be surplus to requirements, dear. Charlotte and Jess have run it together ever since Charlotte came back from Spain and bought the place."

"Spain? Why was she in Spain?" asked Izzy.

"She moved there with her parents when she was young. But they were killed in a car crash—terribly tragic—so she came back to St. Eves."

"Oh, that's awful," said Izzy. "Poor thing."

"Yes, it *was* awful," said Betty. "They were lovely people."

"I think we'd better change the subject," said Harriett. "Here she comes now. Let's make some room at the table."

With the dogs in tow, Charlotte arrived on the terrace to be caught up in hugs and noisy cries of "welcome back" from her regular customers who were enjoying a spot of lunch.

"I've only been gone since yesterday!" She laughed as she made her way to the table, the dogs pulling at their leads to get to Ava, who usually carried treats for them in her bag. "Hi, everyone." She held out a hand to Roy and Izzy and introduced herself. "Sorry I'm a bit late," she said, flopping into the seat. "It's such a relief to sit down these days. And I can't stop eating. Has anyone else ordered?"

"No dear, we were waiting for you," said Ava, as she waited for Pippin and Panda to sit before she passed them each a treat. "I don't suppose you happened to notice if there was any update on Roman Haley on the news before you left home, did you?"

"No, there's been nothing new, just that he's still in a critical condition. It's terrible, isn't it?"

"I think he's a goner," said Roy, bending down to tickle the dogs. "Excruciating stomach pains don't just come from nowhere, do they?"

"It must have been something he ate," said Betty. "I get the most awful wind if I eat something that doesn't agree with me, and the pain just doubles me over."

"Yes, but that's hardly the same, is it?" said Harriett. "That always goes away, doesn't it?"

"Oh yes," said Betty. "Usually after I…"

"Yes, thank you very much, Bet!" interrupted Ava, her eyebrows shooting up at the turn the lunchtime conversation had taken. "I'm sure Roy and Izzy aren't interested in hearing about your gas." She leaned over and muttered to Charlotte. "Although, between you and me, I'm sure if someone lit a match in her general direction, it'd blast her into outer space."

"Afternoon, everyone." Jess appeared at the table and gave Charlotte a hug. "Sorry it's taken me a while to get to you."

"Don't worry, you're obviously in the middle of the lunchtime rush, and we were quite happy admiring the view," said Izzy. "I'm either stuck indoors, or in a traffic jam for most of the day. You're so lucky to work in such a fabulous setting."

"Yeah," said Roy. "And I spend most of the day in a kitchen. This view beats that one hands down."

When all the orders were taken, and drinks had been delivered to the table, an easy conversation developed amongst the group.

"So, how do you two know each other?" asked Betty.

"We met a few years ago at a music festival, didn't we, Iz?" said Roy. "But we lost touch until we met up again last year. You know how it is, I was busy, Izzy was busy, but we eventually got back in touch and arranged to meet up."

"So, are you a chef?" said Charlotte. "You said you worked in a kitchen."

"Nothing so grand," he replied. "What I'd really like to do is be famous for doing something that makes people sit up and take notice, but as that's not likely, I'm working as a kitchen assistant in a care home instead."

He grinned. "I do all the jobs no one else wants to do. You know, preparing the veg, washing up, cleaning. Sometimes I help take the meals round to the residents, which is great—I've been told I've got an excellent bedside manner." He cleared his throat. "I'm looking for another job, though. The care home's only temporary. I used to be a medical supplies salesman, but I was made redundant last year."

"Oh, I'm sorry," said Charlotte.

"Don't be. It wasn't all bad. One of the nurses I know at the local hospital put in a good word for me when the position at the care home came up and I got my details in early. I couldn't believe it when I got the job." He sighed. "Thank God I'd already paid for Becky's course before I was made redundant. There's no way I could have afforded it on the measly salary I earn now."

"Well, whoever she is, Becky's a very lucky girl," said Charlotte. "I hope she appreciates how thoughtful you are."

There was an awkward silence. "Doubtful," said Roy, forcing a laugh. "We broke up last year, just after Izzy had told me about Roman's course and I'd booked Becky onto it as a surprise. She met up with a guy at her school reunion and decided she'd rather be with him than me. Ironically, he looks very similar to Roman Haley, minus the twirly moustache."

"Oh. I'm so sorry. I had no idea." Charlotte's cheeks flushed. "Me and my big mouth. I suppose there's no chance of a reconciliation?"

"Not likely. Our divorce was finalised on Christmas Eve. It was a pretty dismal year all round."

"Oh," said Charlotte, her cheeks flaming. "Well, couldn't you at least have got your money back for the course?"

Roy shrugged. "Some of it, but it hardly seemed worth it, so I decided to come along myself. Not that I'm a Haley fan—I think the guy's an absolute moron—unlike Becky who thought the sun shone out of his backside." He scowled. "I thought I might as well do something, though, rather than mope around thinking about her."

He looked around the table and gave everyone a crooked grin. "Sorry, I'm sure the last thing you're interested in are the specifics of my love life. Or should I say, the lack of it. Anyway, that's about all there is to know about me. Roy Tanner; an ordinary guy who's extraordinarily unlucky in love." He looked away and fixed a stare on the boats, bobbing on the gentle motion of the sea, and Betty filled another awkward silence.

"And what about you, Izzy," she asked, dunking a cocktail cherry into her apple juice. "What do you do with your time when you're not in St. Eves?"

"Well, let's see… I live in a village called Mousehoole, I'm also divorced, I'm a member of my local ladies' cricket team, my pride and joy is my little Fiat that I've just had resprayed lime-green, and I'm a buyer for a tea company." Izzy grinned and nibbled on the lemon slice from her tonic water. "It's only part-time—I job- share with another girl—but I love it."

"Ah, I saw your car in the carpark," said Charlotte. "You tend to see a lot of the same cars every day, so unfamiliar ones stand out. And I don't know anything about cricket, but a tea buyer sounds like my dream job—I'm an absolute tea nut! My mum drank gallons of it when she was pregnant with me, and I definitely got the taste for it. Even when we lived in Spain, where they take their coffee very seriously, Mum and I always managed to sniff out a proper cup of tea."

"A woman after my own heart," said Izzy, raising her glass. "I can't even function until I've had at least two cups of tea in the morning."

"I like tea *and* coffee," said Betty. "It depends on my mood. My mum loved coffee and my dad loved tea. I've still got all his old teapots at home. He used to collect them."

"Really? Oh, I'd love to see them," said Izzy. "I love stuff like that."

"Well, you're welcome any time, love," said Betty. "Here, I'll jot my number down and you can call me. We can arrange something for before you leave. And I can take you to the social club—it'll be nice to have a new face around the place. Be prepared to be chatted up by all the old widowers, though."

Izzy laughed as she slipped Betty's phone number into her pocket. "I'll remember that. And I'll definitely give you a call."

"Oh look, here comes Jess, the food must be on its way." Harriett smoothed her serviette over her lap.

Jess was unusually flustered as she approached the table. "Sorry, your food's not ready yet, but I had to come and tell you that there's just been a newsflash. Roman Haley died an hour ago. And his death is being treated as suspicious."

CHAPTER 7

Majestic in its prime seafront position, *The President Hotel's* elegant ivory façade was bathed in the muted glow of the weak spring sunshine.

Usually, a lone doorman stood outside St. Eves' only five-star hotel, hailing taxis, welcoming guests, and bidding them farewell. Today, though, he was being besieged by reporters who wanted to know if he'd been on duty when the ambulance had arrived, and whether he'd seen Roman Haley being stretchered away.

Ever since the medical staff at the hospital had expressed doubt that the cause of death could be due to something more sinister than natural causes, there was only one question that Nathan, along with Detective Sergeants Ben Dillon and Fiona Farrell wanted answered as they arrived at the hotel. Had Roman Haley been murdered?

"The whole world and his wife's going to have trampled all over the bedroom by now," snapped Fiona. "If there *has* been any foul play, any evidence that may have been left behind is going to be completely contaminated."

As they walked into the entrance lobby, the hotel Manager, Simon Clancy, virtually flung himself at them with relief.

"Oh, thank God you're here!" he said dramatically, as he grabbed Nathan by the elbow and steered him towards his office. "There's a hysterical woman in there," he jabbed a finger towards the door, "and Roman Haley's lying dead in a hospital bed after falling ill at this hotel."

He rubbed his right temple with the pads of his fingers. "Of course, death is nothing we can't deal with... especially not after the last time we had an 'incident' here." He made quotation marks in the air with his fingers as he referenced the time a woman had been pushed to her death from the rooftop restaurant. "But what I can't deal with is *that*." He jerked a thumb at his office door. "She came back from the hospital in a terrible state. I've been trying to get some sense out of her, but she's so distraught, she can barely speak. She was wailing so much, I thought it best to stick her in there. At least she's out of the way of any guests."

"Who is she?" asked Fiona.

"Monique Hathaway, the grieving personal assistant. It was her who found him." Simon pursed his lips before dropping his voice to a whisper. "In *her* bed, if you don't mind, not his. That's one thing the news report got wrong, but I'm in no hurry to put it right. I don't want people thinking *The President* is *that* sort of hotel. The last thing we need is to be inundated with bed hoppers."

Simon was a mean-spirited stickler for the rules, and the fact that Roman had slept in someone else's bed, rather than his own, seemed to bother him more than the fact that he was dead. "Anyway, can you please sort her out?"

Nathan nodded. "Okay. Fiona and I will have a word with her. Ben, can you get up to the room and see what's going on? We'll catch up with you in a while."

"If you could get rid of her asap, I'd appreciate it," said Simon, as he ran his hands over his bald head and down his cheeks, giving him the appearance of a mournful Bloodhound. "I need my office back."

———————

Once she'd calmed down, Monique blew her nose forcefully and pulled off her false eyelashes.

"I was at the hospital and they told me to come back here. They said there was nothing I could do and I should try to get some sleep, seeing as I'd been there all night." Her eyes widened. "How they expect me to sleep after what's happened, I don't know. Although, even if I could, I can't get into my room."

"Yes, sorry about that," said Fiona. "We're checking it, so you won't be allowed back in until we've finished. We'll be as quick as we can, but I'm sure you understand the need for us to be thorough. I'm sure Mr. Clancy will move you to another room but, in the meantime, is there anything in your room you need urgently? Medication, for instance?"

Monique shook her head. "No, there's nothing. I've got my phone—that's all I need for now. I can buy anything else I need."

"I know this must be very difficult for you, but can you tell us what happened last night?" asked Fiona.

Monique blew her nose again and rubbed her eyes. "After we got back to the hotel, Roman went to his room to shower and change and then he came to my room at around six. We were supposed to be going out for dinner, but his stomach pains were getting worse so he decided he didn't want anything to eat. I've never known him to skip a meal, so he must have been really bad."

"Did he say how he was feeling?"

"Dizzy and sick, with terrible stomach cramps. He was in the bathroom for ages and when he came out, he was shaking and he looked grey. He said he just wanted to go to bed and sleep it off, so I left him and went down to the hotel restaurant." She picked at a hangnail on her thumb. "You're probably thinking I should have guessed there was something seriously wrong, but I honestly thought he just had a stomach bug."

"And what happened later?" asked Fiona. "Take your time, there's no rush."

Monique took another tissue from a pack in her pocket and gulped.

"I got back around half-past ten and he was in bed, lying on his side. I thought he was asleep but when I went to the bathroom, I had to walk past him and I saw that his eyes were half open. He'd thrown up all over the pillowcase and there was so much sweat pouring out of him, his hair was stuck to him and the sheets were soaked—they were clinging to him. I still thought he must have some kind of bug, or something, but when I spoke to him, he didn't respond. I shook him and I just knew something was wrong. It was as though he was paralysed—he couldn't move—so I called reception and they got an ambulance."

She began to sob again. "I feel so awful. If only I'd got back from the restaurant earlier, he'd have got to the hospital quicker, but I got chatting to some of the other guests, and lost track of time. Roman might still be alive if I hadn't."

"Do you remember who the guests were?"

"Abigail and John—they were on their honeymoon—and a businessman called Tony. We got chatting at the bar, and I ended up staying for longer than I should." Monique frowned through her tears. "And I've just remembered something. At the hospital, they asked me what Roman had to eat yesterday. I couldn't think straight at the time but I've just remembered that all he had was Eggs Benedict for breakfast in the hotel dining room, and then he ate in the restaurant again at lunchtime—he had a double bacon burger and fries. After that, all he had was bread and cheese at the tasting session."

Nathan frowned. "The what?"

"The tasting session. It's what we call the last half hour of the day at the culinary school. It's when all the students taste each other's baking, but if Roman's around, he goes along too." Monique looked tired, and gripped by anxiety. "I mean, when he *was* around, he *used to* go along." She sighed. "Do you think you'd be able to let the hospital know? About what he ate, I mean."

"Of course," said Fiona. "One more question, if you don't mind." She flicked back in her notebook. "Why didn't Mr. Haley go back to his own room if he was feeling so bad? Why did he get into *your* bed?"

"Because we were in a relationship," said Monique. "I can assure you, I'm not in the habit of allowing just anyone into my room, let alone my bed." She stared at her hands, clasped in her lap. "Roman didn't like anyone to know about it, though. He didn't like his staff mixing business with pleasure, so he didn't want them to know that's exactly what we were doing."

"Okay, thank you." Fiona tapped the end of her pencil against her chin. "Look, as you were probably closer to Mr. Haley than anyone, can you give us any idea of who might want to do him harm?"

Monique gave her an incredulous look. "Almost everyone he met, I should think. He had a knack of instantly rubbing people up the wrong way. The only person I ever heard him being nice to was his Mum, but that's only because she was even worse than he was. Honestly, she was an absolute dragon of a woman. I'm surprised she didn't breathe fire."

She wiped her eyes again. "And there's Olivia Floyd-Martin, of course. There was definitely no love lost between those two. Word has it she was absolutely furious that Roman had opened a school here. She didn't even want to take part in the tasting session yesterday. Mind you, I don't blame her. She must have hated being a guest in the school she thought should be hers. Not that Roman cared what she thought—he only invited her because he knew it would get under her skin."

"What do you mean, she didn't want to take part?" asked Nathan.

"Well, Roman invited her to the tasting, but she left without eating anything. He was getting stuck in, but Olivia just stormed out."

Nathan and Fiona exchanged a glance.

"I thought it was odd," said Monique. "You'd have thought that, as she'd taken the trouble to go over to the school, the least she could have done was participate. Of course, Roman was delighted that she was upset. He must have listened to it on tape ten times when we left the school. He used to love reliving his 'triumphs', as he called them."

Nathan frowned. "Have I missed something? What was it that Roman listened to on tape?"

"Sorry, I should have explained," said Monique. "I used to tape everything for him so he always had proof of his conversations. People were forever accusing him of saying things he swore he didn't, so it was the only way he could be sure. After Olivia stormed out on Monday, Roman replayed the whole thing when we left." She put a hand into the inside pocket of her jacket. "See? I taped everything on one of these." She held up the old-fashioned dictating machine.

"I used it during the day, and Roman sometimes took it at night to record his thoughts on. Anyway, the conversation with Olivia shouldn't be too far back, let me see if I can find it." She rewound the tape and a whirring noise filled the silence. "Here we are, this should be about the right place." She pressed a button and Roman's and Olivia's short conversation drifted through the speaker, accompanied by a background of crackle.

"So what happened after Olivia said, 'This was a mistake. I should never have come'?" asked Fiona, shooting Nathan a perplexed glance.

"She just stormed out," said Monique. "She obviously never wanted to be at the school in the first place and she couldn't get out fast enough."

"Would you mind if we took that recorder with us for a while? There might be something on there that'll help us to figure out what happened to Mr. Haley."

Monique nodded and peered at Nathan through swollen eyelids. "I doubt that very much, but you can keep it forever for all I care. If I never see the damn thing again, it'll be too soon. I mean, who uses stuff like this these days? It went out with the ark." She dropped the dictating machine into the evidence bag Nathan had fished out of his pocket. "Roman was a complete technophobe—he couldn't work anything that was made after the eighties—trying to teach him how to use a mobile phone was a nightmare. Anyway, I've got loads of his tapes if you want them, too?"

"They might be helpful. Do you have them here?"

"They're in the bedside cabinet in the room. Second drawer down, I think. Keep them, if you want. I doubt I'll be needing them any more."

"One more thing," said Fiona. "Did Mr. Haley have any family? Apart from his mum."

Monique shook her head. "Actually, his mum died a couple of years ago, so there's no one now." She put a hand to her mouth which didn't quite cover her cavernous yawn. "I need to find Mr. Clancy and see if he can put me in another room. I really need to sleep."

"Well, thanks for talking to us," said Fiona. "You've been very helpful. As I said, I'm sure Mr. Clancy will be happy to move you to another room and, hopefully, your personal belongings should be ready for you to collect soon. Someone will be in touch to let you know when, and you can sign for them to get them back."

Monique nodded. "I'd better go and find somewhere else to get my head down." She rubbed a bloodshot eye and went in search of Simon Clancy.

"We need to speak to everyone who was at the cookery lesson on Monday," said Nathan. "And that includes Olivia Floyd-Martin."

CHAPTER 8

"Welcome to the lunchtime news, I'm Ayesha Dooley. We are continuing with coverage of our main story today, which is the death of TV personality and food critic, Roman Haley. Throughout the day, tributes have been pouring in as the plot continues to thicken regarding the circumstances surrounding his death. With more on this ever-developing story, we cross now to our reporter, Andrew Somerfield, who is outside St. Eves' General Hospital. What can you tell us, Andrew?

"Well, Ayesha, a source at the hospital told me earlier that it's believed Mr. Haley may have been deliberately poisoned, but that has yet to be confirmed. The same source told me that hospital staff tried for hours to save the life of the TV star but were unable to do so because his body wasn't responding to any treatment. According to the source, the symptoms Mr. Haley was suffering from were similar to those seen in rare cases of poisoning, but the substance that would cause those symptoms has yet to be established. I repeat, these statements have not been confirmed, but that appears to be the opinion of a number of hospital employees I've spoken to, all of whom wish to remain anonymous.

"To be sure that all possible sources of the suspected poisoning are established, the kitchens at The President Hotel were closed early this morning, as well as Mr. Haley's culinary school. Both premises are being inspected by the Environmental Health Agency, as they are the only two places in which Mr. Haley ate

*on the day he became ill. A thorough inspection will be
carried out, and the kitchens will remain closed until
the investigations have been concluded.*

*"As things stand, it's looking very much like Mr.
Haley's death will be attributed to foul play but, as I
said, this has yet to be confirmed. What I can tell you
for sure is that Mr. Haley's sudden death is a terrible
shock which will reverberate throughout the
community, and our thoughts are with his friends and
fans at this sad time. Of course, as soon as I have more
news, you'll be the first to know. For now, though, this
is Andrew Somerfield, reporting from St. Eves' General
Hospital. Back to you in the studio."*

Fiona turned down the volume on the TV in the
incident room. "What exactly did the doctor who spoke
to you say, Chief? Didn't she give any idea at all as to
the cause of death?"

Nathan shook his head. "Not exactly, but she
did say that none of the obvious reasons for his
symptoms checked out. She said she's only ever seen
all those symptoms presenting at the same time once
before, years ago, in a case of poisoning from which the
patient didn't recover. Obviously, she won't commit to
diagnosing anything, but she's concerned enough to
think the death is suspicious, as opposed to accidental
food poisoning, or something less sinister. Did you
have any luck with tracking down the guests Monique
spoke to in the bar?"

Fiona nodded. "Just like she said, a very lovey-
dovey, newly-married couple, and an auditor who's
here for a couple of days on business. The couple made

their reservation months ago, and the guy was transferred here on Monday from a bed and breakfast that had double-booked and didn't have a room for him. They appear to be genuine hotel guests, with no previous connection to Monique, or what happened to Roman."

Ben drummed a pen against the desk. "I know there's a lot of talk about this running feud between Roman and Olivia, but I can't believe she'd resort to murder over it, can you?"

Fiona shrugged. "Well, we know she's been volatile enough to cause people harm in a fit of temper in the past, but poisoning isn't something someone would do on impulse, is it? It's premeditated. She may react violently to a situation in the heat of the moment, but to take the time to plan a murder? I'm not so sure."

"Is there a rush job on the post-mortem, chief?" said Ben.

"Isn't there always? Although the toxicology reports might hold things up, so keep your fingers crossed for a quick result." Nathan scratched his chin, his nails rasping against the stubble. "Right, what's next?"

————————

Having stopped at her café for a mid-morning mug of tea and a jam tart, Charlotte was walking the dogs back home down the marina.

She was in no rush, and took her time, stopping to say hello and chat with customers and friends along the way.

"I'd better get off," she said, after a long catch-up with Will Goss, the owner of *The Bottle of Beer* pub. "These two need feeding."

"Be sure to tell Nathan to drop by one of these days, won't you?" said Will, with a cheery grin as he clasped his hands on top of his shaved head and flexed his back.

"I will. Although I've no idea when that'll be, what with everything that's going on. Anyway, good to see you."

As she went on her way, a figure coming towards her began to look more and more familiar. It wasn't often she saw Olivia Floyd-Martin in civvies instead of her gleaming chef's whites, but as she drew closer, she realised it was her.

At six foot, three inches tall, Olivia's shoulders had sagged so much, she looked a foot shorter. Her spiky bleached hair was flat to her head and her expression was one of anguish rather than irritation, as it so often was.

"Hi, Olivia. You don't look too happy? What's up?"

Olivia ran her hands down her face. "I had a call from Simon Clancy first thing this morning, suggesting it might be a good idea if I took some time off," she croaked, her voice hoarse and strained. "He said, 'Under the circumstances, we think it would be better for everyone concerned if you took a break from *The President*—just until things calm down a bit.'" She smacked her palms against the side of her head in frustration.

"And then I had to go to the police station to give a statement of my version of events, seeing as I was one of the people who saw Roman the day before he died. I've been walking around for hours since then, not knowing what to do with myself. You know how much that job means to me, Charlotte. I don't need the money, but if I can't cook for people, I'm lost."

"Why do you have to take some time off?"

Olivia scowled. "Let me give you a clue. Two words, four syllables. First word begins with R, second word begins with H."

"Ah, I see," said Charlotte.

"Honestly, I'm so mad, I feel like punching something."

"Well, I don't think that's going to help matters, do you?" Charlotte handed Olivia Pippin's lead. "Come on, we're going to walk the dogs back to my place and when we get there, you can tell me all about it."

Olivia gave her a wary look. "Back to your place? Are you sure that'll be alright? What with Nathan being the DCI, and all?"

"Of course it'll be alright," said Charlotte. "Why wouldn't it be? You haven't done anything wrong, have you?"

"No, but I reckon there are a lot of people who think I have. Just standing here, talking to you, I can feel the dirty looks."

Charlotte scanned the crowds of people sitting in cafés and bars all along the marina, many of whom looked away when she caught their eye, but many of whom continued to stare at Olivia and talk in hushed voices. She shrugged. "Let them think what they want, and let them look. If you say you haven't done anything, then that's good enough for me. And if you come back to my place, there'll be tea and cake." She gave Olivia a sidewards glance. "But only if you're interested, of course."

Olivia's stomach rumbled and she tried to silence it with a hand. "Actually, I'm really hungry. I haven't eaten yet."

"Well, come on then. Be careful you don't get caught up in Pippin's lead, though," said Charlotte, as the old terrier gambolled around Olivia's feet like an excitable pup. "The last thing he needs is you tripping up and squashing him flat. Now come on, turn that frown upside down and let's go. Tea and cake await!"

———————————

After Olivia had made light work of Charlotte's Raspberry Drizzle Cake, she started on a large slice of fruit cake.

"It's a good thing I did a batch of baking the other day," said Charlotte, tipping up the almost-empty cake tin and peering inside. "You weren't kidding when you said you were hungry."

"Sorry," mumbled Olivia. "I always eat a lot when I'm anxious."

Charlotte put down two mugs of tea, and leaned across the table. "Right then, what's going on?"

Olivia chewed and talked at the same time. "Well first of all, I swear I didn't have anything to do with Roman's death, but I told the police they have to find out who did, and quick, because I'm not sure I'll be allowed to go back to work until the murderer's been caught." She took another giant bite of cake and swallowed it in seconds.

"After all I've done for that hotel, this is how they repay me. What happened to innocent before being proven guilty? Simon told me he didn't think it was a good idea for me to be working in the restaurant until the cause of Roman's death has been established and the killer has been caught. He said people talk, and it won't be long before word gets around the entire town that I had a grudge against him. He said if people think I had anything to do with him being poisoned, they'll be reluctant to eat at the hotel."

Charlotte nodded. "Well, that's a perfectly understandable reaction, don't you think?"

"Yes, I know that, but I didn't do anything!" protested Olivia, throwing up her hands. "I don't know how anyone who knows me could think I would."

Charlotte raised both eyebrows and chose her words carefully. "If you don't mind me saying, you're never going to win most affable employee of the month award, are you?"

Olivia responded with a glare. "Look, I know how bad it looks for me that Roman's dead. Everyone at the hotel was talking about it yesterday after that news report. Not to my face, of course, but I've got ears." She slammed a fist on the table. "Just look at the evidence. We hated each other's guts. He opened a school in my hometown which I was livid about. I walked out of his stupid school without eating a thing after he'd invited me publicly to his stupid tasting session. He ate food that had come out of *my* kitchens twice on the day before he died. He had severe stomach pains and was violently ill, and then he took a one way trip to the big old cookery school in the sky."

She pushed herself up from the chair and began to lumber back and forth across the tiled floor. "Whatever everyone thinks, I'll bet my last penny that the people scouring those kitchens, and all the stock in them, won't find one bit of evidence that will implicate me." She flopped down in the chair again with a thud and twiddled her multiple ear piercings. "Just because we'd had a stupid grudge match going on for years, doesn't mean I killed him, but I know everything points to me being the guilty party. I'm not an idiot."

"And *are* you a guilty party?" asked Charlotte, watching her closely, and remembering all the things Harry had said about her spiky relationship with Roman.

"Of course I'm not, but I *feel* guilty just because I know everyone thinks I had something to do with it." She sighed and cradled her heavy head in her hands.

"Out of interest, why *did* you walk out of the tasting session without actually tasting anything?" asked Charlotte.

Olivia's fleeting look of embarrassment was replaced with one of determination. "I didn't want to eat anything, because I couldn't stomach it. I wish I'd never said I'd go to the bloody thing, but I did it to save face. That school should have been mine. It's what I've wanted for years and Roman knew it—he only invited me to make me feel bad.

"You know, when I walked through the door, I felt physically sick, but I didn't want him to know that. I thought it would be easy to just do the tasting, play nice for half an hour, and then leave, but I just couldn't, so I walked out." She gritted her teeth and her knuckles turned white. "There's no one else who could get to me like he could—look at me, I'm shaking just thinking about him, and he's not even here any more." She puffed out a long breath.

"Was that the first time you'd had any contact with him since he'd been in St. Eves?" asked Charlotte.

Olivia nodded. "To speak to, yes. Before then, I'd seen him around in the restaurant and the hotel, but we hadn't spoken. He didn't make any attempt to approach me, and I was glad. Probably just as well that he didn't, because I would have wanted to plant my fist in his smarmy face. Not that I would have, of course."

"Did you see him after the tasting? Later that evening at the hotel?"

"No. And I was so relieved when he didn't come in for dinner. He'd been in every night and I've never felt so stressed sending food out of the kitchen. I've cooked for royalty and rock stars, but that was a breeze compared to cooking for Roman." Olivia wiped her clammy palms on her trousers. "Anyway, that's everything off my chest." The hostile expression on her face faded. "Thanks. You're a good listener."

"You're welcome," said Charlotte. "If you need to chat, you know where to find me. More tea?"

CHAPTER 9

"You don't really think Olivia had anything to do with Roman's death, do you?" said Charlotte as she and Nathan took the dogs on a late walk.

Nathan shrugged a shoulder. "I'd like to think not but, honestly, I don't know. She's been such a loose cannon in the past, it's not easy to forget everything she's done."

"Well, I don't think she's involved." Charlotte called out to Pippin and he stopped digging in the sand and ran towards her. "Don't you remember how fantastic she was when we got married? She played a huge part in making sure everything was perfect for us, and nothing was too much trouble—I'll never forget that. And when Molly was born, she turned up on the doorstep out of the blue, with that beautiful hand-painted nameplate for her bedroom door."

"Yes, she was great, but you know I can't let personal stuff like that get in the way of the investigation," said Nathan. "And she's hardly done herself any favours, has she? Even now, after all the therapy she's had, she still flips her lid from time to time. What's to say that seeing Roman Haley in St. Eves, in the school she thought should be hers, didn't tip her over the edge? You've got to admit, she's got a mean streak."

Charlotte nodded. "Yes, I know, but when I saw her today, she swore she didn't have anything to do with it. She said she knows that most people have probably already made up their minds that she's guilty, but if she says she wasn't involved, then I believe her."

"Oh, you didn't say you'd seen her," said Nathan. "Where was that?"

"I bumped into her on the marina and then I invited her back to the house for a cup of tea."

Nathan stopped walking. "She came to the house?" The look on his face told Charlotte he wasn't pleased.

"Yes, she came to the house. We were hardly going to stand and talk about things in the middle of the marina, were we? And don't get all Detective Chief Inspector about it with me, Nathan. It's not as though she's a serial killer, is it?"

"No, but she's a suspect in the very high-profile murder case of a very popular TV personality. All things considered, I don't think it looks good that you're entertaining her at tea parties in our home. And I'm sorry about getting "all Detective Chief Inspector", but it sort of comes with the job."

Charlotte ignored the comment. "It wasn't a tea party," she said, with a frown. "And don't patronise me."

Nathan sighed and pulled her into his arms. "I'm sorry. I didn't mean to. It's just that, however innocent she may sound, we don't know for sure if she's guilty or not. And you know I'm not usually one for keeping up appearances and pulling rank, but it really wouldn't look good for me if it came out that she *did* have something to do with Roman's death, and she'd been sipping cups of tea around our kitchen table."

Charlotte nodded against his chest. "You're right. I didn't think of it like that. I'm sorry. I won't ask her round again until you've solved the case." She pulled her coat around her. "I still don't think she's involved, though—call it a gut feeling—so I'm not going to avoid her."

Nathan nodded. "Okay. And I promise not to get all Detective Chief Inspector again. He kissed her on the nose and whistled the dogs. "Come on, let's go home and talk about something other than Roman Haley and Olivia Floyd-Martin."

"I've lost count of how many favours you owe me now, Nathan," said Pathologist, Wendy Myers, with a half-grin.

Nathan held up his hands. "Any time you want to call them in, you just let me know. So, what can you tell me?"

"Well, as we thought, it's a case of foul play. Mr. Haley's death was caused by ingesting a substantial quantity of raisins which contained a solution of Aconite tincture, which caused the symptoms exhibited before he died. He must have had a very strong constitution. Having seen the number of raisins in his stomach, I'm surprised he didn't succumb to the poison long before he did."

"Aconite?"

"It's a poison derived from the wild Aconite plant. If that's not familiar, you may know it by its more common name of Wolf's Bane or Monkshood. It has the most beautiful flowers—purple, usually—but it can be so deadly in the wrong circumstances. However, in the hands of someone who knows what they're doing, it's possible to extract Aconite in various forms which can be used perfectly safely as a natural remedy—it's used quite widely in homeopathic medicine. However, if the poison is extracted from the root in its pure form, it's deadly, as was the case here."

"Is there any way it could have got into the raisins accidentally, or as part of a natural process? Cross-contamination in their natural habitat, for example?"

"Not a chance," said Wendy. "Those raisins were deliberately contaminated with poison—injected, most probably. And, as I understand that other people ate the raisins without any ill effects, it looks very much like Mr. Haley was purposely targeted. I'm very sorry to say, Nathan, but it looks like you've got another case of murder on your hands."

———————————

"See, I told you it wasn't Olivia," said Charlotte, when Nathan kicked off his shoes, left his clothes where they fell, switched off the light and climbed into bed at quarter-past two in the morning.

"Well, we don't know that for sure, although it does look less likely after the post-mortem results." He yawned and snuggled up to Charlotte.

Charlotte sat up and switched on the light again. "Less likely? Impossible, I'd say. How could it be her? If the poison was in the raisins, they must have come from the culinary school. Mini raisin loaves were one of the things they made—I saw it on Harriett's itinerary."

"I agree that would be the obvious crime scene," said Nathan, "but we heard this afternoon that none of the stock at the school was dodgy. Everything from the sugar to the raisins was squeaky clean, so they must have come from somewhere else."

"You mean someone planted them in the room with the ingredients the students were going to be using for the lesson?"

"Looks that way. Which points to the two tutors, primarily, but it's far too early to say for sure. It could just as easily have been one of the students, or anyone else who had access to the room before Roman Haley ate the bread. Unfortunately, any evidence that may have been left by whoever planted the poison will be long gone by now."

"You can hardly blame yourself for that," said Charlotte. "You weren't treating it as a murder investigation initially, were you? How were *you* supposed to know he'd been poisoned? Didn't you say that even his assistant thought his stomach pains were due to a stomach bug?"

Nathan nodded and yawned widely. "That's true, but not very helpful. Now, can you turn off the light, please? Sorry, but I've got a really early start."

Charlotte flicked the switch and lay in the dark with her eyes open. Not for the first time, she began to go over what she knew about the investigation.

Who had wanted Roman dead? And why?

———————————

The next morning, after she'd finished her pre-natal exercises, Charlotte settled herself at the kitchen table with a mug of tea and a notepad and pen.

She wasn't planning on getting physically involved in the investigation—she had no intention of putting either her baby, or herself, at risk—but she could at least put her ideas down on paper and give them to Nathan. They'd helped in the past, there was no reason to doubt they could help again.

She cast an idle glance at the silent TV and watched the recently-crowned winner of a talent show hold a four-way conversation with his ventriloquist's dummy, and two bemused breakfast show presenters.

The doorbell rang, sending Pippin and Panda running to the front door, skidding on the wooden floor and barking at the visitor.

"Yoo-hoo, dear, it's only me," Ava shouted through the letterbox. "Sorry to disturb. Can I come in? I won't stop for long."

"You can stay as long as you like," said Charlotte, giving her a hug. "I was just having a cup of tea. You want one?"

"Love one, thank you, dear." Ava unwound the scarf from her neck and hung up her jacket before following Charlotte into the kitchen. "How's the little one?"

"Pretty quiet, apart from a few drop-kicks and a Mexican wave," said Charlotte, with a grin, as she poured tea into a cup and opened a tin which contained the remainder of the homemade fruit cake Olivia had done her best to demolish. "Are you on your own?"

"Well, Derek's rehearsing, as you know, Betty's gone on a day trip to a rubber glove factory with the retirement home social club," Ava pulled a face, "and Harriett's just locking up the car and giving Leo a quick call. I left the front door open because she's coming in to say hello, but she's not stopping because they've got a ginseng class in an hour."

"Ginseng?" said Charlotte.

"Yes, you know, that martial arts thingy they've started doing."

Charlotte chuckled. "You mean Ju-Jitsu?"

Ava clicked her fingers. "That's it! You know, I have no idea why, but that name just will not stay in my head. No matter, I've brought you a present." She delved in her bag and handed Charlotte a package.

"Aaw, that's so sweet of you! Thank you." She squeezed it and it yielded slightly under her fingers. "Ooh, feels interesting."

"I hope you like it. It was Betty who gave me the idea." Ava beamed as Charlotte tore off the wrapping paper.

"Oh," said Charlotte, her smile fading a little. "It's a rubber ring. Thank you... I think."

"It's to help with any piles that may be lurking, my dear," said Ava, looking very pleased with herself. "I'm sure I don't need to tell you, they can be the bane of a new mother's life after all that pushing and shoving. And when it's deflated, you can carry it around in your bag. If you need it, you can just whip it out wherever you are, and in a couple of puffs, voila! Instant comfort. And when you're not using it, you can fold it up and keep it in that little black pouch. Very discreet, I thought.

"Anyway, I blew it up for you before I wrapped it, and had to put my head between my knees in the car because it made me terribly light-headed. That's because I don't have a very big lung capacity—they told me so when I went for my top-to-toe medical check-up. All the other parts are in perfect working order, though." She crooked her little finger as she sipped her tea and left a perfect pearly-pink lipstick imprint on her cup.

Charlotte grinned as she looked at the rubber ring, and remembered the present Ava had given her when she was pregnant with Molly. A book entitled, *How Not to Be a Pain in the Butt When You're Expecting*. "Thank you, Ava. I'll keep it in my bag, just in case."

"What are you up to, anyway?" asked Ava, peering at the notebook on the table.

"Not much," said Charlotte. "I was just thinking about what could have happened to Roman."

"Hmpf, aren't we all, dear. We were talking about it on the way here. I don't suppose Nathan's let slip anything that you can tell us about the investigation, has he?"

Charlotte grinned. "Nice try, Ava, but no." As much as she thought the world of Ava, she would never divulge anything that Nathan might have shared with her with anyone.

Harriett appeared in the doorway. "Morning, Charlotte. You're looking well." She gave her a peck on the cheek and looked her up and down.

"Thank you. Ava was just telling me you've got a ginseng class later?" Charlotte winked and gave Ava a gentle nudge.

Harriett replied with an eye-roll. "I've given up trying to remind her—it's a lost cause." She took a comb and a powder compact from her bag. "I must just use the bathroom. Won't be a sec."

"Ooh, look, there's something on the news about Roman." Ava turned up the volume on the TV when local reporter, Andrew Somerfield, appeared on the screen, standing in front of the culinary school.

"Good morning, Patricia. We have new information coming in regarding the death of Roman Haley. I am now able to report that the post-mortem results indicate he was killed by a lethal dose of poison called Aconite. It was administered into a quantity of raisins which were an ingredient in some bread eaten by Mr. Haley on the day before his death. What makes this news even more shocking is that the bread in question was prepared by students who were taking a course at his very own culinary school."

There was a clatter as Ava's cup and saucer dropped from her hand, hit the table and smashed.

"Blimey, Ava!" said Charlotte, as she jumped in her seat, a hand over her heart. "I know you're keen to see the baby, but I don't think that'll get it out any quicker."

"Oh, I'm sorry, dear," said Ava, her face as pale as the marble worktops. "I didn't mean to startle you. I'll clean it up. And I'll replace what I broke. "

"Don't worry about it," said Charlotte. "It's just a cup and saucer." As she dabbed at the spilt tea with a handful of paper towels, she noticed that Ava had turned ashen, and began to fan her with her notebook.

"What's the matter? Are you feeling okay? Shall I call an ambulance?"

Ava flapped a hand. "No, it's nothing medical… it's that news report. It's made me come over all strange."

"What's going on?" asked Harriett, reappearing and returning her comb and her compact to her handbag.

"You won't believe it, Harriett!" said Ava. "Roman was poisoned by our bread!"

"What are you talking about?" said Harriett. "And what on earth was that crash?"

"Ava dropped her cup and saucer, and I'm a bit worried about her." Charlotte continued to waft the notebook in front of her friend's face. "She's gone ever so white."

Harriett put the back of her hand to Ava's forehead. "Hmm, it's a bit clammy. Perhaps it's the over-exertion of blowing up that rubber ring."

Ava shook her head, "No, it's not." She pointed at the TV. "The news just said that Roman Haley died after eating poisoned raisins… they must have been in those loaves we made."

"I sincerely hope you're joking," said Harriett, with a look of alarm.

"I wouldn't joke about something like that," said Ava. "Look!"

They all turned towards the TV to listen to the rest of the news report.

"I can also report that the inspections on the kitchens at The President Hotel, and Mr. Haley's school, have now been completed, and both premises have been given a clean bill of health, as has all food stock therein.

"What's so puzzling, Patricia, is that we've been told the only two places Mr. Haley ate on the day before he died were the hotel and the school, so it's a mystery as to where the poison came from, and how it came to be in the raisins and, subsequently, the bread. However, the police are extending their investigation to establish answers to these questions and, as always, I'll report again as soon as I have more information. For now, though, it's back to you in the studio."

Ava leaned across the table, as if there were eavesdroppers skulking in the kitchen, and said furtively, "We could have killed him without even knowing, Harriett! One of us could be Roman Haley's murderer! You or I could have made the raisin loaf that poisoned him." She slumped back in her chair and Charlotte wafted the notebook in front of her face again. "Oh my goodness… who will Derek take to the couples' dance competition when I'm sharing a prison cell with a drug trafficker?"

"For heaven's sake!" said Harriett. "Don't be so dramatic."

"I really doubt that either of you are in the frame," said Charlotte, putting down the book and curling an arm around Ava's shoulder. "How could you possibly be? Even if it *was* one of you who made the bread, you weren't to know the raisins were poisoned, were you? All the ingredients belonged to the school."

Ava thought for a while, then nodded. "That's true. I hadn't thought of that. That makes me feel a lot better." She patted Charlotte's hand and managed a smile, the colour returning to her cheeks.

"Maybe Olivia *did* have something to do with it," said Harriett. "She was in and out of the tasting faster than you could blink. I wonder if she stuck some poisoned raisins into one of the loaves on the breadboard without anyone noticing? You know, sleight of hand, and all that."

"Sleight of hand?" repeated Ava, raising a brow. "Be sensible, Harriet, have you seen the size of Olivia's hands? They're like table-tennis bats with giant frankfurters for fingers. There's no way those hands could have done anything surreptitiously, I can assure you." She picked at a piece of fruit cake, and munched thoughtfully on a cranberry.

Charlotte grinned. "Well, I saw Olivia yesterday and after hearing what she had to say, I'm even more convinced she's not involved, despite all the gossip. She said the only reason she didn't hang around at the tasting session was because she didn't want to be there. No other reason."

She threw the dogs a biscuit and they settled down happily. "What was the set-up at the school? Where did you collect all your ingredients from before the class began?"

"We didn't collect them from anywhere," said Ava. "Everything we were using for the day was already set out in canisters on our workbenches when we arrived. All we did was follow along with Gavin. He was the tutor with the attitude problem I told you about—I still don't feel quite right from inhaling all those exhaust fumes." Ava coughed feebly, and finished the rest of her cake. "Shall I pour us another cuppa?"

Charlotte nodded and clicked the end of her pen in and out. "So, you have no idea who made the bread Roman ate?"

Harriett shook her head. "None at all. He was given samples which had been cut from a selection of all the loaves we'd baked, and arranged on a breadboard. By the time of the tasting, no one knew whose bread was whose. We were all told to set aside one mini raisin loaf from our batch, but seeing as he scoffed all of them, we've no way of knowing which was the poisoned one, or who'd baked it."

"You think only one was poisoned?"

"Well, I'd have thought so," said Ava. "Otherwise—unless there's a very delayed reaction— we'd all be toes up by now. We all tried some of each other's bread at the end of the class, you see. So did Gavin and Larissa, because they had to check everything was up to standard before they gave anything to Roman."

Charlotte frowned. "So, everyone ate the raisin loaves, but only Roman was poisoned? How could that have happened?"

"Don't ask me," said Ava, cutting another generous slice of cake. "I just thank God no one else was harmed. We all took home what was left over. Harriett and I shared ours with Bet and none of us have had any ill-effects at all."

"What about Roy and Izzy?" said Charlotte. "Have you heard from them since you last saw them? Are you sure they're okay?"

"Actually, we *haven't* heard from them," said Harriet, "but Roy mentioned that someone told them about a concert in St. Matlock this week that they'd managed to get tickets for—I can't remember when. I suppose we should check at *The St. Eves' Tavern*, just to make sure they're alright, but I'm sure we'd have found out by now if they'd been taken ill, or worse. That blabbermouth landlady, Beverly Brady, can't stop talking for longer than it takes to breathe in."

"Hmm, you're probably right." Charlotte doodled in the margin of her notepad. "So, as I see it, the only way Roman could have been poisoned would have been if someone switched one of the raisin loaves a student had baked for a poisoned one? It sounds to me like there's no other way it could have happened."

Ava nodded. "I suppose so. And the only people who could have done that without anyone noticing are Gavin or Larissa," she said, with her mouth full. "You know, when I think that we could have been in the presence of a murderer, it makes me feel quite weak."

"But, if it *was* Gavin or Larissa, when would they have made the switch?" asked Charlotte, her pen flying across the page.

Ava shrugged. "Either just before Roman arrived, or when we went for lunch. We left our dough in the kitchen to prove, you see. Either one of them would have had ample opportunity to stick some poisoned raisins into one of the loaves. All they had to do was make sure they'd be able to identify it after it was cooked, and make sure it was given to Roman."

She popped what was left of her fruit cake into her mouth and brushed the crumbs from her fingers. "Mind you, although I'm sure Gavin has the potential to poison someone in cold blood, I really don't think Larissa could have had anything to do with it. There's just no way she could be involved in something so terrible. She's such a lovely girl."

"For heaven's sake, we've only know her for a few days," said Harriett. "How can you possibly know what she's capable of? She's hardly going to broadcast the fact that she's the murderer, is she? If it *was* her, she'd keep it to herself, wouldn't she?"

Ava washed her cake down with a gulp of tea. "Hmm, I suppose you're right. So, do you think we should tell the police that Gavin and Larissa were left alone with the dough for a while?"

Charlotte nodded. "Absolutely, I do. Even if someone else has already mentioned it to them, you should let them know so they can make a record of it. Can you think of anything else you haven't already told them that might be of help?"

"Actually," said Harriett, a frown clouding her face, "we didn't tell them about Gavin and Monique sniping at each other, did we, Ava? D'you remember how he called her 'Monique the Sneak', and she told him Roman knew he and Larissa were seeing each other? And she said his days were numbered and he wasn't being considered for the Manager's position any more?"

Ava nodded. "And did you tell them you overheard Gavin and Larissa talking in the kitchen about him being a shareholder in the school? And that Gavin said he wouldn't be responsible for his actions if Roman fired him because he couldn't afford to lose the salary? Did you tell the police any of that?"

Harriett's cheeks turned pink. "Oh dear. No, I didn't tell them about any of it. I really only told them about the first time Roman and Monique came into the class, and then what happened when they came back again with Olivia." A frown settled in between her brows. "That's quite a lot of things we didn't tell them, isn't it? I hope they won't be cross."

"And you'd better tell them that Larissa asked you not to tell Roman about finding her and Gavin in that compromising position," said Ava, wagging a finger in Harriett's direction.

"What compromising position?"

"They were on the reception desk at the school, and they weren't checking the bookings diary, if you know what I mean," said Harriett.

Charlotte chuckled. "Yes, I think I can guess."

Ava's eyes widened. "You don't think we'll be arrested for withholding information, do you? It's an offence in a murder investigation, you know."

"Of course you won't!" said Charlotte. "Just tell them you'd like to add something to your statement that you've just remembered. I'm sure they'll be fine about it. They'll probably be over the moon that you're giving them such a lot of new information." She flicked off the TV and picked up her handbag. "And I'm sure they won't be in the slightest bit cross. We can go to the station now and you can both tell them what you forgot to tell them before."

"What? Now?" said Ava, looking flustered. "We can't. We can't go now. Harriett's got a kamikaze class in half an hour."

Harriett raised her eyebrows and exchanged an amused glance with Charlotte. "Well, the *Ju-Jitsu* class can wait for today, Ava. I think this is more important. Now, just let me call Leo again to let him know he'll have to go on his own, and I'll be ready to leave."

Ava dabbed her mouth to make sure there were no rogue cake crumbs sticking to her lipstick and forced a smile.

"I suppose I should be relieved. Just think, we could be on the brink of solving Roman Haley's murder!"

CHAPTER 10

Fiona pulled up a chair next to Nathan in the incident room.

"Chief, Ava Whittington and Harriett Reeves have just been in to add to their statements. They've raised a theory on how the poisoned raisins got into the bread without anyone else being affected by them. And from what they told us, it seems that both Gavin Doyle and Larissa Reece could have had motive enough to want Roman out of the way." She handed the file to Nathan.

"What did Gavin and Larissa have to say?"

"Pretty much the same as each other," said Fiona. "According to them, the class went smoothly. Roman arrived with his assistant, Monique, at around quarter-to ten, they broke for lunch at one until two, then carried on with the lesson until Roman, Olivia, and Monique arrived at half-past four. Olivia didn't hang around for longer than a couple of minutes, Roman stuffed his face with bread and cheese, and then the class ended just before five, after Mr. Haley left. Gavin and Larissa stayed behind to clean the kitchen, then they locked up and went home."

"Did they admit to being in a relationship?" asked Nathan.

Fiona nodded. "Although we didn't know they'd had to keep it a secret from Roman until Harriett told us. Not that it was a secret in the end, mind you, because he saw them together, but only Gavin knew that initially. He didn't tell Larissa about it until the day before Roman's death. Have you got to the part in Harriett's statement about the conversation she overheard between Gavin and Larissa?"

Nathan looked up. "Seems to me that both their lives have been made a lot easier by Roman not being around any more."

Fiona nodded. "Do you think his shares will pass to Gavin? It makes me wonder exactly how much he stands to benefit from Roman's death."

"I'm guessing the share value would have dropped considerably as soon as the news broke," said Nathan, "and there's no guarantee that Roman's shares would have passed automatically to other shareholders." He sat back in his chair, deep in thought. "But, for now, it seems that Gavin Doyle has plenty of motives for murder."

———————

Detective Constable Carl Tibbs blew out a breath of resignation as he peered into one of the boxes containing the tapes from Roman's dictation machine. Over the past couple of days, he'd listened to eight tapes, and there were still plenty more boxes to go through, containing hundreds more.

He'd started at the most recent, in the hope they'd be the ones that would hold the biggest clues but, so far, he'd heard nothing of any significance, just the random musings of the egotistical restaurant critic turned TV star.

He flicked a tape out of the machine and replaced it with another, wishing he was out and about, in the thick of all the action, rather than stuck behind a desk listening to Roman's monotonous voice droning on and on. He sighed again and pressed the 'Play' button on the dictation machine, sending Roman's voice through the earphones again.

"Re. Gavin Doyle, to say I'm disappointed in him is putting it mildly. I will not tolerate my staff lying to me, especially after I gave him every opportunity to own up to being in a relationship with Larissa. As he will soon find out, there are no second chances with me. I must say, I'm having fun stringing him along. He obviously thinks I have no intention of replacing him, because I've done nothing since I saw the two of them together. What he doesn't realise is that I won't be firing either of them until I've secured suitable replacements. Then, it'll be bye-bye to them both.

*"Poor Gavin. I don't know how he's going to cope without a regular wage coming in—not with the mess his personal life is in. It's going to be very difficult for him **and** Larissa, but they should have thought about that before they tried to get one over on me.*

"When I think of how devastated he's going to be when I break the news, I get a warm fuzzy feeling inside. I might even have to ask Monique to stop recording for a moment so she can snap a photo of his poor, anguished face. The day I tell him his career with me is over can't come quick enough. And then, of course, there'll be the fun of dealing with Larissa. She's going to crumble when I make the details of her nasty little secrets public and everyone finds out what she did.

"Re. replacements for them both, Olivia Floyd-Martin has some excellent staff in her kitchens. She won't appreciate me stealing them from under her nose, of course, but she'll just have to put up with it. I think it's time I asked Monique to discreetly vet a few of the ones who could take over from Gavin and Larissa with the minimum of training.

"And speaking of Monique, I hope she's ready for me. After all, she owes me the biggest debt of gratitude of all. If she ever forgets that, I shall take great pleasure in making her suffer so much, her life won't be worth living. End of notes for today."

The tape came to an abrupt end. Carl rewound it and listened again.

It seemed that Roman had an axe to grind with all his employees, but had one of them really been so desperate to keep their job, and their secret, that they'd been prepared to cause him harm?

What kind of mess was Gavin's personal life in?

And what were Larissa's 'nasty little secrets'?

Carl scratched his head and made some notes, rewinding the tape and playing it again.

Had Olivia found out that Roman had been intending to pilfer the staff from her very own kitchens? She was already a suspect in Roman's murder due to their long-standing grudge, but it seemed there could be even more reason for her to have wanted him out of the way.

And why did Monique Hathaway owe Roman such a huge debt of gratitude?

Carl took the tape over to Ben. "Have you got a minute, Sarge?" He played the tape twice. "It sounds like Gavin, Larissa, Olivia *and* Monique, could *all* have credible motives for wanting Roman dead."

Ben nodded. "Most definitely. For a start, we need to know what Gavin and Larissa aren't telling us because it sounds like they've both got something to hide. And we already know what Olivia thought about Roman opening a school in St. Eves. I dread to think what she might have done if she'd found out he was planning on taking her kitchen staff, too."

Carl nodded. "And Roman says Monique was in his debt for something, but what? As she was probably closest to him, I think we need to do a bit of digging to find out."

Ben slapped the young detective on the shoulder. "Good work, Carl."

———————

Monique Hathaway smiled at Nathan across the table in the interview room.

"Before I answer any questions, I'd like to apologise for the other day. I was in a terrible state, and probably babbling without making much sense, but you were very kind to me."

"No problem. I'm glad you're feeling better."

Monique nodded. "I've been going to the gym and swimming a few lengths in the pool every morning. Exercise always has a mildly sedatory effect on me, which is helping. Working for Roman is... sorry, *was* very stressful, and I suffer with anxiety sometimes.

Anyway, you were going to ask me about the tape you just played, I presume?"

"Just a few questions," said Nathan. "I'm interested to know why Mr. Haley thought you should be so indebted to him?"

"Could have been anything," said Monique, with a shrug of her shoulder. "Maybe just because I worked for him, or because I was his girlfriend. You may have noticed he wasn't the most modest of people." She laughed. "He used to tell me all the time that I had the job and the man everyone wanted."

"I see," said Nathan. "Although if that's why he believed you should be in his debt, it's odd that he'd be so intent on meting out such a severe punishment if you were to forget. Don't you think? He says on the tape that if you ever forgot what a huge debt of gratitude you owed him, he'd take pleasure in making you suffer so much, your life wouldn't be worth living. That's rather extreme, wouldn't you say?"

Monique shook her head. "You didn't know Roman. He demanded absolute loyalty from all his employees, even me... *especially* me, probably." A smile played on her lips. "And you're reading too much into his words. When he said he'd make sure my life wasn't worth living, he most likely meant that if I ever forgot how grateful I should be, there'd be no nookie for a month, or something like that. It's the kind of thing he'd say—he had a weird sense of humour."

Nathan nodded. "Mr. Haley also refers to a plan he had to employ some of Olivia Floyd-Martin's kitchen staff. He says he was going to ask you to vet them. Did you? And was there any chance that Olivia might have known about it?"

Monique shook her head. "If Roman hadn't died, I would have started checking out some of the staff by now, but I didn't get that far."

"So there was no chance that Olivia would have found out about it?" said Nathan.

Monique pushed her glasses up the bridge of her nose. "Definitely not. Although even if I *had* started the vetting process, she *still* wouldn't have found out about it because I'm very good at my job. I'm very thorough, and very discreet. I've *always* been very discreet."

"I can't imagine there was much you didn't know about," said Nathan. "You were Mr. Haley's most trusted employee, after all."

Monique nodded. "No, there wasn't. And yes, I was."

"Did he always ask you to vet his staff?"

"Yes. He insisted on it. And wherever possible, he preferred to employ people who had a few skeletons in their past. He used their secrets to manipulate them, you see. He liked to have that hold over them—it made him feel powerful."

Nathan put his elbows on the table and rested his chin against steepled fingers. "And did *you* have secrets?"

Monique laughed. "No, I didn't. I'm pretty boring, really. I don't have any skeletons in any cupboards but even if I had, Roman would have found out about them. He insisted on getting to know me before he offered me the job, you see, so there wasn't a thing about me he didn't know." She took off her glasses to polish them on her shirt.

Nathan watched her. "I'm sure I don't need to remind you that even the smallest piece of information could lead us to Mr. Haley's killer. Even if *you* don't think it's important, it could be crucial to the investigation. And I'm sure I don't need to remind you that it's an offence to withhold information that might help us to solve his murder."

Monique smiled. "Yes, I'm aware of that."

Nathan nodded. "Good. It's as important that we eliminate the innocent from our enquiries as it is that we find the perpetrator, but it's much easier for us to do that if people cooperate with us."

Monique looked at her watch. "Do you think I'll be here much longer? I dislodged one of my fillings on a piece of toast this morning, so I'd like to get to an emergency dentist as soon as I can."

"You can go now, but we may need to speak to you again. As you know so much about Mr. Haley and his business, you could be very helpful to the investigation."

Monique smiled. "Well, if you need me, I'll be at *The President*. Roman and I were already booked in for another month, you see." She blinked repeatedly and twirled a loose lock of hair around her finger. "I'm going to be far too upset to even think about leaving the hotel for a while, let alone St. Eves. Even if I went home, I don't think I could settle without knowing who killed him, so I'm staying put until you've found his murderer. Even if I have to extend my stay, it'll be a final act of loyalty to Roman."

Nathan returned the smile. "I'm sure we'll be in touch."

"Is it true that you have shares in Roman Haley's culinary school?" asked Fiona, calmly.

"Who told you about them?" Gavin spluttered.

"Why didn't you mention them before," said Fiona, ignoring his question.

"Because I didn't think it was relevant." The sulky chef glared at her from across the table.

"You didn't think telling us that you possibly stand to gain from Roman's death was relevant?"

"No. I mean yes. I mean..." Gavin became flustered. "What I mean is, if I'd told you I had shares in the school, you'd have immediately thought I was guilty of something. I didn't even *want* to work for him." He rubbed the pads of his fingers against his eyelids. "Look, when he first asked me to come to the school, I had no intention of leaving the job I was in. I was happy where I was, I was earning good money, and I had a great team."

"So what changed your mind?"

"He offered me shares in the school. And he offered to quadruple my salary."

Fiona whistled through her teeth. "That's quite a carrot."

"Exactly," said Gavin. "And Roman wanted Larissa to work for him, too. He liked her—she made him laugh and he knew she was a hard worker. We spoke about the opportunity and we both agreed we'd be mad not to take him up on the offer."

"Were you and Larissa together back then?"

Gavin shook his head. "We only started seeing each other after we came to St. Eves. We had no intention of getting together but we spent so much time in each other's company while we were getting the school up and running, it just kind of happened. Things were going great until Roman found out."

He scowled. "We'd been careful for months and then he saw us out together. It was Larissa's birthday and we'd both had a bit too much to drink. It wouldn't have taken a genius to work out we were more than friends." He looked Fiona in the eye. "Larissa gets very affectionate when she's tipsy."

Fiona met his stare. "And that caused you a problem with Roman?"

Gavin nodded. "Yeah, but not as much of a problem as I thought it would. He told me he'd have to decide what to do about it, but I'm pretty sure he was going to let me off. He couldn't afford to lose me *and* Larissa so soon after the school opened, you see. He wanted continuity and he wouldn't have had that if he'd replaced us both, would he?

"In any case, where would he have found anyone who was experienced enough to take over from us at short notice? Monique tried to wind me up by saying he was considering taking on some of Olivia Floyd-Martin's kitchen staff but knowing how hostile their relationship was, I reckon she'd have done everything she could to have stopped her people defecting to Roman's side."

Fiona nodded and clasped her hands on the table. "We have reason to believe that Mr. Haley might have been in possession of some sensitive information about you—about your personal life. Is that right?"

Gavin shifted in his seat, not meeting Fiona's eye. "Sensitive information? Who told you that? What kind of information?"

"Well, I rather hoped you'd tell me," said Fiona. "It's always better when we get our information straight from the horse's mouth, as it were. Of course if we can't, we ask around... see what we can find out."

Gavin said nothing for a while. Then he sighed. "Let's just say my finances aren't looking particularly healthy right now."

"I thought you said Mr. Haley had quadrupled your salary?"

"Yeah, he did. But when my money-grabbing cow of a wife found out, she thought she'd hit the jackpot. She thought I had an inexhaustible supply of cash because I worked for Roman. She wanted her share in maintenance payments, and he knew it." His face darkened with another scowl.

"You're divorced?"

"No, we're separated, but we've got two kids," said Gavin, "and Victoria, their mother, is absolutely bleeding me dry with child support. Even though *she* was the one who had an affair, *I* was the one who decided it would be better for everyone if we separated. The atmosphere at home was toxic. It wasn't good for any of us, most of all the kids, so I left." He paused, his jaw and his fists clenched.

"I felt so guilty afterwards, though, I agreed to a ridiculously high maintenance payment—much more than I needed to. Not that I begrudge paying it, mind you. I'd give my girls my last penny, but whatever I give their mum is never enough. And, in any case, I doubt very much that most of what I give her is being spent on them."

"They're not being neglected, are they?" said Fiona.

"Oh no, nothing like that," said Gavin. "Quite the opposite, in fact. Victoria buys them everything they want in the way of pretty dresses and shoes, getting their hair and nails done—all the girly stuff I wouldn't have a clue about. Every time I see them, though, they tell me she's been whining that I don't give her enough money, so she can't afford to buy them the stuff they need for school.

"Last month, I found out from my eldest that Vic's having the house redecorated, and they've had a new bathroom. Now, you tell me, where's the money coming from for that? They've already had new windows and a new drive this year, and they're all going to Portugal next month. You know who's paid for all that?" He jerked a thumb back on himself. "This mug, that's who. It's no wonder there's not enough money left for the kids' school things."

He puffed out a long breath. "What I should do is talk to Victoria about it, and tell her I'm not giving her any more money than what was agreed, but I know that if I do, it'll turn into a blazing argument and she'll try to turn the kids against me, out of spite." He ran his hands through his hair and looked thoroughly miserable. "Roman had me over a barrel, and he knew it. He said if I ever stepped out of line, he'd make sure my family life suffered."

Fiona frowned. "Because he'd fire you, and you wouldn't be able to keep up the child support payments?"

"Exactly," said Gavin. "I don't have the words for that guy—he was a disgusting human being—and Monique isn't much better."

"Oh?" Fiona raised an eyebrow.

"If it wasn't for her, Roman wouldn't even have known about the situation with my kids. She was his spy—didn't you know? She was always running back to him like a little lapdog, telling tales and dropping people in it at every opportunity, and she used to vet all his staff before he took them on. If he wanted someone to work for him, she'd dig around in their personal stuff and find out everything she could about them. If they had any secrets they didn't want anyone else to know, they wouldn't stay secret for long."

He laughed, bitterly. "Believe me, if anyone had something to hide, Monique would find it and give the information to Roman. He liked to have a hold over his employees, you see. He'd reel them in until it was difficult for them to break ties, then he'd tell them they'd better always be loyal to him, or he'd see to it that they suffered. If I was a dancer, I'd do a jig on his grave."

"So why did you give him reason to fire you by starting up a relationship with Larissa?" asked Fiona.

"Because I didn't think he'd find out."

"And what's going to happen to you now that he's gone? About your job at the school, I mean?"

Gavin spread his hands and shrugged. "Right after Roman died, we weren't sure *what* was going to happen, but we've decided to carry on as we are for the time being. We already had bookings till the end of the year but we thought people would start cancelling because Roman isn't around any more. The exact opposite happened, though. The phone calls and emails haven't stopped with people wanting to book a place on one of the courses. It seems that the school's popularity hasn't died with its namesake, thank God."

"But you still stand to benefit from the shares you hold in the school?"

Gavin nodded. "But that doesn't mean I had anything to do with Roman's death, does it?" He looked at the expensive watch on his wrist. "Look, do you think this is going to take much longer, 'cos I really have to get going. Until the police give the school the all-clear, Larissa and I will be working from home to confirm all the new bookings, and reschedule the ones we haven't been able to honour since the school's been closed. We'll be opening for business again as soon as we can, and we've got a ton of things to get ready before then."

"Almost finished," said Fiona, making a note on her pad. "I also need to ask you about the sequence of events after the students went for lunch on Monday."

Gavin frowned. "What do you mean? What sequence of events?"

"I mean, what happened after the students went for lunch? Can you run through it for me?"

"Oh, I see. Well, Larissa told the students that lunch was set out for them in the staff dining room, and they all took a break for just over an hour. They were back at their benches by two."

"And did you also go into the dining room?"

"No, I had my lunch in the kitchen, with Larissa. We don't usually eat with the students."

"And while you had your lunch, where was the dough the students had made?"

"It was in the kitchen, proving."

"So you and Larissa were alone in the kitchen with the dough for the raisin bread?"

"Yeah, but not just the raisin bread, *all* the bread." Gavin's expression changed. "Just a minute. Are you insinuating that Larissa or I did something to that dough?"

Fiona raised her shoulders. "I'm merely asking where it was while the students were having lunch, and who had access to it."

Gavin shook his finger in front of her face. "Listen, you've got nothing on me—nothing at all. Just because I told you I won't be shedding any tears over Roman's death, doesn't mean I killed him by stuffing him full of poisoned fruit. And, anyway, if I *had* done that, how could I have been sure that someone else didn't eat it by accident?"

"Well, if you *were* the perpetrator, you'd know which loaf you'd poisoned and make sure it was saved for Mr. Haley. Not that I'm insinuating that, of course," said Fiona. "I'm merely answering your question." She gave him a thin smile. "If you plan on leaving St. Eves, perhaps you could let us know, Mr. Doyle?" said Fiona. "We may need to speak to you again."

Gavin gave her a sneer and brought his hand to his forehead in a mock salute. "I will, but as I've got nothing to run away from, I won't be going anywhere. If you need me, you know where to find me."

———————

In another interview room, Larissa brushed the perspiration from her top lip as she sat across the table from Ben.

"I swear, I didn't touch the flippin' dough! And even if I *had* wanted to get rid of Roman—which I didn't—I wouldn't have done it with that Aconite stuff. You can't just walk into a shop and buy it, you know. Not the dangerous stuff, anyway. It has to be extracted by experts."

"You seem to know a lot about it," said Ben.

"I Googled it after I saw the news report," she said. "Along with most of the country, I should think. I'd never heard of it before. Look, I promise you, I haven't done anything wrong." Her face turned pink as she fidgeted in her chair. "How long is this going to take?" she asked, before a fat tear splashed onto the table.

"You're upset?" asked Ben.

"What do *you* think?" said Larissa, through heaving sobs. "You think I had something to do with Roman's death, don't you? Why else would you be speaking to me?"

"We're not *just* speaking to you, Miss. Reece. We're speaking to everyone who might be able to tell us something that'll help us solve this case. *Is* there anything you can tell us?"

Larissa shook her head and continued to sob.

"Look, if you know anything that may help us in this investigation, I'd recommend you let us know," said Ben, kindly. "If you don't, we can find out from other sources, but it would really be better if you told us yourself."

"I'm not hiding anything from you, because there's nothing to tell." Larissa lifted her head and put a hand up her sleeve to pull out a tissue.

"Are you sure?"

"Of course I'm sure. I'm just upset because Roman's dead."

Ben nodded. "I see. Well, some information has come to light which we'd like you to help us understand."

"What information?"

"It seems that Mr. Haley was aware of something you wouldn't want anyone else to know about? Something he may have been planning to make public? Could you tell me what that might have been?"

Larissa's expression turned from forlorn to fearful, but she said nothing.

Ben fixed his eyes on her. "Can you tell me what he was referring to?"

Larissa began to cry again. "I have no idea. Roman was very suspicious of people. He probably thought we were all keeping secrets from him." She wiped her eyes with the raggedy tissue. "If that's what you want to know, I'm sorry, there's nothing I can tell you."

Ben gave her a dubious look. "Okay, that's all for now, but we may need to speak to you again."

Larissa nodded as she pushed out her chair and blew her nose again. She waited until she was well away from the police station before collapsing into a heap on a bench. She fumbled in her bag for her phone and dialled a number with shaky fingers.

"I had to tell a whopping lie, Gav," she said, gulping down the fresh air as if her life depended on it, "but I think I got away with it."

"She's lying," said Ben. "What was it Roman said? 'She's going to crumble when I make the details of her nasty little secrets public.' Why would he say something like that if there wasn't at least some truth to it? Let's face it, when he made that tape, he didn't know it was going to be heard by anyone else, did he?"

"Larissa obviously thinks she's put you off the scent by pretending she had no idea what you were talking about," said Fiona.

Ben nodded. "I don't doubt that Roman Haley was a suspicious guy but, at the moment, I'm inclined to believe him rather than her. And I won't rest until I find out what it is she's keeping from us."

———————

"Do you think this will take long?" said Izzy. "It's just that Roy and I are going to a concert in St. Matlock tonight. I don't know where I'm going, so I want to leave in plenty of time in case I take a wrong turn, or something. I don't have Sat-Nav in my car, so we're going to have to rely on Roy-Nav and a road map."

"No, it won't take long, just a few minutes probably," said Nathan, pleasantly.

"Well, I can't tell you much, I'm afraid." Izzy threw him a flirtatious grin. "We made the dough, using the ingredients that were on the bench, and following what Gavin told us to do. Then we went to lunch, went back to the kitchen to give the bread a second prove, and then we baked it.

"When the bread was ready, we all tasted some of everything, then Roman turned up, pigged out, and then we all went home—or back to *The St. Eves' Tavern* in mine and Roy's case." She scratched her head. "And that's about it, in a nutshell."

"Did you see anything suspicious?"

"Well, Roy's ponytail was a little suspect, but apart from that, no, nothing."

A smile hovered at Nathan's lips.

"Unless you count Olivia Floyd-Martin coming to the tasting, and then leaving without actually tasting anything," said Izzy. "That was a bit weird."

"Okay, thanks for your time, Miss. Davenport. If you think of anything else that might help with our inquiries, please let us know. We'll get in touch if we need to speak to you again."

———————

Roy Tanner sat across the table from Nathan with a wide smile plastered across his face.

"I just turned up at the school and followed along with everyone else. Baking's not my thing, see, so I didn't have a clue what was going on. Do you bake, DCI Costello?"

"No, I don't. Did you see anything suspicious during the day you spent at the culinary school, Mr. Tanner?"

"Suspicious?" Roy rubbed his chin with his big hand. No, I didn't see anything suspicious at all. Mind you, we were all too busy getting on with stuff. That Gavin's a hard taskmaster, so even if there had been something suspicious going on, I doubt any of us would have noticed."

He laughed. "Have you ever tried kneading dough by hand? I tell you, it's not easy, even for a big bloke like me. It certainly kept me occupied, I can assure you of that, as I'm sure it did everyone else. No, I certainly didn't see anything suspicious."

"Okay, thank you, Mr. Tanner. We'll be in touch if we need to speak again. If you remember anything that could be of interest to us, please let us know, won't you?"

———————

Later that evening, after Monique had had her tooth refilled, and had finished a four-course dinner in the rooftop restaurant, she relaxed in the hotel bathtub, up to her chin in bubbles.

She reached an arm over the side of the tub and picked up the bottle of vintage Champagne she'd ordered from room service. Pouring herself a glass, she lay back and sipped her drink, the bubbles fizzing on her tongue.

She gazed at her surroundings. It was about time she had some pampering. After everything she'd been through, God knows, she deserved it.

She smiled and raised her glass in a toast. "To you, my darling Roman. May you rot in hell."

CHAPTER 11

There was a shuffling of chairs and papers as the team assembled for the latest briefing.

"Right, now that we've taken statements from everyone, let's take a look at where we are," said Nathan. "Regarding Olivia Floyd-Martin, although she may have the most obvious motive on the surface, how would she have got the poison into the bread? We've considered that she could have contaminated the bread when she arrived for the tasting session, but how plausible is that? And is she *really* a killer? Are we missing something? If so, what?" He looked around the table, his eyes coming to rest on Carl, the station's youngest, newest, and keenest, detective. "Carl, I'd like you to take that on. Dig around, ask questions, see what you can find out."

Carl's face lit up and his cheeks flushed when the rest of the detectives catcalled and cheered. "I'm on it, Chief."

"Good. Right, Monique Hathaway doesn't appear to have any obvious motive but as we know that Roman Haley liked to employ people who had at least one vulnerability he could use to blackmail them with, I wonder if she's hiding something? I want everything we can find on her, okay? Fiona, if you can get onto that, please?"

She nodded. "Will do, Chief. Also, with regard to Gavin Doyle, his story about his ex-wife appears to check out—she's bleeding him dry—but I'm still working on it. Apart from a couple of speeding fines, we've got nothing else on him, but he had some strong motives for wanting to see Roman dead. It suits Gavin well to have him out of the way, leaving him to run the school, with no worries about his salary being stopped, nor his shares in the school at risk. That said, we've got no proof that he's guilty of anything. I'll report back when I have more info."

"Okay, thanks. What have you got, Ben?"

"Well, Larissa Reece's story is flaky, to say the least. I'm convinced she's lying about something. She's trying to put us off the scent, although off the scent of what, I have no idea, Without knowing what she's hiding, I can't say if she had a motive for wanting Roman dead, or not, but I'm still checking her out, so I'll let you know what I find."

Nathan nodded. "Regarding Izzy Davenport and Roy Tanner, neither of them have any obvious motives. Again, early background checks don't throw up anything of concern but, as with everyone, we'll keep looking. I want you all working together closely on this."

He tapped the picture of Roman Haley that was stuck to a giant whiteboard. "Someone killed this guy in broad daylight, in front of multiple witnesses. Who the hell was it?"

———————

"How'd you get on?" Fiona asked Carl, as he flopped down into a chair in the incident room and swung round to face her.

"Not bad. I spoke to Greta Borasinski. She's the Head of Housekeeping at *The President*."

"Yeah. And?" Fiona looked up at him while she was typing out a report, her fingers never missing a key.

"She's been off sick since the day Roman Haley was taken ill, but she said that the day before he arrived at the hotel, she overheard a huge argument in Simon Clancy's office, and the person doing most of the shouting was Olivia Floyd-Martin."

Fiona stopped typing. "What were they arguing about?"

"She said Olivia was screaming and swearing at Simon, asking why Roman had to stay there. She asked him why he couldn't have told Roman the hotel was full and sent him somewhere else."

"And what did Simon say?"

"He told her that people would come to the hotel just for a glimpse of Roman, and it would be a bad business move to turn him away. After that, Olivia went into a full-blown rant. She flung open the door and told Simon he'd better hope she didn't bump into Roman around the hotel because if she did, there'd be a bloodbath of epic proportions. Then she slammed the door behind her so hard, it rattled in its frame," said Carl. "She sounds like a delightful woman."

"She's had some issues, but she's not all bad," said Fiona, summing Olivia up in a nutshell. "Probably like most of us."

She went back to her report and was disturbed again seconds later when Ben shouted from the other side of the room.

"You are *not* going to believe this!"

"What's up?"

"Come and look!"

Fiona and Carl, along with everyone else in the room, huddled around the desk, peering at the grainy CCTV image.

"What are we looking at?" asked Fiona, screwing up her eyes.

"It's the recording from a camera in the market square, just across from the school. I've been checking for anything that might be helpful, from the day the tradesmen finished work, until the day Roman was poisoned. The camera's on the opposite side of the square, so we've got a pretty good view. This footage is from the Wednesday before the school opened, taken at twenty-past one in the morning."

A figure in dark trousers and hooded jacket could be clearly seen prowling around the perimeter of the school, looking through every window before rattling the handle on the front door.

"Looks suspect," said Carl.

"Certainly does," said Ben. "And you wait till you see who it is."

The figure slouched against the wall before turning and lumbering back across the square. As it approached the camera, the light from a nearby streetlight was enough to illuminate the face of the suspicious prowler and clearly identify it as Olivia Floyd-Martin.

———————

"Well, obviously, I didn't tell you because I knew how it would look." Olivia crossed her arms in a show of nonchalance, but squirmed on the chair.

"There seems to be a lot of that going around at the moment—people not telling us the whole story." Fiona exhaled an impatient sigh. "What were you doing, anyway?"

"I was curious to see the school but I was hardly going to ask for a guided tour, was I? I was just looking around."

"At twenty-past one in the morning?"

"I was stressed out. I wasn't sleeping well. And I didn't want anyone to see me. I didn't even know there was a camera there—there never used to be."

"It hasn't been there long. Roman Haley had it installed," said Fiona. "The thing is, Olivia, when you first came in to give us your statement, you said, and I quote, 'Accepting Roman's invitation to the tasting was a huge mistake. I don't know why I went, because it was the last thing I wanted to do. I had no inclination to go anywhere near the place before, and I haven't set foot near it since, so I can't help you with what happened to Roman after I left. All I can tell you for sure is that he couldn't get the food into his mouth fast enough. And that he was enjoying watching me squirm.'" Fiona raised an eyebrow in Olivia's direction. "You can see why I'm having trouble understanding why you'd say you had no interest in going anywhere near the school, but then this footage turns up of you all over it."

The groove between Olivia's eyebrows deepened as her mood darkened and she threw her hands in the air. "When is anyone going to appreciate how hard it was for me to have Roman bloody Haley hanging around this town? And when is anyone going to believe that, as much as I might have wanted him to disappear, I did. not. kill. him."

She threw herself against the back of the chair and folded her arms, a mutinous grimace on her face.

Fiona returned the grimace with an impassive stare. "We've also been told that you were overheard having a hells-bells of an argument with Simon Clancy, prior to Roman Haley's arrival at *The President*, which concluded with you telling him he'd better hope you didn't bump into Roman around the hotel because if you did, there'd be…" she flicked over a page in her notebook, "a bloodbath of epic proportions."

Olivia's face turned scarlet, and she took a controlled breath, as if she was trying her hardest not to blow her top.

"Look, whether you believe me or not, you've got no proof that I did anything wrong. It's not a crime to look through windows, you know. If you've got something on me, arrest me, otherwise, leave me alone." She pushed the chair away from her and stood up, towering over Fiona. "Can I go now?"

———

"Well, it turns out Roman Haley was a nastier piece of work than we knew."

Nathan fell onto the couch, put his head on Charlotte's lap, and closed his eyes. "And, as all the stock checked out clean in the hotel *and* the school, someone must have brought in the poisoned raisins the day Roman ate the poisoned bread at the tasting session. Who that was, though, we don't know. I feel like we're getting nowhere fast at the moment."

"You'll get a lead," said Charlotte, switching off the TV and gently stroking his cheek. "You always do."

Nathan opened his eyes. "You said you'd met Roy Tanner, didn't you?"

Charlotte nodded. "Ava and Harriett brought him and Izzy to the café. Why?"

"I interviewed him today. I wondered what you thought of him."

"I thought he was very nice," said Charlotte. "Why d'you ask?"

Nathan pushed himself up. "That's just it. He *is* very nice. *Too* nice, almost. I can't put my finger on it, but there's something about him."

"What's wrong with being nice? You're getting far too cynical in your old age."

"Yeah, I know. It comes with the territory." Nathan yawned. "I wish I could be like you, Charlotte. I wish I could take everyone at face value but, unfortunately, I can't. If someone's *too* nice, all it does is make me suspicious."

"Did you interview Izzy, too?"

"Yes. Again, she seems pleasant enough but not over the top, like Roy. He just seemed like he was trying much too hard. They both answered all the questions, but neither of them gave any clues that take us further forward with the investigation, and neither of them have an apparent motive. We'll wait and see if the background checks give us anything to go on, but I wouldn't like to bet on it."

"Are they still staying at *The St. Eves' Tavern?*"

"Until after the weekend, although they went to a concert in St. Matlock tonight and they're not back until tomorrow. They were more interested in setting off in time for that than they were about Roman Haley popping his clogs."

"Well, apart from seeing him on TV, and the short time they saw him at the school, they didn't know him, did they?" said Charlotte. "They didn't have a connection to him like the others did."

"You're probably right," said Nathan, swinging himself off the couch with a chuckle. "I'll tell you something that made me laugh today, though. We were watching Roy from the office window, squeezing himself into Izzy's tiny Fiat before they set off for the concert. His knees were literally up to his chin—that must have been the most uncomfortable car journey of his life."

He held out his hand to pull Charlotte up. "Anyway, come on. Let's go to bed and I'll give you that back rub I've been promising you for ages."

CHAPTER 12

Ava, Harriett and Betty studied the menu at Porcinis, the vegetarian Italian restaurant on the marina.

"What are you having?" asked Ava. "There are some wonderful smells coming out of the kitchen, but I've never been here before, so I have no idea what anything is."

"I think I'll have the set menu," said Harriett. "Minestrone soup, aubergine parmigiana, and the lemon tart."

"And I'm having tomato, olive and basil bruschetta, followed by the mushroom risotto, and then the tiramisu," said Betty, nibbling on a tray of antipasti.

"Hmm, well seeing as my knowledge of Italian food stretches to spaghetti Bolognese or lasagne, I think I'll just take pot luck and order what sounds the most adventurous," said Ava. "I'm going for a Caprese salad with pesto, sweet potato gnocchi with tomato and spinach sauce, and Zagablione with fresh fruit. Or shall I have the cannolis? It all looks so delicious on the menu."

"It *is* delicious," said Harriett, closing her menu and pouring a glass of sparkling water. "Even Leo loves the food here and you know how much he loves his meat and two veg. Honestly, it's to die for."

They ordered and sat back to watch life on the marina go by.

"I say," said Ava, looking over the top of her glasses. "Isn't that Roy and Izzy over there?"

A tall figure strode down the marina front, his small companion taking two steps to his one. They wore rucksacks on their backs and, as they drew closer, it became apparent that they were unkempt and tired-looking.

Betty waved to get their attention. "Hello, you two. Where've you been?"

"Hi!" said Izzy. "We've just got back from St. Matlock." She crouched down next to Betty with Roy towering above her. "I'm so glad we managed to get tickets for that concert at such short notice because it was brilliant, wasn't it, Roy? Mind you, there were no tents left, and we didn't have our own, so we had to sleep in the car." She pulled a face. "Not to be recommended when the car is as small as mine, and your travelling companion is six foot six."

"Oh dear," said Ava. "Are you alright, Roy?"

Roy shook his head and dug his knuckles into his shoulders in an attempt to pummel his stiff muscles back to life. "It seemed like a cracking idea last night after four pints of cider but let's just say I realised the error of my ways when I woke up this morning, feeling like I'd been folded in half. Not that I had more than an hour's sleep, mind you. Bloody car. I'd have had more room if I'd slept in a matchbox. And I don't know how strong that cider was, but my head's killing me. I feel like my brain's too big for my skull."

"Don't say nasty things about my car!" said Izzy. "It got us to the concert and back again, didn't it? And I didn't hear you complaining when it kept us dry from the rain last night."

Roy put his hands to his head and moaned.

"Would you like a glass of sparkling water?" asked Harriett.

"No thanks. We're going for breakfast at Charlotte's Plaice," said Roy, looking a little more cheerful. "The thought of it is the only thing that's kept me going since we set off this morning. A full English breakfast with lots of hot buttered toast, and a nice big mug of tea. And then we're going back to *The St. Eves' Tavern* to get showered, and I'm going to bed. But I'm not doing *anything* until I've had some breakfast." He rubbed his hands together.

"Oh dear," said Ava. "I hate to disappoint you, but Charlotte's Plaice is closed today."

Roy and Izzy's faces fell. "You're kidding!"

"It's closed *every* Saturday," said Betty.

"I don't believe it," said Roy shrugging his rucksack off his back. "Where else can we get a good brekkie?"

"Well, we could go back to the *St. Eves' Tavern* and have breakfast there," said Izzy, "but it's not great. The fried bread looks like it's done twenty lengths in the pan before it's put on your plate, and it's *still* swimming in oil, and the bacon's really limp and insipid."

"Why don't you have something here?" said Harriett. "It's not breakfast, but they do a fabulous set-menu for only £10. Here, have a look."

"I'm not sure we're dressed for a restaurant," said Roy, sniffing his underarm. "And I'm sure I don't smell too good."

"You could always splash on some of that aftershave you were wearing last night," said Izzy, with mock sweetness. "It was strong enough to fell a charging rhino at twenty paces, so I'm sure it'll cover up a little B.O."

Roy shot her a sarcastic smile. "Well, I had to do something to mask the smell of your sheepskin boots. After we got caught in the rain, they stunk like a damp yak."

"Now, now, you two, that's enough bickering," said Ava. "You could probably do with combing your hair, and a shave, but I'm sure they won't mind what you look like. Here comes our waiter—I'll ask him."

A young man in a white shirt and tight black trousers approached, carrying three plates. "Your starters, ladies," he said, in a heavy Italian accent, placing the plates on the table. "I bring you the pepper."

"Thank you, young man," said Ava, "but before you go, I want to ask you something."

"Madam?" The waiter lowered his chin and fluttered his dark eyelashes.

"These people are our friends. They look a little dishevelled, and they're a bit whiffy because they've slept in a car all night and haven't had a shower yet, but we can vouch for them, can't we girls? They might look like they are, but they're really not the type of people to eat and run off without paying their bill. Do you think you'd be able to find a table for them?" Ava used her polite, but bossy voice. The one she reserved for when she absolutely wouldn't take no for an answer.

The waiter looked Roy and Izzy up and down before gesturing to a nearby table for two. "Here for you is good?"

"Here for us is perfect," said Izzy, gratefully, and sank into the soft cushion. "Grazie mille."

The waiter's blank expression transformed into a smile and he gave Izzy a little bow. "Prego, Signorina."

"Yeah, thanks." Roy put down his rucksack and rubbed his chin through his patchy stubble. "And thanks, Ava. That was good of you."

Ava gave him a saint-like smile and started on her salad. "Don't mention it dear. I'm glad we saw you, actually. I wanted to ask you how you got on when you spoke to the police. I assume you *have* spoken to them?"

Izzy nodded and took a breadstick from the container on the table to dig in the butter dish. "We spoke to them yesterday, but there wasn't much we could tell them. I still can't believe the bread one of us baked was what poisoned Roman. I mean, how the hell did *that* happen? Thank God it wasn't one of us who ate it." She shuddered. "It was all we talked about on the drive up to St. Matlock, wasn't it, Roy? We were listening to a local radio station in the car and the presenters were saying they reckon Olivia Floyd-Martin's the prime suspect. Not sure I agree with that myself, though."

"And what do you think, Roy?" asked Betty.

He shrugged. "Dunno, really. I guess the obvious people to have put the poisoned raisins in the bread are Gavin and Larissa, but I can't see them having done it. Gavin seems like a good bloke and Larissa reminds me of my sister, who wouldn't hurt a fly. She even went vegan to save the animals."

He tossed an olive into the air, catching it in his mouth. "As far as Monique's concerned, I've heard she's pretty devious but as it's come out that she was Roman's girlfriend, I can't see her doing him in. And I don't know Olivia but from what I've heard, she strikes me as the type of person who'd come straight to you if she had a problem and sort it out face to face, not do something sneaky like poison your food." He caught another olive. "Of course, that's just a guess—like I said, I don't know her."

"I think you're probably right," said Ava. "She does tend to grab the bull by the horns, as it were. She's certainly not one to shy away from conflict."

"Although she didn't taste a thing at the session, did she?" said Harriett. "And we all know how much she loves her food."

"Well, maybe she *did* do it," said Betty, "but she only meant to put enough poison in the raisins to upset Roman's stomach for a few days."

"'Upset his stomach for a few days'?" repeated Ava. "Betty, dear, in case you've been asleep since Monday, those raisins caused Roman Haley to keel over and go kaput."

"Yes, I'm aware of that," said Betty, "but even the best laid plans can backfire sometimes. When I was at school, Jimmy Sluman put itching powder in Richard Finegan's plimsolls and poor Richard had to have a month off sick because he had the most terrible allergic reaction to it. His whole body swelled up like one of those Pufferfish and he had to have an emergency tracheotomy."

"That's very interesting, Bet," said Ava, "but what does some poor boy's tracheotomy from decades ago have to do with Olivia?"

"If you'll let me get a word in, I'll tell you," said Betty, munching on her bruschetta. "Anyway, Jimmy wasn't to know that Richard was going to have such a bad reaction—he was only larking around—but he kept his mouth shut when the headmaster went to every classroom, trying to find out who was responsible. It was only because Jimmy's mum found the itching powder packet under his bed when she was tidying his room that she realised what had happened, and went straight down to the school to tell the headmaster."

"What happened to Jimmy?" asked Izzy. "Did he get three thwacks of the cane, or whatever it was they used to do in those days?"

"Oh no, he got expelled," said Betty. "If he'd owned up right away, he would have been punished, but he could have stayed at school. The point I'm making is that he didn't *mean* to cause Richard any harm but when it all went wrong, he was too scared to own up. Maybe that's what happened with Olivia—she didn't mean to kill Roman but when he died, she panicked."

"You know, Betty, that's an excellent theory," said Ava. "I think you should tell Nathan."

"*Nathan*! That's it!" Izzy banged her hand on the table. "We've been trying to remember his name. He's the guy who interviewed us yesterday. And quite yummy, I thought. For an older man, anyway."

"Yes, he's lovely," said Harriett. "Such a shame Charlotte doesn't get to see him much at the moment, especially in her condition. Mind you, she never does when he's working on a case like this."

"Charlotte?" said Izzy. "What's Charlotte got to do with him?"

"He's her husband," said Ava. "Did I forget to tell you?"

"Must be the only thing she's forgotten to tell someone all year," Betty stage-whispered to Harriett, with a wink.

"Oh, be quiet," said Ava. "Yes, dear, Charlotte and Nathan are married."

The smile almost slipped from Izzy's face but she forced it back on. "Oh. Well, lucky Charlotte. One sprog, another on the way, both successful, he's a respectable pillar of the community... I'm sure they must be very happy. Sounds like a perfect life to me."

Her sudden change in mood wasn't lost on her dining companions.

"Is something wrong, dear?" asked Ava, as Izzy jabbed the breadstick into the butter dish with rather more venom than suited the occasion.

Izzy shook her head, the tension in her jaw disappearing as she slouched over the table. "Sorry. I get a little uptight sometimes when I hear about people who have fantastically happy marriages. I haven't really got over my divorce yet, although I keep telling myself I have."

"Huh, I know how you feel," said Roy, gloomily, snapping a breadstick in half.

"Oh, I'm so sorry!" said Izzy, giving his hand a squeeze. "I wasn't thinking. Take no notice of me, everyone. It makes me feel better to wallow in self-pity sometimes." She smiled apologetically.

Ava reached over and patted her on the shoulder. "It's alright, dear, and there's no need to explain to us. It can't be easy when your dream of a perfect marriage crumbles to nothing before your very eyes—it must be terribly distressing. Marriage can be hard work but with the right man, it can last for many blissfully happy years."

She gave Izzy a sympathetic smile. "Still, there's plenty more fish in the sea—it's just a matter of reeling one in. Have you thought of dating sites? I hear there's been a resurgence in their popularity recently. You don't want to leave it too long, though. Women start to sag after a certain age, but men seem to get better as they get older, so you'll need to get out there before all the good ones are snapped up and you're left with the dregs. You're such a lovely girl, it would be a terrible waste if you ended up unloved and alone."

It was left to Harriett to break the awkward silence.

"Good grief!" she said, shaking her head, briskly, and shooting Ava a withering glare. "First of all, I found the love of my life just a few years ago, Izzy, so I don't think you need to worry *just* yet about being left on the shelf. And, second of all, promise me you'll never become an agony aunt, will you, Ava? The poor girl needs comforting, not driving to suicide."

Betty nodded, wisely. "She's right, Ava. I know you mean well, but you really need to work on your delivery."

"What have I said?" Ava's eyes widened as a hand flew to her chest. "I was simply trying to empathise. I didn't mean to upset you dear." Her look of concern was so genuine, it made Izzy giggle.

"Really, it's okay—I'm fine. Like I said, I just get a bit tetchy about the divorce sometimes. Like now, when I'm tired and hungry, so thank goodness someone's coming to take our food order."

The waiter arrived back at the table, his long eyelashes and dark Italian good looks not wasted on Izzy.

Roy gave her a sly look. "Looks like you've found an antidote for your crush on Nathan the hunky detective."

Izzy stuck out her tongue. "It's *not* a crush. And even if it was, and he wasn't married, I'm going home soon, so there wouldn't be much time to do anything about it, would there? Anyway, can we change the subject please?"

"Did you get your refund for the course?" asked Harriett.

Izzy nodded. "Larissa came to *The St. Eves' Tavern* to let us know she'd arranged it. She looked awful."

"Hardly surprising," said Roy, "seeing as her boss was poisoned right under her nose. She told us that the stock at the school had been given the all-clear, so that was a weight of her and Gavin's minds, but she still looked really stressed."

"Well, Roman's death must have come as a terrible shock," said Ava. "You can't blame the poor girl for not looking her best." She turned to Izzy. "By the way, aren't you going home soon? I thought you and Betty were supposed to be arranging to see each other."

Izzy nodded. "I'm leaving on Monday, so we're getting together tomorrow, aren't we, Betty? I'm going round to see her dad's old teapot collection."

Ava lifted an eyebrow. "Don't get too excited, will you?"

CHAPTER 13

"Oh my God! Just wait until Olivia sees this," murmured Charlotte as she shook out *The Sunday Herald* and read the print emblazoned across the front page.

Exclusive! We interview Gordon Buckingham, who suffered dreadful, and life-changing, injuries at the hands of the prime suspect in the murder of Roman Haley, Olivia Floyd-Martin. Full story on pages 2, 3, and 4.

It's a well-known fact that Olivia Floyd-Martin, the Executive Chef at St. Eves' President Hotel, has a hot head on her burly shoulders, but not everyone knows that she has a streak so mean, it left restaurant critic, Gordon Buckingham, fighting to live a normal life.

In fact, he still walks with a limp and suffers constant pain; the legacy of the injuries he sustained in a cowardly and unprovoked attack by the now world-famous chef, during which she threw him through a plate-glass window.

Our reporter, Michelle Durban, spoke to Gordon at his home recently.

Gordon Buckingham is a quiet unpretentious man. He lives alone in a modest house, in an equally unassuming neighbourhood, on the outskirts of the village of Little Acorns. I ask him what life is like for him these days.

"Well, some days are a bit of a struggle," he says, "but my sister and my carers do a fantastic job of

looking after me, and making sure I have everything I need. I couldn't cope without them, that's for sure."

I ask him about his wife, Melanie, who left him a few months after the accident.

"She couldn't cope with it—couldn't cope with me, I suppose. She said she loved me so much, seeing me in pain was too hard for her to deal with. I was devastated when she left, but I didn't blame her. She was quite a bit younger than me, you see, and I can't imagine the pressure it must have put on her. Anyway, life must go on, so you just have to do your best to forgive, or it can become unbearable."

Over a cup of tea, and homemade lemon biscuits, Gordon shows me the diaries he kept before his accident, when he was enjoying life as a restaurant critic. The diaries contain reviews of every restaurant he'd ever critiqued, its chef, every course he'd eaten with a mark out of ten for each dish, and a total mark for the whole dining experience. "I loved keeping those records," he says, "and looking back to see how restaurants had improved, or not, since my last visit."

One of the last entries in the diary Gordon was using at the time is a review for The Old Barn in the village of Shottingford—a village about ten miles from Gordon's home—which is the restaurant at which he had his accident. The mostly empty pages which follow that critique are a constant reminder to Gordon of what happened. "I would have continued with the reviews, but it was a bit difficult to get to many restaurants with a fractured hip and a shattered kneecap," he says, with a wry smile.

It shows the true mettle of the man that despite his accident, and consequent injuries, he bears Olivia Floyd-Martin no ill will. As we settle down to chat, I ask him to share his thoughts on Ms. Floyd-Martin, and the accident that changed his life.

"I don't blame Olivia at all," he says, completely without malice. "She was a genius then, and she still is now. Working in a top-class kitchen is extremely demanding and the pressure the staff work under is immense. That's something that not many people outside the industry realise."

I remark that he surely isn't excusing her behaviour. He smiles, and responds in his quiet voice. "I don't expect you to understand. Everyone I know has wanted me to sue the backside off that woman, but that's not me. You see, I loved my job as a restaurant critic, but what made it so enjoyable were the chefs who worked so hard to produce such wonderful food and ambience in their restaurants. Olivia was one of those chefs.

After the accident, I just couldn't bear to see her punished for what she did. She had too much to offer the culinary world for her talent to be snuffed out, and if I'd pressed charges, I feared she would have gone to prison, which would most likely have been the end of her career. I could never have forgiven myself if I'd been the one to deprive others of her talent."

I ask Gordon why the police hadn't carried out their own investigation, and brought charges against Ms. Floyd-Martin. "Oh, they did carry out an investigation," he replies, "but they couldn't find enough evidence against her for a conviction. None of the people who witnessed the incident wanted to get involved and give a statement, you see, so they all claimed they'd been looking the other way when it happened which meant the police had very little on which to base their case."

In an unusual move, the police asked Gordon if he would like to suggest any form of retribution for Ms. Floyd-Martin. When I ask him about this he says, "Olivia needed help, not punishment, so I was delighted to be given the opportunity to suggest an alternative to the more conventional penalties which are handed out to offenders. She agreed to have the anger management therapy I'd suggested, which I believe helped her then, and has continued to help her since. In fact, I heard from friends in the industry that she calmed down considerably after the treatment began."

I suggest that his decision not to press charges against Ms. Floyd-Martin were magnanimous in the extreme. "Not really," he says, with a smile. "Look, I'm no saint—I did what I did for my sake as much as hers. If I'd been the one responsible for cutting her career short, I would never have forgiven myself. The guilt would have eaten away at me, and holding onto resentment is never good for one's health—it can be so terribly damaging. For that reason, I would implore any of your readers who may feel a desire to take retribution against Olivia on my behalf to cast all such thoughts from their minds. Anger and revenge will not help me, and it will not help them.

"I have made my peace with Olivia in my heart, and the decision to do so was an easy one, really," he tells me. "You see, as I've already said, forgiveness is the only way."

It is truly incredible that someone who has been through such hardship can have so much compassion in their heart.

Charlotte wiped the tears from her eyes as she read the rest of the interview, which went into detail about the night of the accident, and Gordon's subsequent injuries. The pages were peppered with old photographs of Gordon and Olivia, and more recent ones of him in what looked to be his living room, and Olivia on the steps outside *The President Hotel*, shoving an angry palm into a photographer's face as he tried to take her photo.

She put the paper on the coffee table and blew her nose before putting her feet up on the couch and sipping her mug of tea. Although she'd heard snippets about the attack over the years, she'd never realised quite how bad it had been. She wondered if Olivia really appreciated how fortunate she'd been that Gordon Buckingham had never brought charges against her.

Her phone rang and Ava's face flashed up on the screen. She blew her nose again and put on a cheery voice. "Morning, Ava. Everything alright?"

"Fine, dear, just fine."

"Are you sure? You sound out of breath?"

"Yes, I'm on my morning speed-walk. Sorry to call so early, but I wondered if you'd done your exercises yet? If you haven't, I thought I could come and join you and pick up something for breakfast on the way? Does that fit in with your plans?"

"Sounds good to me," said Charlotte. "Nathan's at work, and I don't have any plans apart from meeting the bus at the school when Molly comes home from camp later. Then we're going out for a pizza. Apart from that, though, I'm free all day."

"So you don't mind if I pop round?"

"Do you even need to ask? I'll see you in a bit."

"Are you absolutely sure you don't mind me hanging around so much?" said Ava, as she puffed along with Charlotte's early morning pre-natal exercises. "With Derek away at rehearsals, I'm at a bit of a loose end, you see. I caught up with Harriett and Betty for lunch yesterday and it was lovely to get together, but Betty's got Izzy going round today, and Harriett, Leo and Harry have gone on one of those retirement home day trips. I think I told you, didn't I?

"They invited me along, of course, but I ask you, dear, why on earth anyone would volunteer to go on one of those deathly boring coach trips, I have no idea. They've gone to a shoelace factory today." Her eyebrows quirked in opposite directions. "A *shoelace* factory! Honestly, I'd rather have a root canal without anaesthetic while I was watching paint dry. D'you know what I mean?"

Charlotte giggled and flopped onto the couch. "Yes, I can't say I've ever been a big fan of coach trips.

Especially if I sit near a wheel—it gives me horrible travel sickness. By the way, have you seen *The Sunday Herald* this morning?"

"No. I was out before the paperboy called round. Why? Anything worth reading in there?"

Charlotte handed her the folded newspaper. "Here, you take a look at that, and I'll get us some tea and fruit juice and pop those chocolate croissants you bought in the oven for a couple of minutes."

Ava's eyes widened as she read the headline. "Oh, good Lord! The scandal is never ending!" She slipped her glasses on and began to read.

———————

"I'm surprised he's never given an interview before," said Ava, as she used the pad of her index finger to pick up croissant crumbs from her plate.

Charlotte shrugged. "Maybe he just wanted to forget about what happened. You can hardly blame him, can you? If I'd been through what he's been through, I know I wouldn't want to dwell on it. In any case, the newspapers probably weren't interested in him before now because it wouldn't have been such a big news story. Olivia hasn't always been so well known, but now she's recognised wherever she goes and she's a suspect in a TV megastar's murder. *The Herald* must be thrilled that it got the scoop."

"Poor man, you have to feel sorry for him," said Ava, looking over the paper again. "Fancy his wife leaving him after everything he'd been through—what an awful thing to do. He must have had a terribly miserable life."

"Well, thankfully, he doesn't sound very miserable now," said Charlotte. "He says he let go of any resentment he had towards Olivia for the sake of his health, doesn't he? And you know what they say about forgiveness—it's like a huge weight's been lifted off you."

"Hmm, I suppose that's true, and he does say his sister and his carers look after him well." Ava took off her glasses and folded the paper. "That's good. I'm glad he's not on his own. Everyone needs someone to care about them, you know."

"Yay! Mummy!" cried Molly, as she jumped off the coach steps, a toothy grin stretching from one ear to the other. "No baby yet, then?" she said, reaching her arms as far around Charlotte as they would go, and resting her head on her stomach.

"Not yet, poppet, but soon." Charlotte bent to hug her. "Oh, it's so good to have you home, Mol. And Daddy says he's very sorry, but he couldn't come to meet you. He's going to try to get home for a while later, though, okay?" She stepped away and looked Molly up and down before hugging her again. "So, tell me all about it—did you have a good time?"

"Oh my gosh, Mummy," said Molly, slapping a palm to her forehead. "We had the best time *ever*."

Charlotte chuckled. "I see your tooth came out eventually."

Molly nodded and stuck her tongue through the gap. "Erin accidentally hit me in the face when we were practicing our dance routine for the end of camp concert, and my tooth went flying across the tent." She giggled. "She didn't mean to do it—it was an accident—but it hurt a bit. I was glad, though. I'd been wobbling it for ages but I didn't want to pull it hard. I've been keeping it safe in my pencil case."

"That's a good place to keep it," said Charlotte, pulling out into the evening traffic. "Baby teeth are so small, they can easily get lost."

Molly nodded. "Mummy?"

"Yes, sweetheart."

"I put my tooth under the pillow in the tent, but the tooth fairy didn't come. Erin said it's because she only comes to your house, not to camp. Is that right?"

"Yes, that's right," said Charlotte.

"Oh, I see," said Molly, her forehead creased in a curious frown. "Why's that?"

"What? Er, well, the tooth fairy only knows where you live. You know, your *home* address, not where you are when you go off to camp."

"Huh? So she doesn't even know my tooth's come out yet?" Molly said, with a dubious expression.

"Probably not," said Charlotte.

"But I thought fairies knew *everything*. The last time one of my teeth fell out and I lost it, you told me not to worry because the tooth fairy would find it and bring my money to the house that night. And she did, too. That's what you told me—that fairies know everything."

"Oh. Did I?" Charlotte slapped a hand on her thigh. "Ah, yes, sorry, poppet, I forgot for a minute. Mummy's brain is all over the place at the moment because she's having a baby. Yes, you see, the tooth fairy always *knows* you've lost your tooth, but it isn't, er, until you leave it under your *own* pillow that she comes to collect it. I know she'll come if you leave it under your pillow tonight."

The answer satisfied Molly, the creases between her eyes disappearing and a smile curling her lips.

"'kay, Mummy. Come on, let's go and see Pippin and Panda. I missed them so much."

"And then a pizza, yes?"

"Yaaaaay!" Molly threw her hands in the air and danced in her seat. "Mummy?"

"Yes, darling?"

"You know some pizzas have stuffed crusts?"

"Yes."

"What are they actually stuffed *with*?"

"Well, I've never had one, but I think it's just cheese."

"Nothing else?"

"I'm not sure, I don't think so, but we can find out at the pizza place if you like?"

"'kay." Molly nodded and stared out of the window. "I got bit by a mosquito when we were at camp." She held out her arm. "It's got a scab on it now, though, so it doesn't itch any more."

"I know it's difficult," said Charlotte, "but you should try not to scratch bites."

"Why?"

"Because they can get infected, and they can leave scars."

Molly nodded. "'kay. Mummy?"

"Yes."

"Do mosquitos bite other mosquitos?"

Charlotte laughed and reached over to squeeze Molly's hand. "I have absolutely no idea, but we'll look it up when we get home, shall we?"

"'kay."

Charlotte was still smiling when they arrived at the restaurant. It had only been a week since Molly, with her inquisitive mind and her constant barrage of curious questions, had been away.

Sometimes, keeping up with her could be exhausting but, as Charlotte looked at her skipping along beside her chattering away at the speed of a horse-race commentator, she knew she wouldn't have it any other way.

———

"'lo, Oliver," said Molly, as she answered Charlotte's phone. "I got back from camp today and we've just had a pizza as a special welcome home dinner. Mummy just had cheese and tomato but I had pepperoni and sweetcorn. My Daddy says sweetcorn has no place on a pizza but I like it.

"Daddy has weird things on his pizzas. He has anchovies and those nasty looking artichoke thingies, but Daddy calls them fartychokes." She giggled. "Huh? Oh, yes, she's upstairs, just a minute." She skipped to the bottom of the stairs and called up. "Mummy! Oliver's on the phone."

When she'd been a baby, Molly hadn't been able to say Olivia, instead plumping for Oliver, which she could utter without any problem at all, and the name had stuck. She sat on the bottom step and explored the inside of her nose with her finger.

Charlotte appeared at the top of the stairs, chuckling as she made her way down. She sat down next to Molly and took the phone, putting her hand over the microphone. "Take your finger out of your nose, please," she said, "and go and wash your hands, there's a good girl. Hi, Olivia. I had a feeling I might hear from you today."

"You would have heard from me earlier if I hadn't only just got up," said Olivia, in a raspy voice. "I couldn't sleep last night so I've been catching up all day. Have you seen *The Sunday Herald*? That interview with Gordon Buckingham?"

"Yes, I read it this morning," said Charlotte. "I have to say, all things considered, he seems like a very reasonable man."

Olivia said nothing, her voice faltering when she eventually replied. "I feel awful, Charlotte. Really bloody awful. I've hardly thought of him since... since all that business, but now I can't *stop* thinking about him."

"It's not a bad thing to be feeling remorseful after what you did to him, Olivia—it was horrific. And, if I was you, I'd be thanking my lucky stars that the bloke I'd thrown through a window was so good-natured."

"I am," said Olivia. "That's why I feel so bad. In fact, I wanted to ask you a huge favour, if it's not too much trouble."

"Go on," said Charlotte, warily.

"If you're feeling up to it, I wondered if you'd take me to see him? According to the newspaper, he still lives in Little Acorns village, which is only about two hours away. I could go on the train, but I really don't want to go on my own, so I wondered if you'd take me?" she repeated. "I'd really appreciate it if you could. I'll pay for the petrol."

Charlotte hesitated. She felt torn. As much as she wanted to help Olivia, she wasn't sure if going to see Gordon Buckingham was a good idea. Talking to a newspaper reporter was one thing, but seeing his attacker on his doorstep might provoke a completely different reaction altogether, even if he *had* forgiven her. He'd looked very frail in the picture the newspaper had used and the last thing anyone needed was for him to keel over with fright after taking one look at Olivia.

"*Please*, Charlotte. I really need to do this."

Charlotte sighed. "Alright. Shall we go tomorrow and get it out of the way? The earlier the better, but it'll have to be after I've dropped Molly at school. And I'll need to get back in plenty of time to pick her up at half-past three."

The relief in Olivia's voice was palpable.

"Thanks, I owe you one. I'll call round to you tomorrow at around nine-thirty—will that be okay?"

"That'll be fine. I'll see you then. Oh, and Olivia, do you mind if Ava comes along? She's coming over in the morning."

"The more, the merrier," said Olivia. "I'll see you tomorrow."

CHAPTER 14

"Whatever does she want to see him for?" said
Ava, as she wiped her shoes on Charlotte's doormat the
next morning. "It's not as though he said anything
derogatory about her in the interview, is it? I hope she
doesn't want to cause any trouble." She frowned as she
studied Charlotte's stomach for signs of imminent
childbirth.

"Of course she doesn't," said Charlotte. "Quite
the opposite, actually. She's been feeling pretty down
and lonely lately, so it cheered her up when she read
how decent he was about her. I got the impression she
wants to apologise."

"Hmpf, clear her conscience, more like," said
Ava. "She probably saw how amenable he was to that
newspaper reporter and thought she'd take her chance
while he's in a good mood."

"Maybe." Charlotte shrugged as she switched
the radio on low for the dogs to keep them company,
something she'd always done for Pippin if he was left
home alone, and a habit she'd never got out of once
Panda had come to live with them.

"I'm not so sure Olivia's going to get the same
reception, though," said Ava. "He obviously didn't feel
threatened by the reporter who went round to interview
him, but Olivia's an entirely different prospect. We all
know how intimidating she can be."

"That's what I'm worried about," said Charlotte.
"I know he said he's made his peace with her, but what

if the shock of seeing her does him some damage? Shock can be really dangerous, you know."

"Well, whatever happens, I'm jolly glad I'm coming along too," said Ava. "I don't think you should be driving in your condition without someone in the car who'd know what to do if you went into labour. That baby could pop out at any minute—how d'you expect you'd handle *that* if it was just Olivia with you, hmm? You may like to remember who delivered your last baby when she decided to make an appearance a month early." She arched a brow and cast Charlotte a knowing glance.

"As if I could ever forget," said Charlotte, with a grin. "Oh, look, here comes Olivia now. That's good, she's early."

Not having had time for breakfast before she left home, Olivia had brought along a large dish of cold cottage pie to eat in the car. "Morning both," she said. "Do you mind, Charlotte? I'm not used to getting up so early so I didn't even have time to make some toast."

"As long as you don't spill any," said Charlotte, "or the dogs will go crazy the next time they're in here."

"Goodness, you do have a healthy appetite, don't you?" Ava lifted an eyebrow as they set off and Olivia tucked into her breakfast with a large serving spoon.

"I always eat a lot when I'm stressed." She shovelled food into her mouth, barely pausing for breath. "I can't get it down fast enough."

"Evidently," said Ava, drily, as a morsel of solidified mashed potato flew off Olivia's spoon and landed on her handbag. She picked it off with a tissue and pursed her lips.

"Oops, did I get you with that?" Olivia turned and gave Ava a grin that showed off the food in her mouth. "Sorry 'bout that. Good thing it didn't land on your suit—it looks expensive. Very nice." She shovelled in another mouthful.

"Is it from that designer shop in the high street?" asked Charlotte.

Ava nodded. "Do you like it? I got it a few years ago for a knockdown price in one of their end of season sales. I was going to wear it at Harriet and Leo's wedding, but I put on so much weight beforehand, I couldn't get the zip done up. This is the first time I've had it on since I bought it."

"I'd love to wear feminine stuff," said Olivia, with globs of cold gravy and minced beef trapped in the corners of her mouth, "but you don't seem to be able to get clothes like that for women my build; you know, pretty dresses, floaty skirts, stuff like that."

"Of course you can!" said Charlotte. "You can get them for *any* build, and any size. I'm surprised to hear you like them, though. I've never seen you in anything other than trousers and tee-shirts."

"That's because they're practical for work. And that's where I spend most of my time. Well, *used* to spend most of my time. In any case, I wouldn't have a clue where to start with skirts and dresses. I've hardly ever worn a skirt and I've *never* worn a dress. And as

Sherri Bryan

for makeup, well you can forget it. I was a proper tomboy when I was young and I 'spose I've been one ever since."

"Well, once this is all over, and the baby's been born, why don't we go shopping and get you a dress?" said Charlotte.

Olivia blushed. "I'm not sure I'm ready for a dress. Nice thought, though." She spooned the last of the gravy into her mouth before putting the dish in a plastic bag and stretching out her long body. "Right, I think I need a kip before we get there. Just give me a poke if I snore."

She yawned, reclined the seat, and was asleep in less than a minute.

————————

"Are you sure this is where he lives?" Charlotte slowed the car and pulled in to the kerb.

"Apparently," said Olivia, rubbing her eyes and counting down the house numbers until they got to the right one. "After what happened, my Dad found out where he lived and tried to talk me into going to see him, but I wasn't interested."

Ava pressed her nose up against the car window. "Oh dear, it's a bit of a rundown area, isn't it? Do you want me to stay in the car in case someone tries to make off with your wheels, Charlotte? I could honk the horn to raise the alarm."

"I'm sure that won't be necessary," said Charlotte, as she eased herself out from behind the steering wheel. "And stop being such a snob, Ava.

Page 174

Where he lives isn't important, is it? I'm more
concerned that he's going to freak out when he sees
Olivia, or call the police."

Olivia waved her concern away. "Don't worry,
I'm sure he won't do either. He doesn't hold a grudge,
remember? And he won't call the police, because even
though they investigated the case, they didn't think
there was enough evidence to get a conviction against
me. Anyway, all things considered, I think he'll be okay
with seeing me but if he isn't, I'll leave. I just want to
apologise, so we won't be here long. I'm not going to
cause him any aggro."

"That's the spirit," said Charlotte, swinging her
handbag over her shoulder. "Come on then, let's get
this over and done with."

Olivia nodded and walked up the path to the
front door, Charlotte following behind and Ava
bringing up the rear, concentrating on avoiding slipping
down the cracks in the paving stones in her kitten-
heeled court shoes.

She rang the bell and picked absentmindedly at
the peeling paint on the doorframe as she waited for
someone to answer. "I don't think anyone's home," she
said, after a few seconds, and turned to leave.

"Er, not so fast," said Charlotte, holding up a
hand. "If you think I've driven all the way over here so
you can chicken out after getting this far, you're very
much mistaken. Now come on." She dragged Olivia
back to the front door and rang the bell again.

"I'm feeling really nervous now." Olivia tugged at her collar and kicked at a tuft of dandelions with her huge boot.

A minute passed before they heard a shuffling noise on the other side of the door. "Who is it?"

Olivia looked at Charlotte in panic. "What shall I say?" she whispered.

Charlotte rolled her eyes. "What d'you think you should say? Tell him it's you, of course."

Olivia gulped. "Is that you, Gordon? It's Olivia. Olivia Floyd-Martin."

The shuffling slowed. "Olivia?" The door opened a crack, and Gordon peered out. "Good grief! Talk about a blast from the past. What is this? A coach party?"

Charlotte poked Olivia in the back.

"Do you think we could come in?" She stepped awkwardly from foot to foot, not knowing what to do with her hands.

"I'm a friend of Olivia's," said Charlotte, with a smile, and stuck her hand through the crack in the door. "Charlotte Costello."

"And I'm Ava Whittington. Charmed, I'm sure." She waved her fingers at Gordon and flashed a smile. "I've just come along for the drive."

He stared at them, then closed the door, took off the chain, and opened it to let them in. "Come in then." He shuffled off up the hall, his foot scraping against the threadbare carpet. "Don't rush me, I can't walk any faster than this. It's my damn leg. It's like dragging around a sack of potatoes. I've lost count of the number of operations I've had on my flippin' kneecap, and it's still not right. And close the door behind you."

They followed him into the kitchen where he nodded to a kettle, teapot and a cheerful patterned tea cosy; one of the few things in the kitchen that brought some colour to the beige surroundings. "You can make yourself a cuppa if you want, but don't use the yellow cup, 'cos that's my sister's, or the blue or red ones, 'cos they belong to the carers. And don't use the one with the picture of Princess Diana on it, either."

He lowered himself into his armchair and his knee cracked like a gun shot. "Damn thing," he grumbled, glaring at Olivia. "Well, don't just stand there with your mouth open, woman, there's plenty of tea and coffee in the cupboard. Make us a cup of something, or pull up a chair. You decide."

"*I'll* make a pot of tea," said Ava, glad of the opportunity to keep her designer-clad bottom off the worn furniture for as long as possible. "This doesn't really concern me, so you carry on."

Charlotte sunk into the sagging, springless upholstery of a vinyl-covered stool. The old furniture may have seen better days, but everything was spotlessly clean, and a deliciously fresh fragrance scented the air.

"Well? Sit down, sit down!" Gordon motioned to Olivia with a hand and she immediately dropped into the biggest dining chair, making it look like doll's house furniture as she squeezed herself into the space between the armrests.

Gordon looked around at his guests. He was pale—as though he rarely saw the sun—and thin and wiry. His hair floated around his face like wisps of silver candy floss, and his eyes were the palest blue.

He groaned until he was settled comfortably on his pressure cushion, then crossed his hands in his lap and fixed Olivia with a piercing stare. "So, to what do I owe the pleasure? Although I can probably guess what prompted the visit."

Olivia shifted uncomfortably. "I read your interview in the newspaper." She looked around the kitchen, focusing on anything but the man sitting opposite her. "And I know this is going to sound ridiculous, especially after all these years, but I want to apologise."

Gordon raised a spindly eyebrow and leaned forward in his chair, a hand cupped around his ear. "What was that?" he snapped. "I could have sworn you said you'd come to apologise." He kept the small smile that was hovering about his lips at bay, as if he had no intention of making this too easy for the woman who'd caused him so much pain.

Olivia swallowed. "Yes, that's what I said. I've come to apologise. She looked down at her feet. "I had no idea what you'd been through until I saw the newspaper. I've hardly even given you a thought since… since it happened. I'm so sorry. And I want to say thank you for what you did for me—the therapy was a huge help. If someone had thrown *me* through a window… well, let's just say I wouldn't have been so forgiving."

Gordon cocked his head and rubbed at his bony chin. "Ah, yes, forgiveness." His voice mellowed and he reached over and laid his hand on hers. "Now there's the key."

Olivia looked at him and gulped. Even though Gordon had said in the newspaper interview that he'd made peace with her in his heart, she'd half-expected an argument. But he just sat calmly in his chair, the corners of his pale eyes crinkled in a smile.

He chuckled. "I fooled you good and proper with my grumpy old man routine, didn't I? I don't have much to laugh about these days, so I make my own fun whenever I can." He spread his hands and smiled. "Look, I could have held a grudge against you and felt bitter about what you'd done. Goodness knows, I had enough to feel bitter about. I couldn't work for a long time after the accident, you know."

Olivia dropped her head into her hands. "I'm really sorr…" she began to say, but Gordon wagged an index finger to shush her.

"Did you know that I walked to the hospital that evening? I didn't have my car because I thought I'd be having a glass or two of wine with my meal. I had shards of glass all over me, a fractured hip, and a shattered kneecap, but I couldn't feel a thing because I was in shock. It was the adrenaline, see? That's what the nurses told me before they called the police. They were so desperate for me to bring charges against you. But I knew if I made the wrong decision, it wouldn't just affect the rest of your life, it'd affect mine too.

"I knew the police would do their own investigation but, believe it or not, I just couldn't bring myself to see someone with your talent locked up. I know it sounds strange, but I was relieved when they told me they didn't have enough evidence to convict you. They pushed and pushed for me to press charges but I told them I wanted your punishment to be on my terms." He settled a cushion in the small of his back and let out a sigh of relief. "Aah, that's better. Now, where was I? Oh yes… the anger management therapy. You know, Olivia, without that, God only knows where you were headed. I hope what happened at least made you realise how close you'd come to ruining your career."

Olivia nodded. "It did. But I still don't understand why you've never held a grudge against me."

Gordon smiled again. "Because resentment is bad for the soul. I could have brought charges against you and then still sat here for the rest of my days, bitter about what you'd done to me. Your life *and* mine would have been ruined. I couldn't see the point of that, so forgiveness was the only way. Your life carried on and so did mine. I got a compensation payout from *The Old Barn*, and you carried on with your career. I won, you won."

"It said in the newspaper that your wife left you," said Olivia.

Gordon flinched, as if the pain of the memory was still fresh. He nodded. "Yes, that was a difficult time. We were so in love until…" He sighed. "I'm not going to go over everything again—you obviously read about it in the paper—but after she left, I was very down." He winced as he crossed his legs, lifting one over the other. "By the way, you know an apology is only worth its salt if it's sincere, don't you?" He drummed his fingers against his knee. "*Is* it sincere?"

Olivia blushed. "Yes, it is. If I'm honest, a little part of me hoped that apologising would make me feel better about myself, but mostly, I just wanted to apologise because I wanted you to know how sorry I am for what I did. It's not often I say I'm sorry, but I truly am."

Gordon rewarded her with a smile that reached all the way up to his crinkly eyes. "Well that's all that counts, then. And *I'm* sorry for what you must be going through at home. I've been keeping up with what's going on in the news and, even though I haven't been a fan of Roman Haley since what happened between us, it was still a shock to hear of his passing."

"Something happened between you and Roman?" asked Olivia with a frown.

Gordon hesitated before dismissing the comment as if it wasn't important. "It was such a long time ago. I shouldn't have said anything, but sometimes I forget that a lot of people don't know about it. I don't suppose it'll do any harm to tell you, though." He scratched his head and adjusted his cushion again.

"After I was injured, I had to take a break from my job at the newspaper. As you know, it was a long recuperation and I was away for months, but I wasn't worried, because my boss told me my job would be waiting for me when I was well enough to go back to work.

"When I did, though, I found out that Roman had left *The Old Barn*, and my job had been given to him. Apparently, he'd wanted a change of career and when he heard that the newspaper didn't have a restaurant critic, he went to see my boss and persuaded him that he was the ideal person to step in and take over."

Ava stared, wide-eyed, at Charlotte as she poured the tea. "Oh, good heavens! Do you remember the story Harry told us?"

Charlotte nodded. "We heard that Roman left his job as a chef to become a restaurant critic, Gordon, but we had no idea it was your job he'd taken. That must have been awful."

For the first time since Gordon had been talking, Charlotte was sure she saw a glimmer of anger in his eyes, but it passed so quickly, she wondered if she'd been mistaken. "How can you be so calm after everything that's happened to you?"

Gordon smiled. "Like I said. Forgiveness. Although I don't mind admitting, it wasn't easy with Roman. After the accident, and Melanie leaving me, the one thing that kept me going was the thought of going back to work, but he denied me even that pleasure." He frowned, and rubbed a thumb across the deep furrow between his brows. "I heard from a lot of people that he knew damn well that job should have been mine, but he didn't care. Roman was only interested in furthering his career, and he wasn't bothered who he stepped on to get to where he wanted to be."

He let out a long sigh. "If I'm totally honest, I couldn't have done the job anyway. I couldn't drive, it was difficult for me to sit down for long periods of time, and a couple of other long-term injuries which I won't bore you with, all made the job impossible for me. I wanted the decision to give it up to be mine, though, not to have someone else make it for me." He gazed out of the window and gripped the arms of his chair, his knuckles turning white, as he stared, trance-like, straight ahead.

"Are you alright?" asked Charlotte, warily.

Gordon loosened his grip and relaxed. "Sorry. I was lost in my thoughts for a moment."

"Can I ask you something?" said Olivia.

"Of course. You can ask me anything."

"Why didn't you mention anything about what happened with Roman in the newspaper interview?"

"Because they wanted to talk about you. And I don't like to dwell on it." No other reasons." Gordon managed a smile. "Out of interest, do you have any theories on what happened to him?"

Olivia shrugged. "I wish I did. If I knew, I'd be off the hook and I could go back to work, but it's a complete mystery."

"I can't believe the police really think you had anything to do with Roman's death," said Gordon. "I mean, you're a grizzly old bear, but I doubt you're the person they're looking for. Lots of top chefs react to situations with aggression but, in my opinion, it's the passion they feel about the job that makes them do it, not because they're murderers."

"I don't think they *really* think I'm guilty," said Olivia, with a shrug. "But I did hate his guts, and he did open a culinary school in my hometown out of complete spite, so I suppose I can't be surprised to be a suspect… especially with my track record." She half-smiled and ran her fingers through her spiky bleached hair.

"Well, if I can do anything to help," said Gordon, "if I can speak up for you, or whatever, you know where to find me. I don't think you're a bad person, Olivia, but you're a complex character. A genius often has an edge of madness, you know, but that's all some people see. If they just took the trouble to look past it, they'd find the real person."

He held out a hand, which Olivia stared at for an age before gulping and grabbing it with her two. "Thank you. I can't tell you how much I appreciate that."

"You don't have to thank me." Gordon leaned forward in his chair and clutched his knee, wincing until the pain passed. "Sorry, it just creeps up on me sometimes."

"Look, I want to do something for you," said Olivia suddenly. "How would you and your sister like to come to St. Eves and spend a couple of nights at *The President Hotel*? I'll book your travel, adjoining rooms with a sea view, and all your meals will be included, *plus* use of all the facilities. There's a fantastic spa where you can get a massage, or a sauna, or you can use the hot tub. It might help with your aches and pains. It'd all be on me, of course. I won't be there, but I can book everything for you if you give me some dates that would suit. All you have to do is turn up and relax. How does that sound?"

Gordon batted away the offer with a bony hand. "Don't be silly. It's not necessary for you to do that."

"I know it's not *necessary*, but I *want* to do it," said Olivia. "It doesn't even begin to make up for what you've been through but, please, let me do something for you. *Please*?"

Gordon looked at her pleading eyes, then nodded. "Well, that's very generous, and I'd be delighted to accept. It'll be nice to have a change of scene for a couple of days. I'll tell Lara when she gets here later. Thank you."

Olivia heaved a sigh of relief. "No, thank *you*."

Gordon smiled. "No thanks necessary. As I said, forgiveness really is the only way."

———————

"D'you know, I wish I'd done this years ago," said Olivia, with a carefree spring in her heavy steps as she, Charlotte, and Ava walked down the garden path to the car. "Even though I'm the prime suspect in a murder investigation, I feel bloody brilliant!"

"Well, if Gordon can forgive you after what you did to him, I take my hat off to him," said Charlotte, sliding into her seat. "There's not many who would."

Sherri Bryan

"Did you notice that wonderful smell, by the way?" said Ava. "It was like citrus and freshly-cut grass."

Charlotte nodded. "It was gorgeous, wasn't it? Really unusual. I wish I'd asked him what it was."

"Shall I go back and find out?" said Olivia. "It'll only take a minute. I'll…"

"*Oi*! *Floyd-Martin*!" An angry voice blared out from further up the street. "I don't believe it. You've got a damn nerve, showing your face around here."

They all looked in the direction of the voice to see a furious-looking middle-aged woman with mad, bushy red hair striding towards the car.

"Who on earth is that?" asked Ava, craning her neck forward from the back seat for a better view. "Oh dear, she looks awfully common. I hope she's not going to rob us." She zipped up her handbag and locked the back doors, testing them to make sure they were definitely shut. "She looks jolly cross. Maybe she's looking for a fight?"

"Ava! For heaven's sake!" Charlotte caught her eye in the interior mirror. "Just because we're not in the most exclusive of areas, doesn't mean the locals spend their days looking for someone to rob or wrestle." She shook her head and rubbed her back. "Do you know who she is, Olivia?"

Olivia shrugged. "I've no idea, but judging by the look on her face, I'd say she's not very pleased to see me. She certainly seems to know who I am, though." She squared her shoulders and crossed her arms as the woman drew closer.

Two feet shorter than the Amazonian chef, the feisty woman stopped just inches away, with her hands on her hips, and glared at Olivia, her eyes boring into her like lasers.

"What the hell are you doing here?"

Olivia returned the hostility. "Last I heard, this is still a free country, and I can go wherever I like. What's it got to do with you, anyway? And who are you?"

"I'm Lara Buckingham, Gordon's sister," said the woman, her blue eyes flashing. "That's what it's got to do with me. Now, I'll ask you again, what are you doing here?"

"Oh." Olivia scratched her head. "I've been to see Gordon. I wanted to speak to him."

"Did you now? What did you want to speak to him about?"

"I think you should ask him," said Olivia.

Lara kicked her hard on the shin. "I'm asking *you!*"

"Oww!" Olivia doubled up and took a step back. "Are you mental, woman? You can't just kick people when you feel like it, you know."

"The same could be said for throwing people through windows," Lara snapped back. "Or have you conveniently forgotten about that?"

"No, actually," said Olivia, rubbing her leg. "That's why I'm here. I came to apologise. And I spoke to Gordon about you both coming to St. Eves for a mini-break… all on me."

Lara looked dumbstruck for a moment, then threw back her head and laughed. "Apologise? A mini-break? I think it's a bit late for that, don't you? Have you any idea of the hell he's been through over the past years? Have you? No, of course you haven't, because you couldn't have cared less." She put up a hand. "And don't tell me you've turned over a new leaf, or you've seen the light, or whatever the damn reason is for you being here—your pathetic apology is about twenty-five years too late."

She looked Olivia up and down with a sneer. "Did he tell you he had to stop working after the accident? He's never been the same since he went through that window. God knows, I've wanted him to press charges and sue you for every penny, but he wouldn't hear of it. He just wanted to forgive and forget. But that's Gordon for you." She stopped for breath and brushed an angry tear from her freckled cheek.

"You know what? Gordon may not live in the smartest house, in the best area, but he's still too good for the likes of you. You're not fit to breathe the same air he does. Now, why don't you get lost? You're not wanted around here. I wish they'd locked you up and thrown away the key, although you'd be better suited to where Roman Haley's gone—and good riddance to him, too!" She turned on her heel and stomped up the garden path, jabbing her key at the lock. "And you know where you can shove your mini-break!" she shouted, before slamming the door behind her.

"Well, you can't really blame her for feeling that way, dear," said Ava, trying to lighten the atmosphere, as Olivia heaved herself into the car, her recent good mood having vanished. "You almost killed her brother, after all."

"I don't want to talk about it," snapped Olivia, resting her elbow on the window frame and avoiding eye contact. "Can we just get out of here and go back to St. Eves?"

————————————

"Charlotte! How many times have we discussed this?" said Nathan, through a mouthful of toothpaste.

"Can you go and rinse, please? You're making me feel nauseous." Charlotte stroked Pippin and Panda as they crawled up the centre of the bed and curled up beside her.

"You know I'm grateful for your input," said Nathan, as he reappeared, wiping his mouth on the back of his hand, "but I would never forgive myself if anything happened to you while you were out snooping around. You aren't the police, you know."

Charlotte gave him an incredulous look. "Yes, I know that, thank you, and I was *not* snooping around. I just took Olivia to see Gordon and happened to find out a few things while I was there. And Ava was with us, so in the unlikely event I'd gone into labour, she would have known what to do. But, honestly, Nathan, if I'd thought that was likely to happen, I would never have gone in the first place."

Nathan's eyes widened. "Ava was with you? Well, that's just marvellous, isn't it? The whole town probably knows what happened by now." He put his hands on his hips and exhaled loudly.

"Will you please just come to bed?" said Charlotte, with a sigh that matched his.

The dogs jumped down and Nathan got under the duvet, propping himself up on an elbow. "So, what did you find out?" He grinned. "Or were you going to keep it to yourself?"

Charlotte settled herself against her pillows. "Well, I think Olivia's apology went down well with Gordon, but not so much with his sister. I reckon she would have done Olivia some serious damage if she'd flown at her. Honestly, though, Gordon's the most amazing guy. He's so peaceful and full of forgiveness. He completely forgives Olivia for what she did, despite all the long-term side effects of the injuries he has to live with, and he even forgave Roman eventually, although he said that wasn't easy."

Nathan sat up. "Roman? What's Gordon got to do with Roman?"

"I thought that might get your interest," said Charlotte. "Well…"

She related the story Gordon had told them.

"So Gordon and Roman knew each other from years ago? And Roman used to work at *The Old Barn* with Olivia, but then he left, had a change of career, and swiped Gordon's newspaper restaurant critic job from under his nose while he was on sick leave?"

Charlotte nodded. "I think it was more a case of them having knowledge of each other, rather than actually knowing each other, if you know what I mean, and that's only because they both worked in the food industry. But, yes, that's about the measure of it, although Gordon said he didn't hold a grudge."

Nathan's eyebrow shot up. "Well, he would say that, wouldn't he?"

"Maybe, but I believe him." Charlotte punched her pillow to get comfortable. "Mind you, there were a few seconds while we were talking about Roman that Gordon looked absolutely furious, but that's hardly surprising. I suppose talking about him must have dredged up all kinds of emotions."

"You always give everyone the benefit of the doubt, don't you?" Nathan leaned over and kissed her. "Which is only one of the reasons I love you so much."

"If you'd seen him, you'd have believed him, too," said Charlotte. "He's into forgiveness in a *big* way and if you really want to forgive someone, you have to let go of any resentment towards them, see? You can't forgive someone if you're holding a grudge against them, can you?"

"Perhaps not," said Nathan, "but I think I'll stick to good old-fashioned detective methods to establish guilt, if it's all the same to you. I mean, if we believed everyone who pleaded innocence because they'd forgiven anyone who'd ever done them wrong, there'd be criminals running around willy-nilly. We'd never get any of them off the streets."

Charlotte shrugged. "Suit yourself. I'm just giving you my opinion." She yawned. "Bear in mind, though, that Gordon Buckingham is an invalid. He's pretty much confined to his house, he's in pain, he has trouble walking and, most of all, he wasn't even in St. Eves when Roman was murdered. Hardly fits the profile of the person you're looking for, does it?"

"No, but it's new information, and another lead for us to investigate," said Nathan. "And, you've got to admit, it's very strange that the one person who has every reason to hold grudges against Olivia and Roman, is the one person who claims not to."

CHAPTER 15

"How long will you be on crutches?" asked Charlotte.

"Dr. Talbot said I should be back on my feet again in a couple of days. I just need to rest my foot for a while," said Betty.

"How on earth you managed to sprain your ankle in these, I just don't know." Ava picked up one of Betty's very sensible rubber-soled shoes by the lace, and held it at arm's length as if it was radioactive. "They're as flat as pancakes."

"I know, but I was on my way to the clubhouse and I forgot my lucky bingo pen, so I turned back to get it and *I* moved, but my foot sort of stayed where it was. It's the rubber soles, see? They've got such a good grip. My ankle made the most sickening noise. I thought I was going to pass out."

Betty's face paled. "Thank goodness Harriett was home and heard me calling out, or I don't know how long I'd have waited for help. Most of the residents were in the clubhouse, you see. Actually, do you mind if we change the subject? It makes me feel queasy to think about it."

"Of course we don't, Bet," said Harriett. "I'm just glad we could help. It's at times like this that I'm glad we live so close by."

Betty patted Harriett's arm. "That casserole you brought in last night was delicious, by the way. And I haven't had homemade rice pudding in years."

"And you won't have to worry about your dinner for the next couple of days, either," said Charlotte. "I've made you a chicken and asparagus pie, with potatoes and vegetables, and some chocolate crunch. I'll put them in the fridge, shall I?"

Betty nodded. "Oh, thank you, Charlotte, you're a sweetheart. Yes, please, love. And would you mind making us a pot of tea while you're in the kitchen? Maybe we could have a slice of chocolate crunch to go with it?" She put her foot on a stool and let out a sigh. "Aaah, that's better."

"Did Izzy come over to see you before she left?" asked Harriett.

Betty nodded. "We had a lovely afternoon. I showed her all my dad's old teapots, and we chatted for hours. She was telling me she had to take a course to qualify as a tea taster before she could become a buyer. Not just anyone can do it, you know. Her job sounds fascinating."

"Really?" said Ava, faking a yawn. "I imagine it must have been an absolutely *riveting* few hours, talking about tea and looking at old pots."

"Actually, it was," said Betty, ignoring Ava's snipe. "*And* she gave me a lovely present before she left. She gets so many free samples and gifts from her tea suppliers, she makes them into goodie bags for her friends and family.

"Some of the more unusual things aren't really to my taste, though, so I only took what I knew I'd use and I put the rest aside for you, Charlotte. As a tea lover, I thought you'd appreciate them." She pointed to a bag on the counter. "Didn't you say Nathan's having trouble sleeping? There's a box of flavoured tea bags in there, and there are some lemon balm ones amongst them. They're very good for insomnia, apparently."

"That's fab, thank you—and maybe the tea bags will help. I've been giving him camomile tea, but it doesn't seem to be working. He's been coming home late, falling asleep and then waking up after an hour."

"Doesn't surprise me," said Betty. "He must have a million things going round in his head. Speaking of which, how's the investigation going?"

"Don't ask," said Charlotte. "It's frustrating him no end, but I'm sure it's just a matter of time before they find the murderer. I hope so, anyway."

"There are plenty of suspects, though, aren't there?" said Ava. "My money's on Gavin. He's the tutor I told you about, Bet. He's a nasty piece of work."

"Just because you don't like him, doesn't mean he's a killer," said Charlotte.

"You weren't there, dear," said Ava, taking a dainty bite of chocolate crunch. "You didn't see the way his eyes followed people around the room, locking onto them like a heat seeking missile before it blows something to pieces. He was very intense and quite creepy. I told the police to keep an eye on him."

"Talking of creepy, Roy's another one who can't keep his eyes to himself," said Harriett.

"Roy?" said Ava, her little finger making an appearance as she lifted her teacup. "He's such a lovely young man! Why on earth would you say that?"

"He might *seem* like a lovely young man, Ava, but that's what people who are hiding something want you to think. They want to lull you into a false sense of security and then, when you least expect it, they move in for the kill." Harriett looked knowingly around the coffee table.

"I thought you said you liked him?" said Charlotte

"Well, I don't *dis*like him," said Harriett, "but if I found out tomorrow that he was responsible for Roman's murder, I wouldn't be surprised. Nice enough on the surface, but those staring eyes of his give me the shivers. I noticed them during the tasting session when they were stuck on Olivia like a magnet."

"That's exactly how I feel about Gavin," said Ava. "I wouldn't want to bump into him on a dark night, that's for sure."

"I doubt there's any chance of that happening," said Betty, with a chuckle. "I'm sure the feeling's completely mutual."

Ava threw her a sarcastic smile as she stirred her tea. "Haha, very amusing." She gave Charlotte a look that said, *I can't keep this gossip to myself for a moment longer*, then said casually, "By the way, we went to see Gordon Buckingham yesterday. You know, the chap Olivia threw through the window."

"You didn't!" said Betty, a slice of chocolate crunch coming to a grinding halt halfway to her mouth.

Ava nodded. "Olivia wanted to apologise to him. Better late than never, I suppose."

"What's he like?" asked Harriett.

"Very pleasant," said Ava. "Isn't he, Charlotte?"

She nodded. "He seems like a really nice guy. Very genuine."

"Izzy and I were chatting about him when she came round," said Betty. "She read out the story in *The Herald* while I was making lunch—we were both in tears, just thinking about what that poor man had been through."

"Yes, it was upsetting to read, wasn't it?" said Charlotte. "He seems to be getting on with his life, though, and he's got his carers and his sister. His sister wasn't very good-humoured, but you can hardly blame her for wanting to kick Olivia in the shins, which she actually did."

"I thought she was awful," said Ava, her nostrils flared, "standing there in the middle of the street, screaming like a fishwife."

The ringtone of Charlotte's phone sounded from the depths of her handbag but the call cut off before she could answer it.

"Anyone important, dear?" asked Ava.

"It was Olivia. I'll call her when I get home."

———————

"You'll never guess!" said Olivia, when Charlotte called her back later. "Gordon Buckingham and his witch of a sister have only agreed to come to St. Eves after all!"

"Oh, that's great! I have to say, after your encounter with her, I didn't think they'd be coming anywhere near."

"Gordon said she took a bit of persuading but she eventually agreed. I'm over the moon. I've already been on the phone to the hotel and organised everything. And I've told Simon to look after them."

"When are they coming?" asked Charlotte.

"They're arriving next Thursday and staying until after breakfast on Saturday. They said they'd prefer a mid-week break because Lara works a second job stocking shelves at a supermarket on Saturday and Sunday nights."

"I can tell how much this means to you," said Charlotte. "I'm really pleased they changed their minds."

"Not as much as I am," said Olivia. "Look, I have to go, 'cos I've got some stuff to do, but I really feel like my life's about to change. Don't ask me why, but it's about bloody time! I'll speak to you soon."

———————

"Everything alright, Ben?"

"I've found something on Larissa Reece, Chief." Ben pulled a chair up to Nathan's desk and put a file down in front of him.

Nathan read through the pages before closing the file with a grim expression. "I assume this is one of the 'nasty little secrets' Roman was referring to on the tape? I don't know why people lie about stuff like this.

It's obvious we were going to find out about it sooner or later."

Ben nodded. "You think it's a motive for murder?"

Nathan shrugged. "I'd be less inclined to think it was if she'd been honest with us from the start but now…" He picked up an envelope Ben had put on the table. "What's this?"

"It was in one of the boxes of Roman's tapes that Carl's been going through," said Ben. "He gave it to me last night."

Nathan upturned it and two photographs fell out. They were both of Larissa and a man. One showed them embracing on the doorstep of a house, the other, taken through the window, showed them kissing passionately.

"Who's the guy?"

"No idea," said Ben. "But if Roman was interested enough in the photos to keep them, there must have been a pretty good reason. I'm sure Monique must know who he is, but I'd prefer to hear it from Larissa."

"I agree," said Nathan. "Let's get her in for questioning.

———————

"What's this about?" said Larissa, warily.

"I'd like you to clarify a few things," said Ben. "For instance, how you met Roman Haley."

"I think I already told you, didn't I? I was working at a restaurant called The Moonbeam, with

Gavin, and Roman used to come in to eat sometimes. I used to make a sorbet he liked, and he asked to meet me one day. We got chatting, and that was it."

"I see. And then he asked you to work for him?"

"Yes. Well, he asked if I wanted to help Gavin run his cookery school. He asked Gavin first, but he wanted me on board, too."

Ben nodded. "And how long did you work at The Moonbeam?"

"Er, I think it was around six years."

"And before that?"

Larissa's eyes flickered left and right. "Why do you need to know that?"

"If you could answer the question, please?"

"I worked for an outside catering company."

"So you worked for an outside catering company before you started working at The Moonbeam?" said Ben. "Sorry to labour the point, but I need to be sure I've got the facts right."

Larissa nodded.

"I see. It's just that I've been making some enquiries and according to what I've been told, while you were working for the outside catering company, you slipped and hurt your back at an event seven years ago, after which you started claiming invalidity benefit because you were unable to work. Is that right?"

Larissa nodded. "Yes, that's right."

"I see. And when did you stop claiming benefits?"

Larissa dropped her gaze to her lap and said nothing.

"You see, Miss. Reece, according to the records I've found, you started claiming benefits after you hurt your back seven years ago, and you continued to claim them until Roman Haley employed you last year. There's no record of you working anywhere in between... at The Moonbeam or otherwise." He scratched his head with the end of his pen. "You can understand why this is puzzling me."

"You know, don't you?" Larissa started to cry. Great, heaving sobs that shook her whole body. "I thought that with Roman dead, no one would ever need to find out. Please don't tell anyone. I could get a huge fine, maybe even go to prison." She hunted for a tissue up her sleeve and blew her nose.

"Look, why don't you just tell me the truth?" Ben got a glass of water from the dispenser and put it down in front of her. "We'll find out everything anyway, we always do in the end."

Larissa took a sip of water before picking bits off her tissue and dropping them into her lap. "After I hurt my back, I couldn't work, so I went on benefits. I'd never claimed for anything before, and it was such a big lump of money that when I was well enough to go back to work, I didn't want it to stop.

"I knew it was wrong, but when I was offered a long-term job at The Moonbeam that paid cash in hand, I took it because I knew it was unlikely the benefits office would be able to trace it. I worked there for six years, taking a wage *and* claiming invalidity benefit. Whenever I had to have my injury assessed to see if I was fit enough to go back to work, I just faked it. It's not difficult to fake a back injury, you know." She blew out a heavy sigh. "Before I came to St. Eves to work for Roman, I was claiming for just about everything I could. I was up to my eyeballs in benefit fraud."

"And did Roman know about this?" asked Ben.

Larissa nodded.

"And that's the secret he knew that you didn't want anyone to find out?"

She started sobbing again, harder this time. "It's part of it, yes, but it's not the worst of it. It was my sister… my sister and her husband."

"What about them?"

Larissa pulled another tissue from her sleeve and looked up through damp eyelashes.

"Go on," said Ben.

She sighed. "A few years ago, my sister got sick. She was so ill, we didn't know if she would pull through. It was difficult for all of us, but her husband didn't cope with it very well at all. You know how some people can't handle illness, or being in a hospital, even if they're just there to see someone else? Well, that was Aaron. Sandy was in hospital for months, but he made every excuse not to visit her.

Larissa blew her nose and took a deep breath. "Anyway, all this was happening around the time I started working at The Moonbeam. Aaron used to come in and sit at the bar, rather than go to the hospital, and then he'd take me back to my place at the end of my shift. I'm not proud of what happened… when I think of it now, it disgusts me."

"And what *did* happen?" said Ben.

"We had an affair." She put her head in her hands. "We didn't mean to, but once we were in it, neither of us wanted it to stop. I had no idea that Roman even knew about it, though, or the benefit fraud, until I'd been working for him for a couple of months. He told me he knew everything, but said if I was always loyal to him, he'd never tell anyone... but if I wasn't, he'd make sure I paid."

"When I asked him what he meant, he said a call to the Benefit Fraud Hotline would be all that was needed for them to start an investigation, and an anonymous letter to my sister, along with some photographs Monique had taken, would put her in the picture about what Aaron and I had been up to while she'd been in hospital.

"Roman didn't make idle threats, so I was petrified. It was bad enough that he said I could go to prison for claiming illegally for so long, but the thought of Sandy finding out about me and Aaron was so much worse. It would have broken her heart." Larissa raked the curls off her fringe and fresh tears spilled onto her cheeks. "The thought of her knowing what we'd done was unbearable."

"What did you think when you found out Mr. Haley knew about your relationship with Gavin Doyle?" asked Ben. "Did it concern you?"

Larissa's ponytail bobbed up and down as she nodded. "What do you think? As soon as I found out he knew, I guessed it would only be a matter of time before he made good on his threats. I don't mind telling you, I've never been more relieved than I was when I heard the news he was dead."

"I imagine it must have been a weight off your mind when you realised he wouldn't be revealing your secrets after all?"

"You can't imagine," said Larissa. "And I was lucky that someone else got rid of him first, because if they hadn't, *I* would have killed him to stop Sandy finding out about me and Aaron." She dried her cheeks and fixed her eyes on Ben's. "You may think I had motives to kill Roman, and you'd be right, but you have absolutely no proof that I did."

CHAPTER 16

As was often the case in small towns, gossip spread quickly, reaching the ears of maximum townsfolk with the minimum of delay.

It was fortunate for him that local news reporter, Andrew Somerfield, was one of the first people to hear that Gordon Buckingham and his sister, Lara, would be arriving in St. Eves the following day, and staying at *The President Hotel*, courtesy of Olivia Floyd-Martin. He'd missed out on interviewing Gordon in his home, so he was determined to get in first on *this* story.

Thanks to a nosey hotel porter, whom he rewarded generously in exchange for interesting tip-offs or juicy gossip, Andrew already knew what rooms Gordon and his sister would be staying in, along with Gordon's home telephone number, which he'd just called to ask if he'd be willing to give an exclusive TV interview during his stay in St. Eves, in return for a substantial fee.

Gordon had been reluctant at first, but Andrew had used all his persuasive skills to secure a meeting with him at half-past three the following day, in the Garden Lounge Bar of the hotel.

Andrew had also suggested it would be a huge coup if they managed to get Olivia to participate in the interview, although Gordon had told him he'd have to think about that.

Andrew sat back and put his feet up on the desk. If this interview didn't get him the title of News

Reporter of the Year at the local press awards dinner,
he didn't know what would.

————————

"Well, this is very nice, I must say," said
Gordon, as he settled himself on a plush armchair in the
reception area of *The President Hotel*.

"And so it flippin' well should be," said Lara,
determined not to enjoy herself. "I only came so it
would cost Olivia more." She pulled at the collar of her
polyester blouse and gawped at the luxurious
surroundings. "You know we're going to look like the
poor relations while we're here, don't you? I'm sure
people are looking down their noses at us already."

"Oh, why can't you stop complaining and enjoy
it?" said Gordon. "We've never had someone treat us to
anything like this before, so why can't you just relax
and have a good time? If it makes you feel better, you
can hate Olivia if you like, but why wouldn't you want
to make the most of being here?" He waved a hand
expansively in front of him. "Just look at it, it's
beautiful." He took a deep breath and a smile spread
across his pale face. "Even the air smells different."

"Mr. and Ms. Buckingham?" Simon Clancy
appeared, followed by a hotel porter. "I'm Simon
Clancy, the Hotel Manager. I trust you had a
comfortable journey?" He shook hands and indicated
they should follow him. "Please, let me show you to
your rooms."

"Is it right that everything's paid for?" asked
Lara, sceptically, as they waited for the lift. "We were

told it would be, but I doubt it actually is. I'm only asking because I don't want a nasty surprise of a huge bill when we check out because we had something we thought was included, but wasn't."

Simon nodded. "Absolutely everything will be taken care of. That includes 24 hour a day room service, all spa treatments, use of the gym, sauna, hot tub, indoor and outdoor pools, breakfast, lunch, dinner and drinks in our rooftop restaurant, any drinks or bar snacks you may have during your stay in our ground floor Garden Lounge Bar, any films you watch in your room, full use of the minibar and, of course," he swiped the room key and flung open the door, "your suites, with south-facing balconies and sea views. This is Mr. Buckingham's room, but yours is just on the other side of the adjoining door."

Lara's jaw dropped. The huge rooms were light, airy and beautifully decorated, with soft furnishings in neutral colours and an enormous bouquet of orchids on each of the walnut sideboards. She walked through into her room, stroking the bedspread and curtains, feeling the crisp bed linen, the softness of the towels and the deep-pile rugs beneath her feet.

"If there's anything you need," said Simon, handing her a room key, "please just dial 0 and call down to reception. And Mr. Buckingham, I understand from Olivia that you might be interested in a tour of the hotel kitchens? She said she thought you might appreciate it, particularly the kitchen in our rooftop restaurant, which is state of the art."

Gordon's eyes shone. "Olivia knows me too well—I most certainly *would* appreciate it. You just tell me when, and I'll be there."

"Excellent," said Simon. "Would now be convenient for you? After you've had some time to settle in, of course."

Gordon replied with an enthusiastic nod. "That's perfect. I'm meeting someone this afternoon, so that suits me fine. It shouldn't take too long, should it?"

"Half an hour at the most," said Simon. "How about I meet you in the Garden Lounge Bar downstairs in about half an hour?"

"I'll be there."

Simon gave them both the benefit of the smarmy smile he'd been perfecting for years. "I hope you'll enjoy your stay. See you shortly, Mr. Buckingham."

"Oh my, God!" Lara called from her room. "Gordon, have you seen the bathrooms? They're almost as big as your house and mine put together!"

She pushed open the floor to ceiling glass door and stepped onto the covered balcony to take in the view. Gordon was right. The air *did* smell different.

She went back into his room to find him hunting through his suitcase.

"What are you looking for?"

"My swimming shorts. After I've seen the kitchens, you don't think I'm going to sit up here in the room for two days, do you? Come on, woman, get your cossie on! Didn't you hear what Mr. Clancy said about the spa, the sauna, the hot tub, and the pools?"

Lara grinned as she dragged her swimming costume out of the case. "Here, look, there's a card on these flowers." She flicked it open and read the message.

"Who're they from?"

"Who d'you think?"

"Olivia?"

"Yes. Olivia."

"What does it say?"

Lara pursed her lips and opened the card again. "It says, 'Hi Gordon and Lara, I hope you like the rooms. I wish you a very happy couple of days. Best wishes, Olivia.'" She shook her head. "Honestly, what a suck-up. It's so obvious she's done this to get into our good books. When is she going to get it through her thick head that *nothing* will make up for what she did. No amount of crawling around you is going to make things any better, no matter how much money she throws at us."

"Good God, Lara, you're a hard woman to appease at times," said Gordon. "Olivia knows she did wrong and she knows she can't ever put things right, but she's trying to make amends the best way she knows how. Whatever you may think, I think this is a pretty nice gesture."

Lara scoffed. "So it bloody well should be." She picked up the menu for the rooftop restaurant from the sideboard. "And I'm going to make the most of it. For dinner tonight, I'm having caviar to start, with lobster to follow, white chocolate soufflé decorated with gold leaf, and the most expensive bottle of champagne they have to wash it down with."

"You don't even like caviar," said Gordon.

"I do if Olivia Floyd-Martin's paying for it," said Lara. "Even if I don't eat it, I'm ordering it. Listen, Gordon, I've wanted to get my own back on that woman for years, and this is my opportunity. I'm going to get my money's worth while I'm here, you just see if I don't. There's going to be a big hole in her bank account by the time I'm finished. Now hurry up and get your boring tour of the kitchens over and done with. There's a spa downstairs and I can hear it calling for me!"

———————————

Andrew Somerfield knew that Gordon Buckingham and his sister had arrived at the hotel at exactly quarter-to ten that morning.

He knew that Simon Clancy had given Gordon a tour of the kitchens, and that he and his sister had signed in at the spa half an hour after that, leaving there two hours later to visit the Garden Lounge Bar for lunch.

Andrew checked his watch. It was twenty-past three.

He spotted Gordon and Lara immediately. They were the couple who were well on their way to getting drunk, and ordering drinks for the rest of the guests in the bar. He grinned as he imagined the look on Olivia Floyd-Martin's face when she was presented with their final bill.

He'd been told on many occasions that it was his boyish charm people responded to, so he made sure it was turned up to maximum as he strode into the bar.

"Mr. and Ms. Buckingham? I'm Andrew Somerfield. Nice to meet you."

Lara put down the cocktail she was drinking. "You won't tell Olivia how much of her money we're spending, will you?" she said, with a giggle, her guard coming up a little.

Andrew chuckled. "No, not at all. My only interest is securing an exclusive with you as a follow-up to Mr. Buckingham's recent interview in *The Sunday Herald*. It'll go out on TV on this evening's local news as the lead story."

"Ooh, I didn't know it was going to be the *lead* story," said Lara, as she picked up her drink again and pulled a glacé cherry off a cocktail stick with her teeth. "How exciting."

Andrew smiled and turned to Gordon. "Did you think any more about asking Olivia to participate in the interview? As I explained yesterday, I could negotiate a little more for you if she did."

Gordon nodded. "Actually, I called her about it last night, after I'd spoken to you. As I guessed, she wasn't too keen on the idea, but when I explained it would give her the opportunity to put her side of the story across, she was a bit more receptive. She said she'd have to think about it, though, so I told her I'd call her again today to see what she'd decided." He scratched his head through the strands of wispy hair. "I have to say, she didn't sound very comfortable with the idea at all."

Lara swatted him on the arm. "Gordon, who cares whether she's comfortable with it or not? If Mr. Somerfield's willing to give us some more money in exchange for Olivia saying a few words, I'm sure it can be arranged. Go on, go and call her now and see if she's made up her mind. And if she says no, talk her round. Goodness knows, she owes you a favour."

As Gordon shuffled off, Lara reached across and pulled over a chair for Andrew. She patted the seat. "Why don't you come and sit down and you can tell me all about our fee?"

———————

"Did you speak to her?" Lara demanded to know as soon as Gordon came back into the bar.

He nodded. "She'll do it, but she's not very happy about it—I told you she wouldn't be. She didn't do all this for us because she wanted it splattered all over the evening news, she did it because she wanted to do something to go some way in making up for the past."

"But she agreed to meet?" said Andrew.

Gordon nodded. "She didn't want to come here, though, so she suggested we meet in the park. There's a statue with some benches nearby, apparently? Is that okay?"

"Suits me, and I know exactly where she means," said Andrew. "It's usually quiet there at this time of day, which is good when you're doing an OB…

sorry, that's an outside broadcast. Otherwise you get people walking in front of the camera, behind the camera, waving hello to their mum, etc., etc., you know what I mean? Right, I've got a cameraman on standby, so give me five minutes to give him a call and get him over to the park. Then we can leave. Is that okay with you both?"

Lara nodded, and squealed excitedly. "I just need a few minutes to go and freshen up my makeup. I don't want to look like an old frump if I'm going to be a TV star!"

———————

As Olivia dragged her feet through the park, she started to seriously rethink her part in the interview.

She was still a main suspect in Roman Haley's murder, and tensions were running high among his fans, many of whom were harassing her on a daily basis via social media.

She should be keeping a low profile, not appearing on TV with the man from her past to whom she'd caused such serious injuries, telling viewers how she was making amends by treating him and his sister to a mini-break in a posh hotel.

She'd had enough criticism lately. She didn't need to do anything that would put her in the firing line for any more.

Damn it! I'm not doing it. When I get there, I'm going to tell Gordon I've changed my mind.

As she approached the meeting place, she saw Gordon, Lara, Andrew and a cameraman waiting on a couple of park benches.

She saw Gordon turn and raise his arm in a wave. She lifted her arm to wave back, then turned as a sudden movement drew her eye to the clump of trees to her left.

The last thing she saw was a dark mass heading towards her and then... darkness.

CHAPTER 17

"Olivia. Olivia. *Olivia*! Oh, thank God. Doctor, she's opened her eyes."

Olivia closed them again and groaned. "My head's killing me."

"I'm not surprised," said Charlotte. "You've got a lump on it the size of an egg."

"Glad to see you back with us, Olivia," said the doctor. "I'd like to do a quick examination." He turned to Charlotte. "If you could wait outside, please?"

She sat down on a hard chair in the corridor.

She was only at the hospital because her number had shown on Olivia's phone as a regularly called number, and a nurse had contacted her to ask if she could come to collect her.

"It would be better if she didn't walk or drive anywhere, or be on her own for the rest of the day, possibly tomorrow, too," the nurse had said. "She needs rest and sleep, so if you could make sure she gets home safely, that would be wonderful, and if there's anyone who could stay with her—just to keep an eye on her—that would be great."

Charlotte knew Olivia's parents didn't live too far away, but they owned a smallholding which was difficult for them to leave at short notice. In any case, Olivia was always telling her that, after five minutes in each other's company, she and her mum drove each other up the wall. Plus, she didn't like to worry them.

Charlotte sighed. Who else could keep an eye on her? There was only one person she knew of, but she wasn't sure how her husband would take the news.

The doctor poked his head around the door. "You can come back in now."

Olivia was lying on top of the bed with a hand over her eyes. "Is that you, Charlotte?"

"Yes, it's me. How are you feeling?"

Olivia looked at her through barely open eyelids. "Like someone put my head in a vice. When I said I had a feeling my life was about to change, this wasn't quite what I had in mind. What the hell happened? The doctor said I've got a mild concussion."

"You were hit on the forehead by a rock," said the doctor.

"A flippin' big one, too," said Charlotte. "It was on the ground next to you, so Andrew Somerfield showed it to the paramedics in case they needed to see what had caused the injury."

Olivia closed her eyes again. "I remember. I turned round because I saw something moving in the trees. Then something was coming towards me and that was that."

"You were very lucky you weren't hit on the side of your head—on the temple," said the doctor. "If you had been, this story could have had a very different ending indeed. You should think yourself lucky."

Olivia opened her eyes as wide as she could and glared at him. "Oh, yeah, I feel *really* lucky. I've got a splitting headache, I feel like throwing up, and I've got a lump on my head that's almost as big as my *actual* head. And the room won't stop spinning, even with my eyes closed. It's like the worst hangover ever."

The doctor returned her glare with a stern look. "I'm not sure you realise how serious this could have been. If an impact of this force had been just a couple of inches to the left, you could have been killed, most definitely seriously injured. Now, if you'll excuse me, I have other patients to see." He put her chart in the cubby hole above the bed, his white coat swishing against his trousers as he walked quickly from the room.

"Did Gordon's interview go ahead without me?" said Olivia.

"Of course it didn't! It didn't go ahead at all. And after you'd been carted off in the ambulance, Gordon and Lara checked out of the hotel and went home."

"Oh no! They were supposed to be enjoying themselves." Olivia picked balls of fluff from the blanket and scowled. "I must be jinxed. The last time I agreed to something I didn't want to do, Roman kicked the bucket, and now this. I should have refused to take part in Andrew's stupid interview from the start. Then Gordon would still be here, and I wouldn't have the headache from hell."

"You might have a headache, but at least you're alive," said Charlotte. "The doctor's right, you *are* lucky."

"Huh, it's alright for you to say that," mumbled Olivia. "*You* haven't got someone trying to bump you off."

"What? Why would you think that?"

"Why else would someone throw a bloody great rock at my head, *and* try to poison me?"

The thought that someone had been trying to deliberately do Olivia harm hadn't even entered Charlotte's mind—until now.

"Think about it," said Olivia. "If I hadn't walked out of the tasting session, *I* would have eaten some of that poisoned bread because Roman and I would have shared everything. It was no secret I'd been invited, because he announced it at the library roof fundraiser. *The Herald* did a write up on it, remember? And if I hadn't turned my head when I was walking through the park, I wouldn't be lying here talking to you. It's pretty obvious to me that someone's trying to do me in."

"Well, it's possible, I suppose," said Charlotte, being careful not to say anything that might make Olivia even more worried than she already was. "Are you sure you're not being paranoid, though? Especially about the rock. I'd have thought it's more likely to have been kids mucking around, rather than someone lurking in the undergrowth, waiting for you to walk past. I'm not excusing them if it was, I just mean that it might have been a random attack, rather than you being singled out deliberately. Think about it, who could possibly have known you'd be walking through the park at that precise time?"

Olivia frowned. "Well, if you put it like that, it sounds more likely that it was random, I suppose." She touched the lump on her head gently and winced. "If it is kids, and they did this for a bit of fun, it needs to be taken seriously. They need to be thrown in the cells for a couple of days, not just let off with a talking-to and a slapped wrist." She pushed herself up on the bed and swayed gently from side to side. "Right, where's my jacket? I need to get home to bed."

"Just a minute," said Charlotte. "Let me go and check if it's okay for you to leave. I know the doctor said you could, but let me go and check first. And then you're coming home with me." She put up a hand as Olivia opened her mouth to protest. "No arguments, please. At least I can keep an eye on you for a day or two if you're in our spare room. Now, wait here while I go and find a nurse."

And call Nathan to tell him the news.

———————————

"Are you sure Nathan doesn't mind me staying at your place?" Olivia said as Charlotte pulled up outside her old fisherman's cottage, having first stopped at Olivia's so she could pick up some things.

"Of course he doesn't," said Charlotte. It was usually only Molly she told white lies to about tooth fairies, but there was no way she was telling Olivia what Nathan's initial response had been to the news that she was going to be a guest in the Costello home for a couple of days, even though his sense of decency had eventually prevailed.

"Come on, you can put your stuff in the spare room and get settled. You'll have to get used to the dogs. They're family, so they're used to having the run of the house. If you don't want them in your room, though, just tell them they're not to come in and they won't. Right, here we are. We should have most things you'll need but just shout if you can't find something.

"I have to go and pick Molly up from computer class but I won't be long. Help yourself to whatever's in the fridge or cupboards if you're hungry. And get some rest. Watch TV, listen to music, have a bath, get some sleep—whatever you need to do. Okay? Oh, and what I said about the dogs—that applies to Molly, too." She grinned. "See you in a while."

———————

Realising she had more time than she thought, Charlotte took the long route to Molly's school. She didn't want to get there too early and get into conversations with the other mums because she didn't want to leave Olivia on her own for too long. If she took the long way, she reckoned on arriving just a minute or two before Molly came out.

She switched on the radio and a country singer's lilting voice warbled from the speakers. As she sung along, it dawned on her that the traffic was slowing down, the brake lights of the cars ahead like a red snake heading into town.

"Oh damn! Just what I don't need."

The cars in front slowed to a crawl, and she craned her neck to try to see the reason for the delay. She lowered her window and called out to a dog-walker coming from the direction of the hold-up. "What's going on, do you know?"

"A lorry's shed its load all over the road, but it's being cleared now. Should only take a couple of minutes."

The cars began to move again, and as she reached the lorry, she saw its driver and a tall man clearing the road of a number of large breeze blocks. The driver was using a trolley to move the heavy blocks of masonry, but the man helping him was lifting them as though they were made of polystyrene before loading them back onto the truck.

As she drove past, the man turned and she caught a glimpse of his face. It was Roy Tanner.

It's a pity he's not staying, she thought. *Some of that muscle would come in very useful when they get around to fixing the library roof.*

———————

"But *why* is Oliver staying at our house?"

"Because she had a bump on the head and it's best if she's not on her own for a couple of days."

"Hasn't she got a mummy and daddy to look after her?"

"Yes, but she doesn't want to worry them, and we live closer."

"How did she get the bump on her head?"

"Someone threw something at her."

Molly frowned. "Why did they do that?"

"I don't know, but I hope it was an accident."

"You *hope* it was an accident? What does *that* mean?"

"It means I hope it was an accident because it wouldn't be very nice if someone had done it on purpose."

Molly nodded. "Oh, I see. It must have really hurt."

Charlotte sighed. "I expect so, but you can ask Olivia yourself in a minute. Come on, let's get inside quickly," she said, as she pulled onto the drive. "It's got cold all of a sudden." She opened the front door and the delicious smell of food cooking wafted past her nostrils. She followed it into the kitchen to find Olivia standing over the hob, stirring a sauce.

"Don't get excited, it's nothing fancy, just homemade meatballs in tomato sauce with green beans and mashed potatoes. I hope it was okay to get started on dinner? Hi, Molly."

"*Okay*? It's fabulous—thank you! It's not every day I come home to find a world-class chef in my kitchen. Can I do anything to help?"

"No, I think everything's under control."

"Shouldn't you be lying down, or something?"

"I'm only cooking dinner, Charlotte, not lifting weights."

"Wow!" said Molly, her wide eyes fixed on the egg-sized lump on Olivia's forehead. "That's so cool! Did it hurt?"

"Well, I don't remember it happening, but it hurts now. The doctor said bumps on your head often look worse than they are, though."

"Can I feel it?"

"No, Molly, you can't," said Charlotte. "The last thing Olivia needs is you poking at her. You wouldn't want to hurt her, would you?"

Molly shook her head and stepped in for a closer look. "Poor Oliver," she said, before flinging her arms around Olivia's waist and patting her reassuringly on the back. "Don't worry, we'll take care of you till you're better, won't we, Mummy?"

Charlotte nodded. "Of course we will. Now go and get out of your school clothes and get your homework done. Just because Olivia's here, doesn't mean you get a night off."

As Molly raced off with the dogs at her heels, Charlotte left Olivia in peace for a while. She'd noticed her eyes tearing up, even if Molly hadn't. She couldn't imagine what Olivia's life must be like, with hardly anyone to call on.

Charlotte thanked her lucky stars every day to be part of such a close group of friends. Despite the difference in ages, she, Jess, Betty, Ava, Harriett, and her godmother, Laura, had always shared in each other's good times, and bad. They had only to call on any one of the others and, depending on the occasion, they'd be there with hugs, a listening ear and a shoulder to cry on, or party poppers and a bottle of Champagne.

She hoped, in time, Olivia would come to realise that she had friends she could call on, too.

At least one, anyway.

———

"That was absolutely delicious," said Charlotte, putting her knife and fork together on her empty plate. "It was like eating at the rooftop restaurant at *The President*."

"Yeah, they were the best meatballs *ever*. They were even better than the ones out of a tin," said Molly, wiping her finger through the sauce on her plate. "Can you give Mummy the recipe, please?"

Olivia blushed. "It was only meatballs, not haute cuisine, but I'm glad you enjoyed it."

"I'll wash up," said Charlotte.

"No, you won't. I will." Olivia pointed in the direction of the living room. "Why don't you go and do whatever it is you do at this time of the evening, and I'll bring dessert through in a bit."

"Dessert!" said Charlotte and Molly together. "We don't usually have dessert during the week."

Olivia grinned. "It's just apple and blackberry crumble and custard."

Molly grabbed Charlotte's hand as Olivia shooed them out. "I don't know about you, Mummy," she whispered, "but I could get used to this."

———————

When Nathan got home at half-past eleven, Olivia had long gone to bed.

"How's the invalid?"

"Okay. When the painkillers wear off, she doesn't feel too good, but she said she's feeling better than she did earlier."

"That's good. Look, I didn't mean to sound cross when you called to say you'd invited Olivia to stay. I don't have anything against her—I hope you know that. It's just that the timing's not brilliant."

Charlotte nodded. "I know, but if you'd seen her the way I have the past few days, you'd know there was no way she had anything to do with Roman's death. Without her job to be brilliant at, she's so vulnerable. I've never seen her like this before—I never even thought she *could* be like this."

"Well, we're following a couple of new leads," said Nathan, "so if all goes well, she could be back at work very soon. Funnily enough, Simon Clancy called me earlier and asked if I could give him some idea if Olivia was going to be charged with anything. Between you and me, it doesn't sound as if the hotel restaurants are doing too well without her. She's got such a unique style, the customers are noticing the difference."

"And what did you tell him?"

"I told him if he wanted to ask her to go back to work, that was his decision to make, not mine. She's not the only suspect, after all."

Charlotte nodded, a thoughtful expression on her face. "Are you hungry? There's some of the dinner Olivia cooked in the fridge."

"She cooked dinner?"

"The best meatballs and apple and blackberry crumble you've ever tasted."

"Meatballs and apple and blackberry crumble?" Nathan repeated. "Actually, now you come to mention it, I am a bit hungry."

Charlotte grinned and kissed him. "Thought you might be."

"I assume Olivia doesn't remember seeing anything before the rock hit her?" said Nathan.

"She didn't see anyone, but she remembers thinking there was someone there, because the trees were moving. That's what made her look round in the first place," said Charlotte, as she put a plate of food into the microwave to heat. "Is anyone looking into it? Do you think it was a random attack?"

"Probably, but that doesn't make it any less serious, regardless of whether it was kids or adults. Although why anyone would think that throwing rocks at passers-by is an acceptable way to get their kicks is beyond me. And, to answer your question, yes, it's being investigated and someone will need to speak to her."

Charlotte hauled herself onto a stool. "Incidentally, Olivia told me earlier that she thinks she's being deliberately targeted. There have been two occasions now where she could have been killed, but wasn't, due to sheer luck. The thought hadn't even crossed my mind until she mentioned it, but it makes sense, don't you think?"

Nathan mulled it over. "Does she have any idea who it could be?"

"No, I don't think so, although if you asked her, she could probably write you a list as long as your leg of people who'd like to get their own back on her for things she's done in the past."

"Interesting," said Nathan. "All this time, we've been looking at her as a suspect when she could have been a target."

CHAPTER 18

"There's something strange about Monique Hathaway." Fiona tossed her pen onto the desk.

"Like what?" said Ben.

"Well, it's as though she didn't exist from when she lived with her parents, and left school at sixteen, to when she started working for Roman. It's as though she just fell off the radar. There's no trace of her living or working anywhere in between. I don't get it."

Ben shrugged a shoulder. "Maybe her social security number was keyed in wrong somewhere along the line? It happens."

"Yeah, but I can't even find anything under her name." Fiona grabbed her bag and keys. "And I'm so hungry, I can't think straight. I'm going for some breakfast. You want anything?"

Ben shook his head. "Nah, I ate the leftover pizza from last night. Jess and I got a takeaway and ate it in bed, watching TV. I finished it off this morning."

Fiona's nose wrinkled in disgust. "Leftover pizza for breakfast? Yuck, that's nasty."

"Don't knock it till you've tried it," said Ben, belching behind his hand.

Fiona grinned and slung her bag over her shoulder. "You're such a slob, Dillon. Right, I won't be long. I'm going to drive to that place with the organic juice bar. I fancy a nice big banana and blueberry smoothie and one of their bacon and tomato wraps. Be back in about twenty minutes."

———————

Five minutes later, she was sitting on a stool in the window of the café, waiting for her wrap to be made.

"Sorry, you'll have to wait a while. We've got a backlog of takeaway orders to do before yours. I'm on my own till ten—what can I do?" The flustered guy behind the counter gave her an apologetic shrug. "You okay to wait for a bit?"

"Take your time. I'm not in a rush." Fiona took a local paper from the newspaper rack hanging by the door and flicked through the pages. She glanced out of the window, her eyes fixing on the brunette who'd just walked past the café and disappeared into the train station.

Where was Monique Hathaway going after claiming to be so upset, she wouldn't even be leaving the hotel, let alone St. Eves?

"Don't worry about my wrap, there's been a change of plan." Fiona slid off her stool and rushed out of the café to the station, just in time to see Monique making her way along the platform towards a huddle of brightly painted wooden seats.

"I need a ticket to wherever that woman with the dark brown hair just bought one for, please."

The man in the ticket office leaned towards the glass partition and started telling her he wasn't at liberty to divulge the destinations of other passengers, but was soon passing a ticket under the window after he laid eyes on the warrant card she flashed at him.

London?

"Are you sure this is the right ticket?"

The man raised a bushy eyebrow over the rim of his bifocals. "That's what she asked for. She said she wanted a ticket for the most direct route to Paddington." He put a rubber thimble on his finger and began counting a pile of five pound notes. "I've been doing this job for thirty-six years—I think I know what I'm doing."

Fiona cast a glance at Monique, who was now sitting on a seat and reading a magazine. "Sorry, yes, I'm sure you do. Could you tell me when the train leaves, please?"

The man looked up at the old station clock. "In six minutes. It's a long journey, you know."

Fiona's heart sank, the rumble of her stomach reminding her that she still hadn't eaten any breakfast. "How long is long?"

"Just under six hours, give or take a few minutes. Depends on any delays, see?"

She sighed and nodded as she reached for her phone.

"Hi, Ben. I'm going to be a bit longer than I thought…"

———————————

The light was fading when Fiona got off the train at London's Paddington Station. For the entire journey—including one change of train—she'd been careful to keep Monique in sight, but stay well out of her line of vision.

She exited the station and followed her to a taxi rank outside, hanging back for a few seconds before taking the next taxi in line. "Where to, love?" asked the cheerful driver.

She pointed ahead. "Can you follow that cab, please?"

The taxi driver chatted non-stop throughout the fifteen minute drive. She was about to tell him to put a sock in it when the cab he was following pulled into a lay-by outside a vast cemetery, surrounded by a yellow stone wall topped with high railings. Monique got out, but the cab waited.

"Whatcha want me t'do?" asked Fiona's driver, whose name, he had told her, was Rodney.

"Pull in at the end, please. And can you wait for me?" She followed Monique, keeping a safe distance behind, and doing her best to blend in with the people who were visiting graves, or using the cemetery as a short cut.

When Monique came to a stop, Fiona slowed down and pretended to be busy on her phone, keeping her head down and her collar up. She watched as Monique crouched in front of a white marble headstone, and pulled weeds from the surrounding grass, before leaning a card against the memorial

Fiona bided her time. The cemetery would be closing soon. Surely Monique hadn't come all the way from St. Eves just to visit a grave?

Ten minutes later, Monique laid a hand on the headstone before making her way back to the cemetery entrance where the taxi was waiting. Fiona walked quickly to the grave and peered at the engraving on the marble.

In loving memory of Naomi Marie Raeburn.
September 17th 1986 – November 12th 2005
Cherished daughter, sister, granddaughter, niece, and friend.

Taken from our arms, but never from our hearts.

She made a note of the details and read the words in the card Monique had left.

He's gone now, so he can never hurt anyone again. At last, you can truly rest in peace, my sweet Naomi.

Fiona took a photo of the headstone and the card on her phone, then quickly made her way back to the waiting car, keeping Monique in her sights all the way.

"You want me to foller it again?" said Rodney, as she climbed into the back of the taxi.

"Please, but keep your distance as much as you can."

"Right'o," he said, leaning back and picking up the conversation where he'd left off. "You're braver than me. I wouldn't set foot in a cemetery after dark. Did you know there's one not far from here that's supposed to be one of the most haunted places in London?" He gave an exaggerated shiver. "No thank you, very much. Now, my wife's friend's brother's father-in-law, well, *he* claims to have seen a ghost…"

Fiona half-listened as the taxi crawled through the London streets in rush-hour traffic. Eventually, Monique's cab stopped again outside an elegant period townhouse, the headlights illuminating its exposed brick fascia, white painted entrance porch, and huge sash windows. Monique got out, paid the driver, and rang the bell, going inside when the door was opened. The driver settled back in his seat and waited.

"Whatcha want me t'do?" Rodney repeated.

"I don't suppose you know who lives here, do you?" asked Fiona.

He shuffled round in his seat to face her. "You mean *you* don't?"

Fiona answered with a shake of her head. "I'm not from around here. I have no idea."

Rodney sniffed. "Joan Walden, that's who." He noted Fiona's blank look and gave her an exaggerated eye-roll. "Don't tell me you don't know who Joan Walden is?"

"Like I said, I'm not from around here," repeated Fiona, patiently. "I've never heard of her."

"Well, if you're not a local, I suppose you could be excused for not knowing the story," said Rodney.

Fiona sat forward in her seat and fully opened the glass partition that separated the driver from the passenger. "What story?"

Rodney rubbed a finger against his nose. "I'm not one to gossip, but Joan runs a... well, these days, she calls it a hostel for women in need. She takes in women who need somewhere to stay. She's been doing it for years—taking them in and offering them a bed and a hot meal for as long as they need it."

Fiona nodded. "I take it there's more to the story than that, though?"

"Oh, there's more to it, alright," said Rodney, getting into his stride. "For years, the police were trying to prove that she was running a business from the premises. An escort business for wealthy clients. And I don't mean just for escorts, if you know what I mean."

"And *was* she running a business?"

"Well, they never found enough evidence to prove it. No men ever visited the house, y'see, but some of the girls were seen out with very rich gentlemen at very exclusive functions; dinners, film premieres, society weddings, charity fundraisers, that kind of thing. There was never any *proof* that anything untoward was going on, but there was always plenty of talk that there was." Rodney produced a handkerchief the size of a small bedsheet from his pocket, and trumpeted into it. "The men claimed the women were simply their dates for the evening, and the women never said a word. They were all very discreet."

"And what about now?" said Fiona. "Do people still think that this Joan Walden's running an escort service from the house?"

Rodney shook his head. "Not now. She still takes in young women who need a safe place to stay, but she was so traumatised after what happened, I reckon that put a stop to anything improper that might have been going on."

"Something happened?"

"It was dreadful, it was." Rodney bent forward and raised his eyes, pointing up to the fifth floor of the house. "See that small window, right at the top? One of the girls who used to stay with Joan jumped from it.

Poor duck, she was only nineteen." He shook his head and sighed. "Anyway, her parents blamed Joan. They said she'd brainwashed their daughter by forcing her to live in an unnatural environment. They said it wasn't healthy for young women to live in what they called 'a commune'. They reckoned their daughter changed after she met Joan, and that's why she jumped."

The door to the house opened and Monique reappeared at the top of the four steps leading up to the front door. She turned and hugged an elderly woman, whose white hair shone bright in the glow of the outside light.

"That's Joan," said Rodney. "She must be getting on for eighty now."

Monique got into the back of the taxi and waved to Joan who blew a kiss as the car pulled away.

"I'll foller it again, shall I?" said Rodney, and resumed his commentary until the taxi in front stopped five minutes later outside a smart, single-storey hotel with tinted glass double-doors, its floodlit sign announcing that it still had vacancies.

Fiona watched Monique get out of the cab but, this time, the driver didn't wait. Through the glass windows, she could be clearly seen checking in at the reception desk.

"She's probably staying the night," deduced Rodney. "Whatcha want me t'do?"

Fiona considered her options. "Can you take me back to Joan Walden's place, please? I'll make my own way from there."

Rodney drove out of the horseshoe-shaped drive and went back in the direction he'd just come from. "You sure you don't want me to wait for you?" he said, as Fiona got out of the cab.

"No thanks. I could be ages, so I'll call another taxi if I need to." She took a note from her purse. "Keep the change."

"Much obliged," said Rodney, and flashed her his best London cabbie grin.

"One more thing," said Fiona. "I don't suppose you remember the name of the girl, do you? The one who jumped?"

"Course I remember," said Rodney. "It was Naomi Raeburn."

Fiona climbed the few stairs to Joan Walden's front door. Close-up, she could see the paintwork was fresh, and the brass doorknob, bell and letterbox gleamed like gold. She gave the bell a short press with her thumb, shortly to find herself face to face with the woman she'd already heard so much about when she opened a viewing hatch in the door and peered through it.

"Yes?"

"Mrs. Walden?"

"Yes."

Fiona held up her warrant card. "I'm Detective Sergeant Fiona Farrell. I wonder if you could spare me a few minutes to answer some questions, please? I won't take too much of your time."

Joan studied Fiona closely before opening the door and inviting her in. "I don't keep very late nights these days, so I'll be going to bed within the hour. I hope you'll have asked everything you need to know by then."

"I'm sure I will," said Fiona, dragging the soles of her shoes thoroughly against the doormat before following Joan into a large room hung with velvet curtains and furnished with dark wood and vast, faded rugs, their muted patterns a gentle reminder of the vibrant colours they'd once been.

She motioned to Fiona to sit down. "I suppose this has something to do with Monique's visit?"

"Actually, yes, it does."

Joan gave a little nod. "Thought so. I had no idea she was coming, you know. She just turned up unannounced—it was so lovely to see her. She got so little time off when she worked for that Haley chap, I hardly ever saw her, and she couldn't call me because I don't have a phone. I got rid of it a few years ago." She frowned. "Anyway, it was lovely to see her again." She leaned forward in her chair. "I expect you want to ask if I think she had anything to do with Haley's death? She mentioned that the police had questioned her about it."

Fiona was slightly taken aback. She hadn't expected Joan to be quite so forthright.

"I might have a few years on you," said Joan, her grey eyes taking on a mischievous twinkle, "but I'm still able to put two and two together and make four. It seems rather a coincidence that Monique should decide to visit me today, completely out of the blue, and then you turn up on the doorstep less than an hour later."

Fiona nodded. "*Do* you think she had anything to do with Roman's death?"

Joan spread her hands. "Who knows. All I know for sure is that if *I* was her, I'd have got rid of him long before now."

"Oh? Why do you say that?"

"Because he wasn't a nice man, and he didn't treat her very well. In fact, he treated her terribly. Mind you, it wasn't *just* Monique. He didn't treat *anyone* very well."

"Can you elaborate?"

Joan ran her gnarled fingers along the brocade antimacassar on the arm of the couch. "He used people to get what he wanted, especially vulnerable people, but he needed Monique far more than she needed him." She gave Fiona a knowing look. "That girl was bright as a button and razor sharp—still is."

"Do you happen to know when she first met Roman?"

Joan's brow creased. "Some of my memories are a little hazy, I'm afraid. I couldn't say for sure."

"Did she meet him here?"

Joan gave her a wry smile and wagged a knobbly finger. "Look at you, trying to catch me out. No, she didn't meet him here. This house is for women only. Always has been, always will be. There's one room in the extension which is totally separate from the main house, and exclusively for me to receive male guests. No other men are allowed, unless it's a postman, a doctor, or a tradesman."

"Ah, right." Fiona returned the smile. "Well, in that case, can you tell me anything about the accident that happened here in 2005, involving a young woman named Naomi Raeburn?"

Joan's eyes narrowed and her fingers clenched into gnarled fists. She pushed herself up from the couch, her back ramrod straight, the mischievous twinkle in her eyes replaced by a stony glare. "I'm sorry, Detective Sergeant Farrell, but I've already said all I'm going to say about that. I have no intention of answering any more questions and dragging up the past." She pushed the fringe of soft waves from her forehead with a slightly shaky hand.

"You know, my blessed phone rang non-stop for seven days after it happened—reporters were calling day and night. In the end, I pulled the damn thing out of the wall and vowed I'd never have another one. The girls keep telling me I need one, but I have this in case of emergencies." She patted the alarm she wore on a band around her wrist.

She closed her eyes and shook her head. "My apologies, I'm feeling very tired all of a sudden, so I must ask you to leave. If you want to know any more, I suggest you ask Monique. I understand she's going back to St. Eves tomorrow."

It was frustrating for Fiona to leave when she still had so much to ask, but she knew when she'd pushed her luck too far. "I'm sorry, I didn't mean to upset you."

Joan waved away the apology. "It's alright. I'm fine. I have a lot of girls staying with me at the moment, and they pop in to see me every day, which is a comfort. I just need to rest."

Fiona nodded. "Okay, thanks for your time. You've been very helpful." She ran down the stairs and hailed a passing taxi. "Paddington Station, please."

If she travelled through the night, she could sleep on the train and be back in St. Eves by the time Monique returned the following day, by which time, she'll have had the chance to do a little research.

She opened her notebook and looked at the name on the page.

Naomi Marie Raeburn.

Did this girl, who had been dead for over a decade, hold a clue to Roman's killer?

CHAPTER 19

"And that's about all I managed to find out," said Fiona, recalling her impromptu London trip to Ben the following morning.

"So was Monique one of the girls who used to live in Joan's hostel?"

Fiona shrugged. "I'm not sure, but I think she might have been. By the time I wanted to ask Joan about it, though, she was already pretty fed up with me and wasn't answering any more questions. She's a smart old bird, so I'm sure she'd have been able to tell me everything I wanted to know, but when I mentioned Naomi, she clammed up. It's not all bad news, though. Come and look at this."

She spun her chair around and wheeled herself back to her desk. "I've been doing some digging since I got back and it seems that, after Naomi's death, Joan became something of a recluse. Naomi's parents campaigned for years to get her locked up, but there was no evidence that she'd done anything other than give Naomi a roof over her head in 2004, when she left home after an argument with her parents and ended up in London. When they eventually tracked her down, they were convinced she was involved in some weird cult that Joan was the leader of. Here, look at this, which was written before Naomi's death." She pointed to the newspaper article on her computer screen.

Dorothea and Oswald Raeburn continue their tireless campaign to see Joan Walden behind bars. The parents of Naomi Raeburn, Mr. and Mrs. Raeburn are

*convinced that Joan Walden used sinister persuasions
to entice Naomi away from them, and is keeping her
against her will.*

*"There's just no way our Naomi would choose
to live with complete strangers rather than the family
who love her," said Mrs. Raeburn. "I don't know
what's going on in that house with all those young
women but, whatever it is, it's not right, and we want
Naomi out of it. It's true that she left home after a
disagreement, but the things we argued about were so
trivial, I know they could be resolved if she'd just let us
talk to her. The fact she won't is proof that Mrs.
Walden is preventing her from having contact with us. I
just know it."*

*However, when the police called at the house to
speak to Naomi, they were happy that she was not being
held against her will, or mistreated in any way, and the
fact that she is eighteen means that neither she, nor
Mrs. Walden, are breaking any laws if Naomi is
choosing to stay at the house of her own free will.*

Fiona scrolled down the screen. "And here's
another article, which was written *after* Naomi's
death."

*Joan Walden leaves Kensington police station,
surrounded by the young women who have supported
her, and each other, since the tragic death of Naomi
Raeburn.*

*It is still not known why Miss. Raeburn jumped
from her bedroom window, but it is known that she took
her life after having spent the evening at a local
restaurant with a friend, who claims that Miss. Raeburn*

had been in good spirits during the evening, and also when they arrived back at the house, just minutes before she jumped to her death.

Joan Walden has asked that she, and all the girls, be given privacy and time to grieve for Naomi, who was dearly loved by them all.

"Look at the picture," said Fiona.

Ben peered at the screen. The old newspaper image of Joan Walden was grainy and under-exposed but it was still clear enough to make out the faces of some of the girls standing round her in a protective huddle.

"See that one?" Fiona pointed at a girl on the edge of the throng.

Even in black and white, with longer hair, it was unmistakably Monique Hathaway.

"Well, that's definitely her," said Ben.

Fiona nodded. "And, according to Joan Walden, Roman Haley didn't treat Monique very nicely at all. He treated her quite badly, in fact."

Ben looked at the photo Fiona had taken of the card Monique had left by the grave. "'He's gone now, so he can never hurt anyone again'" he read. "You think she wrote that about Roman?"

Fiona shrugged. "Yeah, I think so."

"So, you think Monique could be his killer?"

"It's still just a hunch, and I need to speak to her but, for now, yes, I think it's very likely."

Sherri Bryan

"Oh yes, I'm feeling much better now, thank you. It was only just right after Roman's death that I wasn't feeling myself." Monique smiled across the table at Fiona. "It's amazing what a difference some time, and some fresh St. Eves air can make."

"Yes, it's very therapeutic, isn't it, the St. Eves air?" said Fiona, with a smile. "Well, thank you for coming in at such short notice. I wonder, as you're feeling so much better, if you'd be able to answer a few questions?"

Monique nodded. "Ask away."

Fiona put down the copy of the newspaper article she'd printed onto the table, and pointed to the photograph. "Is that you?"

Monique's face went from having a healthy glow to being the colour of uncooked bread dough. "Where did you get that?"

"If you could answer the question, please?"

Monique sat rigidly in the interview room chair. "Yes, it's me."

"Can you tell me about Naomi Raeburn?"

"Why are you asking me about this?" said Monique, through clenched teeth. "What does it have to do with *anything*? It's all in my past."

"I appreciate that," said Fiona, "but if you could just answer the question, please? I wouldn't be asking if I didn't think this might be relevant to our investigation."

A look of fear crossed Monique's sharp features, and she gulped before starting to speak again in a shaky voice. "I met Naomi years ago, when I lived in London."

"Where did you live in London?"

She paused for a second. "I squatted in a house that was marked for demolition. I'd never seen eye to eye with my mum or my stepdad, so we parted company when I was sixteen. And when I say, 'parted company', I mean they threw me out. I had no money, no qualifications, no job, nothing, so I needed to start earning. Once I had a roof over my head, I turned to the only way I thought I'd be able to make some quick cash. And I was right. I made a lot of it."

"How long did you live in the house?" asked Fiona.

"Four years, give or take. The council were obviously in no rush to knock it down."

"And is that where you met Naomi?"

Monique shook her head. "She lived in a hostel. We met after she saw me pick someone's pocket in a street market, and she followed me back to the house. She told me I should take the wallet to the police station and tell them I found it on the street, and then she took me back to the hostel with her.

"That's when I met Joan. She said she had an empty room, and it was mine if I wanted it, but I didn't. I'd got too used to living on my own. She was kind to me, though. She gave me a sleeping bag, blankets, and some clean clothes, and told me I could go to the hostel whenever I wanted a bath.

"After that, I used to visit Naomi there often. I even used to pop in to see Joan. Naomi and I became really close friends. We were total opposites but we just clicked. She was like a quiet, insecure, little mouse, and I was loud, brash, and full of myself. She was such a good, sweet girl." Monique hung her head and took a deep breath.

"Anyway, she'd been seeing a guy for a while who she was really keen on. He was staying in town for six months to co-write a guide to London's top fifty restaurants. Sometimes, she'd go off to stay with him at his swanky hotel and I wouldn't see her for ages. Then she'd turn up again, on my doorstep, like she was walking on air. She was so happy."

She stopped and gulped down a cup of water. "One day, when I hadn't seen her for a month, she came to the house to tell me she wanted me to meet the guy she'd been seeing. She dragged me off to a cafe we used to go to where he was waiting. That was the first time I met Roman and I immediately knew why Naomi was so besotted. Back then, he was one of those people you just couldn't take your eyes off. And, when he wanted to, he could turn on the charm till you felt woozy—if you were in a room packed with people, he'd make you feel like you were the only person there.

"He took us both to dinner and flirted outrageously with me. I thought he probably flirted with everyone, so I didn't read too much into it. No one was more surprised than me when he turned up at the house one day.

"He said he'd told Naomi he couldn't see her any more, because he wanted to be with me. I should have told him to get lost but I was young and easily flattered. I asked him how Naomi had taken the news and he said she'd taken it well, and that I shouldn't worry about her.

"Then he gave me a thousand pounds and told me he wanted me to spend some time with him—to be his 'special friend', he called it. And that's where it all started. I went out with him and he paid me well for my time. He was odd and quirky—different to the guys I usually met—and he was great company. I stayed at his hotel, he bought me nice clothes, took me to fantastic restaurants, introduced me to celebrities, and treated me better than I'd ever been treated by anyone before."

The melancholy smile vanished from her face.

"But then I found out that Naomi had no idea Roman and I were seeing each other, and not only did she have no idea, she'd been waiting for him to get in touch with her. She'd been so worried that something had happened to him, she went to his hotel, and found me in his room. That was when I realised he'd lied to me about breaking things off with her. He hadn't even had the decency to go and see her to tell her face to face. He'd simply dropped her like a stone.

"I told her how sorry I was, but she was inconsolable. Joan said I should give her some time, so I did. When I eventually saw her again, she apologised for not being around, but said she'd needed some time to get over Roman."

Monique squeezed her eyes shut. "I should have left him as soon as I saw how badly he'd treated her but, at the time, I couldn't see further than the amazing lifestyle I'd been living and I didn't want it to stop."

She put her elbows on the table and cupped her chin in her hands.

"Naomi and I arranged to go out. We went to a local pub, drank too much, danced on the tables to live music, and had the best time. We walked back to her hostel, arm in arm, and promised not to leave it so long before we went out again. Then, she went up to her room, wrote a suicide note, and jumped from the window. I was waiting for a cab to take me back to Roman's hotel when she fell, just a few feet away from me.

"Joan told me later that the note Naomi had left said she couldn't get over losing Roman, and the thought of him with someone else was too painful. She said she thought it would be best for everyone if she wasn't around any more." Monique shrugged. "It was awful. Just awful. Joan was in a terrible state afterwards—we both were—and I spent a lot of time with her. I think it gave us both some comfort."

She nodded to the newspaper article. "After the funeral, Naomi's parents did everything they could to get Joan arrested, but there was no proof of any impropriety, so the police couldn't do a thing. The girls closed ranks around her, and I supported her however I could, but I couldn't stay forever. Roman and I left London soon afterwards, and I only ever went back if we were in the area and I could snatch an hour or so to visit Naomi's grave, and see Joan."

"And you were with Roman until his death?" said Fiona.

"Yes." Monique leaned back in the chair and looked at the ceiling. "Although I wish I'd had the guts to leave him when he changed."

"Changed?"

Monique nodded. "Once I'd got used to the good life, he turned on me like he did everyone else. One evening, over dinner, in a beautiful restaurant, while we were eating wonderful food and drinking fabulous wine, he calmly told me that if I ever left him, or was disloyal to him, he'd tell the press that I used to live on the streets, and the things I used to do to earn money, and then he'd take me back to the gutter where he found me."

She gave a bitter laugh. "I might have been able to cope with that but he told me if I ever disappointed him, he'd give the police the evidence they'd been looking for to prove Joan had been running an illegal business from the hostel. Most of the guys who had dealings with her would have done anything to keep their identity secret, but Roman didn't care who knew that he paid young women to spend time with him. That's why I stayed with him—I was too scared to leave in case he ever told the police about Joan. If he had, I would never have forgiven myself. I already felt responsible for Naomi's death—I couldn't have coped with the guilt if anything had happened to Joan, too."

She ran her hands over her weary face.

"Anything I used to feel for Roman vanished a long time ago, DS Farrell, when I realised how mean and nasty and downright malicious he was. If it wasn't for him, I might have some friends, but everyone hates me because they know he used me to find the secrets they were keeping so he could blackmail them.

The only tears I've cried since he died have been tears of relief. Relief that I'll never have to feel his clammy hands on me again, or smell his garlic breath as he puffed and panted in my face, or kiss him while he had food stuck in that ridiculous moustache, and that I'll never, ever have to touch his disgusting body again. He revolted me in every way—physically and emotionally—but he took me from a life on the streets, and he demanded I show him how grateful I was every single night.

"You think I'm sorry he's dead? You're wrong, DS Farrell. But if you think I killed him, think again. As much as I wanted to stab him while he slept for the way he treated Naomi, I saved that fantasy for my dreams. I don't know who murdered Roman, but it certainly wasn't me." She met Fiona's eyes with defiance. "Is there anything else you need to ask me?"

Fiona shook her head. "No. You can go."

———

In the evening briefing, Nathan counted off the suspects on his fingers.

"As far as we know, there are five people, all with very credible motives for wanting to see Roman Haley dead.

"Gavin Doyle couldn't afford to lose his job because he thought his wife would stop him from seeing his kids if he couldn't keep up with the maintenance payments.

"Larissa Reece, didn't want the benefits office to find out she'd been scamming the system, or her sister to find out she'd been having an affair with her husband.

"Monique Hathaway blamed Roman for the death of a good friend and wanted to protect Joan Walden from a possible police investigation.

"Gordon Buckingham lost the job he loved to Roman Haley, but was miles away when he was killed, and he also had ample motive for wanting to harm Olivia Floyd-Martin, but didn't.

"And, finally, Olivia Floyd-Martin herself. She had a long-standing rivalry with Roman and multiple reasons to want him out of the way, but she's also possibly been a target of malicious activity herself."

Nathan sighed heavily and dug his hands deep into his pockets as he paced back and forth. "We've got the suspects, we've got the motives, but we haven't got the proof that any of them harmed a hair on Roman Haley's head, let alone killed him. Same goes for Olivia.

"Of course, they're all denying they had anything to do with his death, but someone's responsible and if not one of them, then who? I know you're all trying your best, but we need to try harder. Check and recheck every lead we've had so far, and every piece of information. I feel like we're so close but we're missing something, and until we find it, the last piece of the puzzle is never going to slot into place."

CHAPTER 20

"Mummy, it looks really cold out there," said Molly, her hot forehead pressed against the cold window.

"It is. That's why I'm wrapping up warm," said Charlotte, pulling on her windcheater. "I want to walk the dogs before it starts raining too hard, which it looks like it's going to any minute if those black clouds are anything to go by, but I won't be long. I don't like leaving you on your own but if you're coming down with something, I want you to stay in the warm." She kissed Molly on the forehead and smoothed a cool hand over her cheek. "Don't open the door to anyone, understand?"

"'kay, Mummy." Molly dropped, cross-legged, onto the window seat. "Is Ava coming today?"

"I have no idea, but if she wants some company, she might drop by, I suppose. She doesn't like being out in this weather, though, because it makes her hair frizzy."

Molly giggled and did an almost perfect imitation of Ava's voice. "Oh, my dear, I simply can't do a *thing* with it!"

Charlotte chuckled as she clipped the dogs' leads to their collars. "Right, what mustn't you do while I'm gone?"

"Open the door to anyone."

"Correct. I'll be back in about forty minutes."

Charlotte stepped out and turned her back to the gale which was growing in strength. Deciding against their usual beach walk, she took a left turn and headed for the town centre, Pippin and Panda trotting along beside her, unbothered by the wind, and pulling at their leads every time a leaf blew past their noses.

The wind dropped a little when they got amongst the shelter of the buildings, a light drizzle starting to fall. She pulled up her hood, shuddering as she walked into the market square and saw Roman's culinary school, still cordoned off with blue and white police tape.

It was probably something to do with her present condition that the thought his murderer could be walking the same streets Molly rode her bike up and down, and flew along on her roller skates, made her feel nauseous. Even though Molly was never allowed out unsupervised, nutters like the person who had killed Roman Haley were unpredictable at best, and at worst, most likely completely undetectable in a room full of perfectly pleasant people who didn't harbour any murderous intentions at all. The perfect place for someone with nefarious notions to hide in plain sight.

She walked on and pushed all thoughts of murderers from her mind, focusing instead on a couple who were losing a fight with an umbrella bloated by the wind, which eventually blew completely inside out and out of the man's hand. As he started to run after it, he was overtaken by a tall figure, his long strides catching up with it quickly.

Charlotte didn't have to see his face to know who it was. Slightly hunched at the shoulder, with a thick jacket and a long scarf flowing out behind him,

Roy Tanner strode towards her after returning the umbrella to the couple. As he drew closer, his eyes told her he was smiling, even though his face was covered by his scarf from the nose down.

"Morning, Charlotte. I thought it was you." He pulled up his scarf and wiped it across his eyes. "This damn wind's so strong, it's making me cry! Anyway, how's things?" He bent to stroke the dogs and looked up at her.

"Oh, everything's fine," said Charlotte. "I'm surprised to see you still here. I thought you'd have left St. Eves by now. Izzy went back ages ago, didn't she?"

"Yeah. It's a shame, 'cos we got really friendly again—we sort of picked up where we left off. I really miss her, actually." He gave Charlotte a wonky smile. "We're keeping in touch, though. In fact, I said I'd call her later for a chat."

Charlotte nodded. "Out of interest, don't you have to get back to work? Not that it's any business of mine how long you stay here, but won't the care home be missing you?"

Roy shook his head. "I don't work at the care home any more."

"What? Why? Did they object to you taking extra time off?"

"No, nothing like that. I just realised I didn't want to go back, so I handed in my notice. No time like the present, as they say. And *The St. Eves' Tavern* is hardly chock-a-block at the moment, so they've extended my booking. I'm staying on in St. Eves for a while.

"It was probably a little impulsive—although my mother would say irresponsible—but after Roman Haley got bumped off, and Olivia Floyd-Martin had that near miss, it made me realise that you just don't know what's going to happen in life, do you? It's certainly too short to be spending five days a week in a job you don't really enjoy, that's for sure.

"So... I'm throwing caution to the wind! It's been so long since I've done what *I* wanted to do, rather than always what Becky wanted to do, I'm really enjoying myself. I mean, it's not like I don't *need* money coming in, because I do, but I'm sure I can find work somewhere. I can go fruit picking, or work in a kitchen, or do odd jobs—I just know if I don't take this time for myself, I'll regret it." He stood up and groaned as his joints cracked. His eyes crinkled at the corners and Charlotte smiled back at him.

"Well, in that case, congratulations on your new adventure! I'm sure I'll see you out and about. Shame the weather's not a bit nicer—it's hardly the Costa del Sol at the moment."

Roy shrugged. "A bit of bad weather doesn't bother me. When I was a medical supplies salesman, I used to drive all over the country in all kinds of weather. It'll take more than a gale and a bit of rain to keep Roy Tanner off the streets." He winked and stepped back to kick up his heels, bumping into someone who was right behind him.

"Ouch, you clumsy oaf! That was my bloody foot!"

Roy turned to apologise and found himself face to face with Olivia Floyd-Martin, glaring at him from under the fur-lined hood of her quilted coat, which was dripping with rain like a mini-waterfall in front of her face.

"I'm so sorry, I didn't see you. I didn't mean to…"

"Oh, stop going on about it!" Olivia dismissed him with a scowl and a wave of her hand, before turning to Charlotte, a wide smile spreading across her face. "I was just on my way to see you to tell you the news—you'll never believe what's happened!"

"Well, if that smile's anything to go by, I guess it must be good news," said Charlotte.

"It's the *best* news! Simon called me first thing this morning and asked if I'd go back to work!"

"*Really*? That's brilliant!" Charlotte gave her a one-armed hug. "I thought he said you should stay away until Roman's killer had been found?"

"He did, but I think the consequences of not having me around are starting to affect bums on seats in the rooftop restaurant," said Olivia, without a hint of modesty. "He knows that place doesn't work properly without me, Charlotte. No one can run that kitchen like I can. No one's got my taste buds, or the same standards. I mean, it's not doing badly, but there have been a few complaints since I've been away, and there have been a few dinner services where they haven't been fully booked, and that's almost unheard of. Anyway, he wants me to start back tomorrow afternoon, but I'm going back in tonight to do a stock check."

"Tonight?"

Olivia nodded. "Yeah. At this time of year, the kitchen's closed and everyone's gone home by half-eleven, so I'm going in after that. It'll give me an ideal opportunity before tomorrow to check things over without people bothering me every two minutes. And, anyway, I can't wait to get back, so the sooner the better as far as I'm concerned."

"Well, I'm really happy for you," said Charlotte. "I take it Simon must have got it through his thick head at last that you had nothing to do with the murder?"

Olivia shrugged. "Must have done. He said, 'As the police don't seem to be any closer to finding Roman Haley's killer, and despite you being a person of interest in his murder, the majority of customers are desperate to see you back in the restaurant, so we feel it would be best if you returned to work.'" She rolled her eyes. "That guy is such a moron. Anyway, I must get some kip before I go in tonight. I'll see you soon."

She turned and saw Roy still standing behind her and the smile disappeared from her face, to be quickly replaced with another scowl.

"Nasty bruise," said Roy, pointing to her forehead.

"What are you still doing here?" she said, throwing him a filthy look before stomping off through the puddles without stopping for a reply.

"She's a charmer, isn't she?" said Roy, his face deadpan as he looked up at the clock tower which loomed in the middle of the square. "Actually, I'd better get off, too—lots to do. Good to see you."

He smiled and stroked the dogs before pulling his long scarf over his face again, digging his hands into his jacket pockets and stepping up his pace.

Nice guy, thought Charlotte, as she continued her walk.

"I can't abide this weather," said Ava, peering out of the window at the fog that had suddenly descended like a grey blanket over St. Eves. "It makes my lips so dry. And I'm glad I cancelled my appointment at the hairdresser this morning. You know how my hair reacts to moisture, so it would have been a complete waste of money."

"At least the wind's dropped," said Charlotte. "I've been back from walking the dogs for ages and I'm only just starting to get warm."

"Do you think Molly will be alright for school on Monday?" said Ava.

"I'm sure she will. She started feeling a bit dizzy about an hour ago, so she went back to bed, but I'm sure she'll feel better when she wakes up. She's been fighting off a cold for a few days now—everyone in her class has had it—so it was only a matter of time before she caught it." Charlotte yawned and stretched up her arms. "I don't know why, but weather like this always makes me sleepy."

"Why don't you go and have a lie-down while Molly's asleep?" said Ava. "I only popped in on my way back from collecting a prescription to see if there'd been any developments." She nodded at Charlotte's stomach and picked up her handbag with a sigh. "I'm sorry to be such a nuisance and keep dropping in, but I'm at such a loose end at the moment, what with Derek always at rehearsals. And the girls have gone on another awayday. Bet's still limping a bit, but her ankle's much better."

"Where have they gone this time? Anywhere exciting?"

Ava raised a brow. "Charlotte, I don't think anyone could say that I don't like to enjoy myself. I'm always the first one on the dance floor at a party, and the last one to leave it, and you know how much I love to lead a conga. But who in their right mind wants to spend an entire day at a factory that makes wooden spoons, even if lunch is included?" She rolled her eyes as she hunted in her bag for her lip balm. "A wooden spoon factory... I ask you."

Charlotte giggled. "Look, I don't need to lie down. And you don't have to go. You can stay as long as you like. I was just going to sort through some old clothes for the charity shop. Not a very exciting way to spend a Saturday afternoon but it needs to be done and I've been putting it off for ages. You can help me if you like?"

Ava gave her a beaming smile and put down her handbag. "Are you sure? I could make a pot of tea and bring it upstairs? And shall I make us something to eat?

As Charlotte sorted clothes into piles, Ava sat on the bed, flicking through magazines and eating toast and marmalade. "I meant to tell you I saw Roy in the pharmacy when I went to pick up my prescription—I thought he'd gone home. He's been here for absolutely ages, hasn't he?"

"I saw him, too, but not in the pharmacy," said Charlotte, holding up a pair of Nathan's old jeans and studying them closely.

"Don't spend so long analysing everything, dearie, or you won't get rid of anything," said Ava. "'If in doubt, throw it out', that's my motto." She picked up her handbag and started to rummage through it and, while she was distracted, Charlotte slipped the jeans into the 'Keep' pile and continued the conversation.

"I saw him when I was walking the dogs. He said he's staying for a while longer. I wondered if he'd met someone. I can't imagine why he'd be hanging around here on his own otherwise. I mean, I know *we* love it here, but there's not much for visitors out of season, is there?"

"Where would he have met someone in St. Eves?" asked Ava, her forehead crinkling as she smeared peppermint flavoured balm onto her lips.

Charlotte shrugged. *"The St. Eves' Tavern, The Bottle of Beer*, the supermarket, the library, the cinema, the beach… there are loads of places he could have met someone. I'm just guessing, though. I could be completely wrong, but he's so pleasant, it strikes me as strange that he'd be spending Saturday night on his own."

Ava's eyebrow shot up and she snapped her fingers. "That's what he was doing in the pharmacy. Thank goodness I didn't go and speak to him. If he *is* seeing someone later on, I bet I know what he was buying." She threw Charlotte a knowing look and gave her lips another vigorous application of peppermint balm. "Harriett and I thought Roy and Izzy might get together. They were both divorced, around the same age, they seemed to get on so well… they would have made a lovely couple."

"Roy said now they've got back in touch, they're going to keep in contact with each other," said Charlotte. "In fact, he said he was going to give her a call tonight. He said he was missing her."

"Well, she couldn't hang around here forever, could she?" said Ava. "Unlike Roy, she's probably got a life to lead, so once Larissa had refunded her the money for the course, she had no reason to stay, did she? I think she went home the day after she went to Betty's. I can't imagine what sort of care home Roy works for that lets him take off as much time as he likes. I thought he was only staying for an extra few days, not weeks."

Charlotte started rummaging through a pile of shoes. "I think he might be around for a while—he's handed his notice in. Said he wanted to have a bit of fun."

"Handed his notice in? Have a bit of fun?" repeated Ava, in her most disapproving voice, her eyebrows and her little finger raised as she sipped her tea. "I thought he had more sense. When jobs are so hard to come by these days, I can't believe he'd do something so foolish."

Charlotte put a pair of Molly's tiny ballet slippers into a black sack and then took them out again and put them to one side. "I don't think I'm ready to get rid of those yet," she said, when Ava gave her a look. "They were her first pair."

Ava rolled her eyes. "Anyway, whatever Roy's doing with his private life is no business of mine. You know I'm not one to gossip."

Charlotte almost choked on her tea and dabbed her mouth on her sleeve.

"I'm just surprised he's staying around here," said Ava. "I mean, St. Eves is hardly the centre of the universe for a young man like him, is it?"

"He's not *that* young," said Charlotte. "He must be in his forties, surely?"

Ava gave a half-hearted shrug. "However old he is, anyone under the age of sixty is young to me, dear. I'm a few years ahead of you, remember." She suddenly sat up straight against the pillow. "Not that I couldn't give him a run for his money, of course. I might be getting on, but I've still got a few tricks up my sleeve... and I'd beat him hands down in a hokey cokey challenge any day."

Charlotte chuckled and gave Ava's hand a squeeze. "I don't doubt that for a second."

———————

The drizzle from earlier in the day had turned into persistent rain falling from low, grey clouds.

Charlotte clasped a mug of steaming hot chocolate as she settled herself on the window seat in her living room, the dogs at her feet.

"What d'you think of this weather, Pip?"

The old West Highland Terrier looked up at her, his head cocked to one side, then lay back down again when he realised Charlotte wasn't about to give him a treat

"And what about you, Panda?"

Panda didn't move, except to simply half-open an eye from his recumbent position, before closing it again.

As the rain poured down, thrashing against the bay window, the waves rolled, cresting bright white against the grey of the sea and the sky lit up in the distance with streaks of lightning, like giant silver cracks running across a vast black wall.

"I like it when it's like this outside and we're indoors, don't you, Mummy?"

Having been asleep for six hours, Molly had woken up feeling much better. Dressed in her pyjamas and dressing gown, with a book in one hand and her diary in the other, she gave Charlotte a hug before curling up on the armchair closest to her.

"Yes, I love it. It's cosy, isn't it?"

Molly nodded and sipped from the cup Charlotte had left on the table beside her chair. "I like tea," she said. "But I don't like tea that smells of perfume. I just like ordinary tea." She pulled a face. "That camisole tea you give Daddy smells like deodorant."

Charlotte chuckled. "It's camo*mile* tea." She pushed herself up from the seat. "That reminds me, I've been meaning to look at that stuff Betty gave me and take the lemon balm teabags out for daddy. He can have them when we run out of camisole tea." She winked at Molly and ruffled her hair. She took the bag from the kitchen cupboard and settled back down on the window seat.

The bag was filled with a variety of tea-related goodies. Apart from the flavoured tea bags Betty had told her about, there was a novelty tea cosy, a miniature tea caddy containing loose leaf jasmine tea, a box of wild berry tea incense sticks, a pack of ginger-tea flavoured chewing gum, a small canister of lime tea and parsley room spray, and an Earl Grey scented candle.

She took out the candle, then put it back when her phone rang, taking her attention away from the bag and its contents until another time.

———————

It was late when Carl walked into the incident room, his cheeks pink and pinched from the cold.

"Where have you been for so long?" said Fiona

"I've just got back from Shottingford. I've been checking up on Gordon Buckingham."

"And?" said Nathan.

"I'm not sure, but I think I might have found something."

Nathan nodded. "Good work. Come on then, let's hear it."

"Well, Gordon is squeaky clean—he hasn't even had a parking ticket, from what I can see. We already know his connections to Olivia and Roman and, while he certainly has the motives to want both of them dead, we also know that he didn't kill Roman, *or* throw that rock at Olivia.

"However, I did a bit of digging around to see what I could find out, and I came across some pretty interesting details about his sister, Lara. After Gordon's wife left him, she became his primary carer. She gave up her job for five years so she could look after him and she's been bad-mouthing Olivia and Roman ever since."

"In what respect?"

"After Gordon had his accident, Lara wrote hundreds of letters to the newspaper he used to work at, not only criticising them for giving his job to Roman, but also to let off steam about Olivia. Not surprisingly, the paper didn't publish any of her letters, so Lara took her protest to the streets. She marched up and down outside their offices every day, shouting at the top of her voice about how badly the paper had treated Gordon, and how Olivia should be locked up."

"What's the source of the information?"

"I tried to get in touch with the newspaper—it was called *The Shottingford Gazette*—but it closed down three years after Gordon was injured, so I went to have a look around the area to see if I could find someone who might remember anything that would be of use to the investigation.

"I found out that Lara used to be married to a guy called Billy Shelton. According to Enid Gaskin, who's owned the village shop for over forty years, and has the memory recollection of an elephant, Lara's husband was ready to take Olivia to task over what she'd done to Gordon, *and* give Roman a piece of his mind, but Lara persuaded him not to because Gordon didn't want the aggro.

"Anyway, Lara continued to care for Gordon but it put a real strain on her marriage. According to Enid, after Lara moved in temporarily with Gordon, she became so consumed by what had happened to him, and so angry, it wasn't long before her husband decided he'd had enough, so he cleared off, and Lara started using her maiden name again after the divorce."

Nathan shook his head. "They didn't have a lot of luck with relationships, did they? First Gordon's wife did a runner, then Lara's husband."

Carl nodded. "Apparently, when Gordon started to recover enough to get out and about, he used to walk down to the shop on his frame, and he and Enid would put the world to rights. She remembers him saying he would always feel responsible for the break-up of Lara's marriage, and that he'd always do his best to look out for Lara and her family."

"She's got children?"

"Yep. And this is where it gets interesting. When Lara's husband left, one of the kids went with him—they're an Entertainment Manager on a cruise ship now. The other one stayed with Lara, though, and helped to take care of Gordon every day after school, at weekends and during the holidays, and eventually became his part-time carer.

"According to Enid, the kids held a grudge against Olivia and Roman since the age of nine. We didn't pick up on it before, because the surname is different to Gordon's and Lara's, and they're registered at a different address to either of them."

"And who is it?"

Carl shook his head. "You're not going to believe this."

CHAPTER 21

Roy Tanner turned up the collar on his coat and checked his watch. Fifteen minutes to midnight.

If he started off now, it would take him around twenty minutes. He didn't want to get there too early and possibly have to hang around waiting, he just wanted to go in and do what he had to do.

He had no idea how his plan was going to work out, but he was banking on the element of surprise to work in his favour.

One thing was for sure, though. If everything went the way he was hoping, he wouldn't be staying at *The St. Eves' Tavern* for much longer.

He pulled the door of his room shut and set off.

The wind was bitingly cold against his freshly-shaved chin, and he pulled up his scarf, winding it around his neck to keep warm.

If he hadn't been so busy adjusting his clothing, he might have seen the lime-green Fiat drive past, going in the same direction as him.

—————

Charlotte tossed and turned for almost an hour before throwing off the duvet and padding downstairs at ten to twelve to make a cup of tea.

Not only could she not get comfortable, but she couldn't switch off her thoughts. Every time she closed her eyes and tried to sleep, a thought would pop into her mind and keep her awake, no matter how hard she tried to dismiss it.

She took her tea and sat in the dark, on the bay window seat that looked out onto the beach. She opened the curtains a little and stared out into the night. The dim glow of the streetlights along the seafront cast just enough light on the blackness to pick out the white crests of the waves when they broke against the shore.

She put her cup on the window ledge, closed her eyes and willed herself to feel tired, but sleep just wouldn't come, so she switched on the table lamp and tried to concentrate on a magazine.

Ten minutes later, and even more awake than before, she gave up on reading and switched off the lamp. As she gazed out of the window, a figure striding along the seafront caught her eye. As it got closer to a streetlight she recognised who it was, as she had earlier in the day.

The tall man with a slight stoop was Roy.

Where on earth is he going at this time of night?

She watched him for a while, before switching on the lamp again and giving the magazine another try, flicking through the pages. As she looked over an article about who the next James Bond was going to be, her eyelids drooped and she gave in to the delicious feeling of falling asleep where she sat.

Twenty minutes later, a thought in her subconscious jolted her awake. Except this time, she didn't want to dismiss it. This time it had her full attention.

Olivia was convinced that someone was trying to do her harm.

Roy Tanner had been there when Olivia had said she'd be at the hotel tonight. Had he overheard?

If someone *had* intended to kill Olivia with the rock that had hit her on the head, Roy was certainly strong enough to have thrown it that hard. The ease with which Charlotte had seen him pick up the heavy masonry blocks was proof of that.

He'd said he wanted to be famous for doing something that would make people sit up and take notice. Killing Olivia and Roman would definitely do that.

And, he'd mentioned that his ex-wife had left him for an old school friend who looked very similar to Roman Haley.

Charlotte thought quickly. On their own, none of those things would have caused her much concern but, together, they were enough to make her think that Roy might have been responsible for what had happened not just to Olivia, but maybe to Roman, too.

She called Nathan and explained her theory. "I'm probably overreacting but it's odd, don't you think, Roy going to *The President* at this time of night? I know he could just be meeting someone else, but if he's involved in what happened to Olivia, I'm really worried for her. And she said she was going to be in the kitchens on her own, so can you get someone there quickly? What? You've got another lead? Oh, that's great. Okay, I'll leave you to it. See you later."

She called Olivia's mobile but the number rang out before switching to her answerphone message. *"I'm doing something more important, so leave a message."*

"Olivia, please pick up if you're there."
Charlotte immediately redialled but, still, there was no
answer.

She could hardly believe that Roy wanted to
cause Olivia harm, or worse. But what other reason
could there be for him hanging around in St. Eves for so
long?

Her uneasy feeling increased, and she dialled
the number again, only for it to revert to Olivia's
answerphone. As she continued to dial and redial, the
bag she'd put to one side earlier caught her eye. As she
waited for Olivia to answer, she rummaged distractedly
through its contents.

She sniffed the Earl Grey scented candle and
squirted a spritz of the lime tea and parsley room spray
in front of her. Its fresh fragrance perfumed the air and
her eyes popped as her senses immediately jogged her
memory.

It was the same scent she'd smelled at Gordon
Buckingham's house.

In the kitchen of *the President Hotel's* rooftop
restaurant, Olivia hummed quietly to herself as she
made an inventory of the stock in the walk-in freezer.

Unable to keep herself away until midnight,
she'd arrived at quarter-past eleven, had said goodnight
to some of the kitchen staff, and was thrilled to be back
on her own territory.

Her head was still sore, and still bruised, but she
couldn't remember the last time she'd felt so happy.

In her heart of hearts, she'd known Simon
Clancy would come grovelling to her eventually. There
was no one else who could manage the kitchens like she
did, *and* make sure that every plate of food that left
them, without exception, was perfect.

She'd been quite sure that at the first sign that
restaurant standards were dropping in her absence, the
management would overlook the fact that she was a
suspect in Roman Haley's murder and beg her to come
back.

She couldn't help but gloat a little that she'd
been right.

She swore under her breath when her pen ran
out of ink. Stepping out of the freezer to get another
one, she gave a start when she saw a woman with
ginger hair standing in front of the kitchen door, the
phone Olivia had left on the counter in her hand. She
looked familiar, but Olivia couldn't remember where
from.

"You're not supposed to be here. The kitchens
are out of bounds to guests."

The woman laughed. "Yes, and we're far
enough away from guests that no one will hear us." She
waved Olivia's phone in the air. "I've switched this off,
by the way, so we won't be disturbed." She smiled.
"You don't remember me, do you? No, I didn't think
you would. You weren't at the tasting session for long
enough."

Olivia gave her a nod of recognition. "Ah, that's
right—you were one of Roman's students. I knew I
recognised you. Right, well, if you give me my phone

back, we can sort something out. What do you want?"
She snapped her fingers. "Aah, I remember Ava
Whittington telling me that one of the students on the
course was a fan—that must have been you. Do you
want an autograph?"

The woman threw back her head and laughed.
"An autograph? Oh, that's funny!" She stopped
laughing as abruptly as she'd started. "No, I don't want
a bloody autograph. And pretending to be a fan was no
fun, I can assure you."

Olivia gave the woman her most threatening
glare. "Look, I don't know who you are, or what you
want, but all I have to do is call security on that phone
on the wall, and they'll come up here and drag you off
in handcuffs."

"Well, let me tell you who I am. My name's
Izzy. Izzy Davenport." She raised her hand and
brandished a knife. "Oh, don't worry," she said, with a
smile. "I won't use it unless I have to."

Olivia made a dash for the wall phone, but
before she could dial security, Izzy had taken a lemon
from a box on the counter and thrown it in a perfect
overarm arc. It flew across the room, landing exactly
where she was aiming for. Knocking the receiver from
Olivia's hand, it crashed to the floor and smashed into
pieces.

"What do you want?" Olivia said, backing
away, her voice shaking and her hand going
instinctively to the yellow bruise on her forehead.

"Still hurts, does it?" said Izzy. "Good, I'm
glad. Of course, if I'd been on target, I wouldn't be

standing here now. And nor would you, although your absence would have been more permanent, if you know what I mean."

"That was *you*?" Olivia gave Izzy a look of fury.

"Guilty as charged," said Izzy, smugly. "I'm not our cricket team's star bowler for nothing, you know. My aim is impeccable… when the target stays still, that is. I was furious when you turned and the rock hit you on the forehead. I couldn't even hang around for another try because I had to make myself scarce in case the police started looking for who'd thrown it."

She took a step towards Olivia, her eyes filled with hate.

"When I read that interview my uncle gave to the newspaper, it broke my heart. All it did was reinforce how much I despise you, and I knew then that I couldn't stop until you were dead—however long it took.

"The only reason I was in the park that day was because I was *already* in St. Eves. When Mum told me that she and Uncle Gordon were coming to stay here, I knew then that I was going to drive back to finish the job. I had no idea when, or how, I was going to do it, I just knew I had to be here.

"Mum told me that some reporter had been in touch to arrange an interview, and was hoping you'd take part. She said Uncle Gordon wasn't keen about you being involved but she pushed him until he changed his mind.

"On the afternoon they arrived, she called me from the ladies' room to let me know they were going off to do the interview at the place you'd suggested meeting at in the park. She was so excited, she was keeping me up to date with everything, but she had no idea I was in St. Eves, too. It was short notice but once I knew where you'd be meeting, I knew exactly how I was going to kill you. All I had to do was hope I'd find a spot that would be close enough to hit you, but overgrown enough to hide me."

"You're Gordon's niece?"

Izzy nodded. "*And* his part-time carer. Mum and I shared the load for years but when I got married, I moved further away which made it difficult for me to look after him every day, so we arranged another two carers to help out, and I used to do whatever shifts I could. Since I got divorced, though, I've been spending more time at Mum's, so I look after Uncle Gordon when I'm there." A glimmer of sadness flashed in her eyes. "I still live in the house I bought with my husband, but since he left, it's good to get away from it sometimes. It's too empty without him."

"That must have been difficult?" said Olivia, trying to keep the panic from her voice.

Izzy gave her a look that dripped with scorn. "Difficult? You don't know the meaning of the word, you privileged cow. I was only nine when Uncle Gordon had his accident. He was in such a mess, and his bitch of a wife left him while she was still young enough to build another life and have some fun. So mum and me looked after him. I hardly remember him being well. And when I was old enough to be out with friends, or boys, I was helping Mum look after Uncle

Gordon. Helping him get around, and helping him learn to walk again after the countless operations he had.

"What kind of life do you think I had, Olivia? Because of you? And Mum's been through hell, too. Well done, you scored a hat trick." Izzy clapped her hands, a sarcastic expression on her face. "That's three lives you've ruined, because you're responsible for the breakdown of three marriages. My Uncle Gordon's, my mum and dad's, and mine. The strain of trying to have a normal relationship with all this hanging over our heads was too much. It put our partners under too much stress."

"No, you don't understand," said Olivia, not taking her eyes off the blade. "Your Uncle Gordon said he'd forgiven me."

Izzy started to giggle, then gave a great guffaw of a laugh until the tears were running down her cheeks. "Oh, Olivia, that's priceless. My sides ache. Poor, stupid Olivia. *He* may have forgiven you, but did you really think Mum and I had, too?"

"What are you talking about?" said Olivia.

Izzy stared at her. "We'd dreamed for so long about making you and Roman pay for what you did, but Mum would never have done anything about it—it was only ever dreams for her. Not me, though. I couldn't believe my luck when I heard Roman was opening a school in your hometown, and how much easier that was going to make it for me to kill two birds with one stone." Her blue eyes flashed and her breath came quickly as she twirled the knife in her hand.

"As soon as Roman announced he was going to open a culinary school, I got my name on the waiting list. I wanted to be sure I was one of the first because I *had* to see him. I had to be with him in the same room for my plan to work."

Olivia paled and slumped against the wall. "*You* killed Roman?" She tried to swallow, but her mouth was dry. "And your mum's involved, too?"

Izzy shook her head. "No, she has no idea what I did. I knew if I'd told her what I was planning, she'd try to talk me out of it. And my uncle doesn't know anything about it either. He wouldn't understand my particular brand of justice. He doesn't even know I booked up for the course, and nor does Mum. My work takes me away often enough for them not to have wondered where I was. They know nothing about what I've done, nor what I'm *about* to do."

"But how? *How* did you kill him?"

Izzy chuckled. "Well, *how* I killed him was the easy part. I got the poison from someone I met through work. He's a herbalist who makes up special blends of tea for all kinds of ailments. Last year, there was a story in the news about a man who died after eating food which had been laced with Aconite. I'd never heard of it before but we got talking about it and he told me that, in the wrong hands, it can be highly toxic.

"Although Mum and I had been talking about getting our revenge on you and Roman for years, it wasn't until then that I realised it might actually be possible. Until then, it had just been wishful thinking. I persuaded the guy to make me a bottle of pure Aconite tincture. It took a lot of persuasion and a lot of money, but it was worth every penny.

"I booked a place on the earliest course I could. When I read the itineraries and saw that Roman would be attending the tasting sessions for the first few lessons, I knew that would be the ideal opportunity to get rid of him, once and for all.

I already knew from the course itinerary what we'd be making, so I took the raisins I'd injected with Aconite with me, and put them into one of the loaves I baked. Then I made sure that was the one I gave Gavin and Larissa for Roman to eat at the tasting session."

"But *I* could have eaten some of that if I'd stayed," said Olivia.

Izzy sneered. "Yeah, once I found out you'd been invited, that was kind of the idea, but you ruined that, so I had to have a rethink. If you'd hung around and eaten some of the bread, my work would have been done and I'd never have come back to St. Eves again. Mind you, it wasn't all bad. Being around for Roman's last breath was worth it. After that, all I had to do was figure out what to do about you.

"Did you kill Roman because of what he did to your uncle?" said Olivia. "Because he took his job?"

Izzy nodded. "It might seem petty to you, but if you'd seen the look on his face when he realised the job he loved had been taken by someone else, you'd understand why I couldn't just let it be. After what you did to him, and his wife leaving, losing that job almost broke him. I don't think you have any idea how much you and Roman hurt him." She gave a hollow laugh. "If you did, you would never have offered him a pathetic weekend break in the hope it would make everything better." She threw Olivia a hostile stare.

"I *didn't* think it would make everything better!" snapped Olivia. "Nothing could have done that, but I hoped it was a gesture that would show him I was genuine about trying to make amends."

Izzy took a step forward. "You know, when Uncle Gordon told me you'd visited him, and you didn't even know that Roman had taken his job, it made me realise how little you cared about what you'd done. Any decent person would have tried to find out how he was, and what he was doing, but it really was out of sight, out of mind with you, wasn't it?

"Did you know, he's never held a grudge against you, not a shred of malice. Even after what you did to him, he still wanted to help you—he wanted both of you to be able to get on with your lives. But then, when he was stuck at home, with his shattered knee and his aching hip, some days barely able to put one foot in front of the other, have you any idea how difficult it must have been for him to watch you and Roman become more and more successful? He used to read every article about awards you were winning and milestones you'd achieved, but he never felt any bitterness towards you."

Olivia nodded. "But you did?"

"Too right, I did. And, as the years passed and his life went further and further into the toilet and yours and Roman's got more and more successful, my craving for revenge got stronger and stronger.

"Both you and Roman ruined my uncle's life. Between you, you took away his health and the job he loved, and he *still* believed in forgiveness and second chances, because he's a good man. *That's* why he cared so much that you might be locked up for what you'd done."

Izzy ran the flat of the blade against her palm. "You didn't know, did you, that two of the permanent effects of his injuries are that he's all but lost his senses of taste and smell? The senses that are the most important to anyone who loves food. It was gradual to start with but now he barely has either of them any more, because of the nerve damage caused by the impact of his head going through the window."

Her hand curled into a fist. "You didn't just ruin his career and his life, Olivia, you ruined the greatest enjoyment he had left. He can't even enjoy food any more, because he can hardly taste a thing. He has to take six sugars in his tea and coffee before he can even *begin* to taste the sweetness, and he has to cover his meals in salt, because only the most highly flavoured foods are enough to kick-start his tastebuds."

She took a few more steps, the knife glinting in the glare of the kitchen spotlights, raised as if she was ready to strike.

"You know what? I used to be like my uncle when I was young. I used to be kind and forgiving, but you've turned me into a vengeful, bitter, murderous woman, and you took my childhood from me. It's been too long coming, but I hope vengeance will finally bring me some release from the anguish I feel every day of my life. Unlike my uncle, though, I don't believe that forgiveness is the only way… revenge is. I've been planning this for years."

"*Please* think about what you're doing," said Olivia. "You haven't done anything yet, but if you carry out this plan… if you actually do whatever it is you're thinking of doing, you'll go to prison. *Please,* Izzy, you *must* think about that before you do something you can't take back."

Izzy shook her head. "I've done too much thinking. It's time for action now, so you're going to turn around and take a little walk into the freezer. Then I'm going to padlock the door and turn the temperature down to -40 degrees, but not before I've given you this."

She took a bottle from her jacket. "This is the Aconite I used to kill Roman. I want you to put it in your pocket so that when your poor, frozen body is found tomorrow morning, and the police are called, they'll think you were the murderer." She chuckled. "I wish I could hang around until the morning shift arrives. It should be quite entertaining."

"Wait!" said Olivia, the fear making her voice tremble. "Just tell me how you knew I was going to be here? I didn't tell anyone, apart from Simon."

"Actually, you did," said Izzy. "You told Charlotte Costello."

Olivia frowned. "How do you know that?"

"Because Roy was there, and he overheard. He called me earlier and mentioned you were going to be here, and that he was going to pay you a visit." Izzy smiled. "Knowing you were going to be here, on your own, in the middle of the night, seemed like such a perfect opportunity for me to finish what I'd started. I couldn't let it pass me by, so I decided to drive down again and get here first."

"Roy?" Olivia frowned as she made her way, inch by inch, towards the fire alarm on the wall. "You mean the tall, gormless guy? What the hell's he got to do with all this?"

Izzy smiled. "Nothing. He's got nothing to do with it. He's too dumb to be involved in anything like this. He doesn't even know anything about the situation with Uncle Gordon because I never told him… sometimes, it's nice for people not to know everything about you. Anyway, lovely guy, but he's as thick as a brick. It's a shame I'm going to have to kill him, too, but I can't have him alerting anyone to the fact that you're locked in the freezer, so I'll have to make sure he keeps his mouth shut." She touched the tip of the knife to the pad of her index finger and smiled. "Start walking, Olivia."

Without any warning, the door swung open and Roy rushed in. "I'll give you 'thick as a brick!'" he cried, pushing Izzy off balance and sending her sprawling to the floor. Her hands flailed for the knife, but Roy was too quick for her, grabbing Olivia by the arm, and leading her out of the kitchen, and to safety.

"No! *No!*" Dazed from the fall, Izzy staggered to her feet and steadied herself before chasing after them. "I *will* kill you, Floyd-Martin! I *have* to!" With her teeth bared and the knife raised above her head, ready to plunge into Olivia's back, she pushed open the kitchen door which rebounded off Nathan, Ben and Fiona who were on the other side. She struggled to push through them but they formed a solid wall between her and her target, and the knife fell from her hand.

She beat her fists against Nathan's chest, spittle flying from her mouth onto his shirt as she cursed at Olivia over his shoulder. Realising her chase was over, she shrank back, her shoulders dropping in defeat. "Arrest me if you want," she said, holding out her hands. "If you care more about her, and the damage she's done to God knows how many people, than you do about me trying to get some justice for them, then arrest me."

"Actually," said Nathan, "we were going to anyway but, as you're already in St. Eves, you've made our job much easier." As he read Izzy her rights, and snapped a pair of handcuffs onto her wrists, she stood like a statue, offering no resistance. "I was *so* close. So close, but not close enough. Just a couple more steps and she'd have been halfway to dead."

She shot Olivia a chilling glare as she was led from the kitchen, a sudden peal of hysterical laughter piercing the quiet of the night.

———————

"We'll need to take a statement from both of you," said Fiona. "We're going to have to cordon off this area for a while, so can you come downstairs to the lounge bar? And the entire kitchen is going to be out of bounds until we've finished. We've already cut off

access to the lift, so you'll have to use the stairs." She
went off to make a call and they trudged through the
indoor restaurant, out onto the rooftop terrace, and into
the stairwell.

Olivia sent Roy a scowl. When he'd pulled her
from the kitchen, Nathan, Fiona and Ben had just
arrived. "I'm not here to hurt her," he'd said when
Fiona and Nathan had grabbed an arm each. "It's the
nutcase in the kitchen you need to arrest."

As they made their way down the stairs, Roy
slowed his pace and took a step towards Olivia on the
small landing between the twelfth and eleventh floors.

She had him in a headlock in a second. "What's
your game? Why did you tell Izzy I'd be here tonight?
Tell me!"

"I'm struggling to breathe here," gasped Roy.
"Do you think you could let go?"

Olivia loosened her grip. "You'd better not try
anything funny," she growled. "There'll be police
swarming all over this place in a minute."

"I won't, I promise."

Olivia crossed her arms and watched him like a
hawk. "Well?"

Roy rubbed at the red welt on his neck.
"Obviously, I wouldn't have told her you'd be here on
your own if I'd known what a fruitcake she was. I had
no idea what she was planning."

"But why *did* you tell her I was here? In fact,
why did you even call her today if you weren't planning
something with her?" Olivia squared her shoulders and
poked a solid finger repeatedly against Roy's chest.

"I called her because we've kept in touch since she left St. Eves. I was planning on calling her today anyway. We were already friends, remember? And I overheard you tell Charlotte you were coming here at midnight, so I mentioned it to Izzy."

"But *why* did you mention it to her? And *why* are you here?"

Roy sighed. "I told her because she's known how I feel for ages. And I'm here because I wanted to see you."

"You wanted to see me?" Olivia frowned. "I swear, Ron, if you don't start explaining what's going on, I'm going to put you in another headlock."

Roy put up his hands. "Actually, it's Roy, not Ron, but okay, okay." He scratched his nose and looked at the floor. "I came because I wanted to talk to you."

"Talk to me? What about?" Olivia flung up her arms in frustration and glared at him.

He raised his head and chanced a smile. "To ask if you, um, if you wanted to go out some time."

Olivia's eyes became narrow slits in her face. "Go out some time? What for?"

Roy shoved his hands into his pockets. "Blimey, this is hard work. Look, I thought it might be nice to go out for something to eat. Or a drink. Like, on a date. What do you think?"

Olivia looked momentarily stunned, then took a step towards him, her hands on her hips and her face like thunder. "Are you trying to be funny?"

"No. I'm *trying* to be deadly serious." Roy took a step towards her, a warm smile creeping across his face. "I like you, Olivia. In fact, I think you're amazing. I have done from the first time I laid eyes on you... even if you did look mean."

Her mouth fell open, then she blushed scarlet from the roots of her hair. "What?"

"I said, I think you're amazing. I've never met a woman like you before and I couldn't leave here without telling you. That's why I've been hanging around. I've been trying to pluck up the courage to speak to you, but you're not the most approachable of people. I just wish it hadn't taken me so long." He laughed. "I even gave up my job so you'd know how serious I am."

Olivia looked around the stairwell. "Is there a camera somewhere? Is this a joke?"

Roy shook his head and took another step forward. "No joke. If I take another step, do you promise you won't punch me?"

Olivia eyed him warily, but nodded.

He stepped closer and reached into his pocket. In a flash, Olivia had his arm twisted up behind his back

"What are you doing? I *knew* you were going to try something funny."

"No, I wasn't," gasped Roy. "I just want to get my breath freshener out of my pocket before I kiss you... if you'll let me, of course. I had a hotdog for lunch and I can still taste the onions. I went to the pharmacy this afternoon to get it after I found out you'd be here tonight. I promise—you can look in my pocket if you don't believe me."

"You were going to kiss me?" said Olivia, letting him go.

"Well, I was trying to," grumbled Roy, rubbing his arm, "*if* I could actually get close enough without you…"

Olivia grabbed him and locked her lips to his. When they eventually drew apart, she rewarded him with her widest smile. "You talk too much," she said. "And I'm a chef. If you think I'm bothered by a little onion breath, you've got a lot to learn."

Roy pulled her to him with a grin. "Well, in that case…"

———————

The new and improved Olivia Floyd-Martin was the talk of the town.

After the night at *The President*, Roy had checked out of *The St. Eves' Tavern* and moved in to Olivia's flat where they'd spent every spare minute together since then.

No one had been more surprised than Olivia when he'd proposed a week later, slipping an engagement ring onto her finger. "I don't need time to think about this," he'd told her. "I know I want to marry you, so why wait? You just need to decide if you're absolutely sure you want to marry me, but we can have as long an engagement as you like if you need time to make up your mind."

"Are you sure you're not just on the rebound after your divorce?" Olivia had said. "You hear all the time about people who take up with someone else—for all the wrong reasons—after a long-term relationship breaks down."

"I couldn't be more sure," Roy had said. "I promise you."

Since then, Olivia had changed so much, people who'd known her for years were scratching their heads in disbelief. Her kitchen staff, who'd spent so long being fearful in her shadow, were now faced—on a daily basis—with a cheery, encouraging and appreciative Executive Chef, instead of the surly, critical and ungrateful one they'd become so used to.

"You know, I had a feeling things were about to change, and they finally have," said Olivia to Roy. "I feel like I've been given a second chance at life. A chance to get it right this time, so I want to make the best of it. I've got more than enough money in the bank to last a lifetime for the two of us, but I want to use the rest to try to put right some of my wrongs."

"Hold on, don't get carried away," Roy said, with a wink, "you can't have *that* much money."

Olivia gave him a playful punch. "I'm serious, and I've already started thinking about what I'd like to do."

CHAPTER 22

"Me! Getting married! Can you believe it? I'm forty-seven years old and I've only had two boyfriends in my whole life. One asked me out for a dare, and the other asked me out to win a bet."

"Well, that was their loss," said Charlotte, reasonably. "And I know it's early days, but if you'd like to borrow something—you know, for your 'something borrowed'—you're more than welcome. I've got a few things that might suit. No pressure, but the offer's there."

Olivia nodded as she paced up and down. "That sounds good, thanks, but before that, will you help me choose a wedding dress?" She stopped pacing and started chewing at a thumbnail. "Mum's coming with me, but I might as well take Pippin and Panda with me for all the help she'll be."

"Of course I'll help you," said Charlotte. "And I can't wait to meet your mum. When's she coming?"

"Too soon." Olivia put a hand to her chest to slow her breathing. "Why do you think I'm so anxious? I've got the weekend off work and Mum and Dad are both coming down on Friday night to meet Roy. Then Dad's taking him for a pint and a pub lunch on Saturday while Mum spends the day doing wedding stuff with me before they go home. They've got someone keeping an eye on the animals but they don't want to be away too long because one of their goats is about to give birth. Don't get me wrong, I adore Mum, but she's not the most relaxing person to have around. She's got a very robust personality."

"Well, I think it's great that she'll be there to give you her opinion," said Charlotte. "I bet she's chuffed to bits that you've asked her."

Olivia raised an eyebrow. "I doubt her opinion is going to count for much. You can ask her anything you need to know about how to run a smallholding, or cure a constipated cow, and she'll tell you, but she doesn't have a clue about stuff like this. I mean, her idea of elegance is putting her hair in a bun when she's feeding the pigs." She massaged the knotted muscles at the back of her neck. "That's why I need you to be there, Charlotte. Mum's the pin-up girl for the dungarees and wellington boots brigade, I have *no* idea what to look for, and the thought of being in a bridal shop scares me to death."

Charlotte laughed and squeezed Olivia's hand. "Stop worrying! It's supposed to be a happy day. Trust me, it'll be fine. What time do you want me there?"

Olivia heaved a sigh of relief. "Thank you. Well, I'm going to the hairdressers at half-past eight to see what she can do with this." She pulled at a tuft of over-bleached hair. "And the salon's also got a make-up artist who's going to have a chat about the kind of look I want on the day." She rolled her eyes. "Like I have the first clue about make-up. Anyway, I should be finished by around eleven. D'you think you'll be able to come along to the bridal shop afterwards? Say, around half-eleven?"

"Course I will. It'll be fun, wait and see. Nathan's away on a course, though, so I'll have to bring Molly with me. And we'll have to be home by four, because she's got her friends coming round for dinner and a sleepover. Is that okay?"

"Yeah, that'll be fine, and bring Molly along, too. And tell Ava she's welcome if she's free. I know she's been on her own a lot recently and, between you and me, I've grown quite fond of her these past few weeks."

Ava and Molly sat on the ivory-silk covered chairs in *Wedding Thrills* bridal shop on the last Saturday of the Easter school holidays.

The rain was still falling, and storms and high winds had plagued the area for the past week, forcing Ava into a war against hair frizz which, so far, she was losing.

"D'you think Oliver and Roy will have a horse and cart when they get married, like Prince Harry and Megan did?" said Molly, her pink-booted feet swinging and her hands clasped in the lap of her purple quilted leggings.

"That was a horse and *carriage*, Molly, not a cart. They're royalty, not rag and bone men," said Ava, with a chuckle, as she washed down the remainder of a sugared almond with a sip of champagne and grimaced as she caught sight of the steel-grey frizzball covering her head, in a nearby floor to ceiling mirror. "And, no, they aren't. Olivia said they're having an old car."

"An *old* car?" Molly screwed up her nose. "Why wouldn't they want a *new* car for their wedding?"

"No, when I say old, I don't mean a clapped out old banger," said Ava. "I mean old as in classic." She looked at Molly's blank expression. "Never mind, dear, you'll know what I mean when you see it." She tapped Molly's hand. "You know, this reminds me of when we came wedding dress shopping with your Mum. There was me, Betty, Harriett, Laura and Jess. We all went for breakfast at your house first, and then we had the most wonderful morning and afternoon, with a lovely lunch. I seem to recall your Mum tried on fourteen dresses before she found The One. You must ask her to tell you all about it one day."

Charlotte appeared, dabbing at her eyes, her thumb stuck in the air.

"What's wrong, Mummy?" Molly slid off the chair and ran to Charlotte's side.

"Nothing's wrong, poppet, it's just that seeing Olivia in her dress has made me a bit emotional, that's all. They're happy tears, though, so don't worry."

"Is Oliver's mummy crying, too?"

Olivia's mother, Penelope, strode out of the changing room and sat down on the end of the chaise longue with her knees apart under her tweed skirt, and her support stockings crinkling around her ankles. She brushed a hand across her ruddy cheeks—a permanent reminder of the outdoor life she led—and scratched at her unkempt hairdo, which was falling loose from the multiple hair pins fighting a losing battle to hold it in place.

"The last time I cried was when we had to have our Friesian put down," she said in her booming voice, a wide smile pushing up her rosy cheeks and narrowing her eyes. "That's a cow, in case you didn't know." She gave Molly's shoulder a squeeze. "Don't tell anyone, but I cried for four days. I don't shed many tears for the two-legged species, but I'm very fond of our four-legged friends."

Molly nodded, as if she understood, then said, "What about kangaroos?"

"Molly, don't go on at Penelope, please. This is supposed to be a relaxing day." Charlotte put a hand in the small of her back and flinched.

"Oh, don't worry about that," said Penelope, with a hearty chuckle. "It's nice to be around children again. It takes me back to when I used to bounce Olivia on my knee. And that was no mean feat, I can tell you. She was a very solid child—all that fresh air and good food." Her handbag suddenly vibrated and she took her phone from it. "Sorry, must take this—I've been waiting all morning for an update on our goat." She went off, her phone clamped to the side of her face, talking loudly.

"Are *we* allowed to see the dress?" asked Ava. "Or is it a secret until the big day?"

"Do you want to see it?" Olivia called from the changing room.

"Of course we do!" replied Ava. "That's what we're here for."

The changing room opened and Olivia stepped out. Awkwardly, she made her way to the middle of the shop, a nervous smile on her lips. "Well?"

Her elegant, white silk wedding dress with its scoop neckline, fell in folds from under her bust, skimming the floor as she walked. The full-length sleeves came to a point at her wrists, each one fastening with three pearl buttons.

Molly's mouth dropped open. "Wow, Oliver! You look like a proper princess!" She held up a hand for Olivia to give her a high-five.

"Do you like it?"

"It's awesome!" Molly jumped off her chair and walked a circle around Olivia for a closer inspection. "I can't wait until *I* can get a wedding dress."

"Molly, I can't cope with anything else that's going to make me cry today, thank you!" said Charlotte, dabbing her eyes again. "Thank goodness I don't have to think about you getting married for ages."

Olivia gave her reflection another glance in the mirror before stepping forward to inspect her hair and makeup again. The brassy, lavender-tipped highlights she'd favoured for so many years were gone, having been toned down to a subtle shade of honey blonde, and her hair had been styled and swept back from her face, revealing high cheekbones no one knew she had. Her minimal makeup was light and flattering, lending just a little definition to her features.

"I can't quite believe it's me," she murmured. "For the first time in my life, I actually look like a girl. I look so happy, and my skin's glowing." She turned to see Ava standing behind her and steeled herself for an honest critique.

Ava looked Olivia up and down. "That's what they call inner beauty, dear," she said, softly. "And if you have that, that's all you need. No amount of makeup will ever look better. You look stunning, Olivia. Simply lovely."

Olivia gulped. "That means an awful lot coming from you."

"I just say what I see," said Ava. "I never mean to offend but, love me or hate me, I always tell the truth." She gave Olivia a wink. "And, believe it or not, I've grown quite fond of you these past few weeks."

Olivia chuckled.

"What's so funny?" asked Ava.

"It's nothing," said Olivia, catching Charlotte's eye. "I just remember saying exactly the same thing about someone not too long ago."

Ava stepped back and took another look at the dress. "Well, is that the one, then?"

Olivia checked her reflection once more. "Yes, I think it is."

———————————

"I don't believe it. It's actually stopped raining," said Charlotte, looking at the sky. "Mind you, I don't think it'll be long before it's pouring down again—look at those clouds coming this way. We must have had more rain this month than we've had all year."

Ava nodded absentmindedly. "What are you
doing tonight?" she asked, as she followed Charlotte
out of the bridal shop.

"Jess is coming round for dinner," said
Charlotte. "We haven't seen each other much recently
and we're getting withdrawal symptoms. Molly's going
to be preoccupied with her friends and Nathan won't be
back from that course he went on yesterday until late.
And Ben's on the same course, so Jess is on her own,
too. Why? What are you doing tonight?"

Ava shrugged. "Well, I'm not expecting Derek
back from dance rehearsals till around ten, and Bet and
Harriett have gone on another godforsaken coach trip,
so I've got no plans, either. I was just going to ask—as
I've spent so much time at your place recently—if you
and Molly wanted to come round to me for a change. I
could have cooked dinner, and you could have relaxed
with your feet up. We could have watched a film, or
TV, or just chatted. But if Molly's got friends coming
round, and you've already got plans..."

Charlotte put an arm around Ava's shoulder.
"Look, why don't you just come round to my place?
Jess won't mind—none of us have seen much of each
other recently, have we? We can *all* have a proper
catch-up."

"Are you sure? You're not going to get fed up
with me, are you? I mean, wouldn't you and Jess prefer
to have some time on your own?"

"Don't be daft," said Charlotte. "We can see
each other any time. And how could I ever get fed up

with you?" She gave Ava a hug before looking back to Molly who was saying another goodbye to Penelope.

"So, will you be at Oliver's wedding?" Molly asked, holding onto Penelope's hand.

"Of course—I'm the mother of the bride, you know—so I'll see you again then."

"Will you bring photos of all your animals, especially the baby goat?"

Penelope chuckled. "I will, if you'd like to see them."

"Yes, please, I would." Molly nodded before slipping her hand from Penelope's and treating her to a gappy grin. "I'd better go now 'cos my friends are coming over later."

As Olivia climbed into her mother's mud-spattered Land Rover, she called across to Charlotte. "I don't suppose you're free tonight, are you? After Mum and Dad go home, Roy's going back to his place to pick up some of his stuff to bring it back to mine. He won't be back until tomorrow, so I wondered if I could come round to have a look through the things you said I could choose my 'something borrowed' from." She grinned. "Now I'm in the wedding mood, I'd like to prolong it for as long as I can."

"Of course you can. I'll be in all evening, so come round whenever you want. See you at the wedding, Penelope—I'm glad we had the chance to meet beforehand."

"Likewise, Charlotte, likewise. And thank you for looking after my Olivia. She's told me all about how good you've been to her." Penelope settled herself in the driver's seat. "Right, seat belt on," she said, in her booming voice. "Are you sure you don't need a piddle before we set off?"

"Mum, I'm forty-seven years old." Olivia rolled her eyes and looked out of the window to hide her embarrassment.

"Forty-seven, schmorty-seven," retorted Penelope. "You're still my little girl. Well, we'll be off then. See you all soon." She drove away, tooting her horn and waving madly from the window.

"Nice woman," said Ava. "Quite eccentric."

"Yes, isn't she?" Charlotte giggled, then rubbed her back, wincing with pain.

"Are you alright?"

"Yes, I'm fine. It's just trapped wind, I think."

"Are you sure, dear?" said Ava, looking excited.

"Yes, I'm sure. It doesn't feel anything like the last time, so I doubt very much it's the baby." Charlotte looked at the sky, which was rapidly filling with dark clouds. "Come on, let's get in the car before we get soaked."

———————————

The heavens opened again just as Charlotte arrived back at home.

"Come on, you two. If we make a dash for it, we shouldn't get too wet."

"I'm done worrying about it, dear," said Ava, picking her way carefully through the puddles. "My hair's beyond redemption but I'm going to be amongst friends who won't care what I look like, so I'm not bothered." She bent to fuss over Pippin and Panda who'd run to the door to meet them. "You're not taking them out for a walk in this rain, are you?"

"No way," said Charlotte. "They can use the garden until it eases off a bit. I took them out the other day when the rain was really heavy and the puddles were almost as deep as the dogs are high, and there was no way I could have carried both of them. I thought they were going to have to swim home. *And* I almost went over on my ankle when I stepped off a kerb into a hole I couldn't see because it was underwater." She gave the dogs a cuddle, hung up her coat and put on her slippers. "Right, Molly, go and give your room a quick tidy and I'll come up and check the bunk beds have got clean linen on them. Then I'll get dinner on the go. Won't be a sec, Ava."

"What can I do, dear? How about I light the fire and make us a nice cup of tea?"

"That'd be lovely," said Charlotte. "I think I'll have a peppermint one, see if I can get rid of this indigestion. And there's some cake in the tin if you want some. We won't be eating for a few hours."

———————

Charlotte rubbed her stomach and blew out a deep breath. "Didn't Olivia look fabulous in her dress?"

Ava nodded as she held a match to the pile of logs. "Honestly, if I hadn't have known it was her, I'd have walked past her in the street, she was unrecognisable. All those years she's shuffled around with a permanent scowl, and hair and clothes that wouldn't have looked out of place in one of those zombie movies."

She stepped back from the flames and put the guard in front of the fireplace. "There, that's better. We'll be warm and toasty in no time. Come on, doggies. There's a rug for two here with your names on it."

Pippin and Panda bounded in from outside, shook themselves, and settled down in front of the fire.

"I meant to tell you," said Ava, filling the kettle. "Harriett saw Monique Hathaway last week. She'd just checked out of *The President* and was on her way to London to see an old friend who she thought might need her help. Something to do with the police asking questions about something that happened years ago, so she was going to stay with her. She seemed much happier, Harriett said."

"That's good," said Charlotte, chopping onions and wiping her eyes. "I suppose you saw the news in yesterday's paper about Larissa Reece? What do you suppose will happen with the cookery school now that she's being investigated for benefit fraud?"

"No idea," said Ava. "Although I'm sure she only owned up to it because she thought the police would take it further once Roman's murder investigation was over if she didn't. Maybe the benefits office will show her some leniency? If she gets a fine, she may be able to carry on working at the school, but if she gets a prison sentence, who knows? In the meantime, I suppose Gavin will carry on running the school with the other staff."

She checked her hair in the mirror and grimaced, flipping through a recipe book as she waited for the kettle to boil. "I wonder what she meant when she was asked if she regretted what she'd done, and she said she only had one regret in her life, and it wasn't the benefit fraud?"

Charlotte shrugged, and leaned against the kitchen counter, rubbing her back.

"D'you mind if I put the TV on for a minute?" said Ava. "I want to see if the weather forecast will give me some idea of how long my hair's going to resemble a bird's nest." She flicked on the TV, just in time to catch the last item on the news, and pointed excitedly at the screen. "Look! It's a picture of Izzy!" she said, turning up the volume.

"Joseph Shelton, the brother of Izzy Davenport, the woman accused of murdering television personality and food critic, Roman Haley, was seen arriving at his mother's home earlier today, where he spoke briefly to our reporter, Toni Finlay. What can you tell us, Toni?"

"Well, Patricia, Mr Shelton has taken emergency leave from his job as an Entertainments Manager on a cruise ship, and will be taking his mother, Lara Buckingham, back with him. When I asked him how his mother was, he said she was at her wits' end, but coping as well as can be expected, under the circumstances.

"He said his sister's arrest has deeply affected the whole family, but wasn't prepared to say anything else on the matter, apart from asking for privacy from the press as his family come to terms with the situation.

If I manage to speak with him again, you'll be the first to know but until then, back to you in the studio, Patricia."

"Thank you, Toni. And now, the weather for the week ahead..."

"I'm glad he was able to come home," said Charlotte, after the forecast. "His mum must be feeling dreadful, so it's good she'll have him with her." She sprayed the kitchen with lime tea and parsley room spray. "And if it hadn't been for this stuff, it would never have occurred to me that Izzy might have been involved in what happened.

"If it had been a more common scent, I wouldn't have given it a second thought. It was only because it was so unusual that I thought not many people would have it, so it struck me that there might be a connection between her and Gordon. I could never have known the extent to which she was involved, though, especially as I'd already convinced myself that it was Roy who'd killed Roman and was trying to do the same to Olivia."

"You know, it just goes to show, you never really know what people are like, do you?" said Ava. "Izzy seemed perfectly well-adjusted to me, but nothing could have been further from the truth. All that trauma with her uncle, the breakdown of her parents' marriage, and her own divorce, was just too much for her. I can't help but feel a teensy bit sorry for her. So much pressure on a young girl turned her into a homicidal maniac."

She shuddered. "And when I think of what the police found at her house after they arrested her, it gives me the chills. All those letters she'd written to Roman since she killed him, telling him she'd be making sure Olivia, her dad, her ex-husband, and Gordon's wife would be joining him soon. Seems like she had a hit list of everyone she held a grudge against. Thank God she was stopped before she went on a killing spree."

"Well, she won't be able to hurt anyone else now," said Charlotte. "Although it's Gordon I feel sorry for." She tipped chopped onions and garlic into hot oil and their scent wafted up into the kitchen. "I know Olivia said she'd like to help him out with practical stuff that'll make his life easier, if she can, but I bet he's going to miss having Izzy around. Whatever she did, she looked after him for years, and she's still his family."

———

Two hours later, while Ava was snoozing in front of the fire, Olivia arrived, the taxi which brought her sending a spray of water all the way from the kerb to the front door as it drove off.

"It's like a disaster movie out there," she said, untying the hood of her anorak which was fastened tightly under her chin. She hung up her coat and glanced in the mirror at her pale face. "I would have loved to keep my makeup on, but I didn't want Roy to see it, so I wiped it all off in the car on the way home. I kept my hood up, though, so he didn't see my hair. I'd like to try to keep that looking presentable till the end of the day, at least." She took another peek at herself before following Charlotte into the living room. "Funny, I've never been a big fan of mirrors, but I haven't been able to stop looking in them today."

The screech of excited laughter and the thundering of three sets of footsteps on the stairs signalled the arrival of Molly and her friends, Erin and Esme, in the living room.

"'lo, Oliver," said Molly, breathlessly. "Mummy, when will dinner be ready, please?"

"Are you hungry?"

Three heads bobbed up and down.

"Well, I've only got to cook the pasta, so you three can eat in about fifteen minutes, and we'll eat later. That okay?"

"'kay." Molly turned to her friends. "Come on, let's get back to the dancing till it's ready."

More laughter and whispers accompanied the thundering of three sets of footsteps up the stairs. A door slammed and the muted sound of music and giggling started up again.

Ava stretched in the armchair. "Oh, hello, Olivia. I must have dropped off." She squinted at her watch. "Good heavens, it's half-past six. Honestly, what sort of dinner guest am I? I all but invite myself round, and then I fall asleep." She pushed herself out of the chair, the leather creaking as it relaxed. "Can I help with anything, Charlotte?"

"No, but you can get yourself a glass of wine, or a cup of something, and get something for Olivia, while I get the kids' dinner on the go. You know where everything is. And, Olivia, the 'something borrowed' box is on the table, if you want to take a look through it. And can someone get the door, please? It'll probably be Jess."

Ava opened the front door to see Harriett and Betty outside, looking like drowned rats. "What on earth are you doing here?" she said, ushering them in.

They stood on the doormat, water dripping from them into a puddle around their feet. "We went on that trip to the candle factory and we were on our way to lunch when the coach got stuck in some mud," said Betty, shaking the rain from her plastic hat. "That was four hours ago."

"The driver had to call the AA to get us out," said Harriett, shivering. "And then, to top it all, he couldn't even take us all the way home, because he had a call from his office to tell him there's a tree blocking the main road, so he'd have to take the long way round."

"And goodness only knows how long that would take in this weather," said Betty. "So we got off the coach when it dropped some people off outside *The President*, and thought we'd wait it out here until the rain eases off a bit."

"Is that alright with you, Charlotte?" said Harriett. "You seem to have a houseful already."

"Of course it's alright." Charlotte beckoned them in. "The more the merrier. Come upstairs and get out of those wet clothes—you can change into something of mine and I'll put your things in the dryer. And if you haven't had any lunch, you must be ravenous. Come on, let's get you something dry to wear and then I'll make you a sandwich. Or you can have some tea and cake, if you prefer." Charlotte looked around the room. "Look, on second thoughts, why don't you *all* stay for dinner? You too, Olivia. The weather's disgusting, but it's warm and dry in here. What d'you say?"

Betty, Harriett and Olivia exchanged glances.

"Are you sure we won't be imposing?" said Betty.

"Are you sure you'll have enough?" said Harriett.

"Are you sure you don't mind?" said Olivia.

"Oh, good grief! Talk about dither!" said Ava, throwing her hands in the air. "I'm setting three extra places, and that's final!"

CHAPTER 23

Jess arrived half an hour later to find Olivia and Ava looking through the box of mementoes, Betty and Harriett chatting in front of the fire dressed in Charlotte's clothes, and Molly, Erin and Esme sitting around the kitchen table, discussing the merits of putting Cheddar cheese on top of your spaghetti sauce, as opposed to Parmesan.

"I like Cheddar," said Molly, slurping up a strand of spaghetti between her lips. "Parmesan smells like feet."

"Not if you get the *actual* cheese, like Mummy does," said Erin. "It's quite nice. It's only the dried stuff that smells like feet."

"Well, I don't like either," said Esme, sticking a spoon into a jar of mayonnaise. "I like *this* on my spaghetti."

She shook a white blob onto her plate, sending Molly and Erin into a fit of uncontrollable giggles.

"Mayonnaise on spaghetti? *Eeeewwwww!*"

Charlotte rolled her eyes and held out her arms. "Welcome to the madhouse!" She laughed and pulled Jess into a hug. "It's good to see you," she said. "There's a few extra for dinner—I hope you don't mind?"

"Course I don't," said Jess, kicking off her shoes and dropping a kiss on top of Molly's head as she passed by to taste a mouthful of spaghetti sauce from the pan on the hob. "Mmm, that's delicious. God, the weather's vile out there. Talk about April showers."

She put the bottle of wine she'd brought with her into the fridge and poured herself a glass from the open bottle on the counter. "Everyone seems to be playing very nicely together in there," she whispered, nodding towards the living room. "It's like Olivia's had a personality transplant."

"I know, it's great, isn't it?" Charlotte grinned and took a gulp of her tea. "Shame it's taken a tragedy and all these years for us to get to know the real Olivia. She was saying just now that being with Roy's done wonders for her confidence. It's amazing how she's blossomed since she's had someone telling her how great she is for just being her, rather than because she's an amazing chef. D'you know what I mean?"

"Mummy, can we get down from the table, please?" said Molly.

"Yes, poppet. Just rinse your plates off and put them in the dishwasher, will you? And then you can take some strawberries up with you, if you want. They're in the pink tub in the fridge."

Charlotte and Jess sat down at the vacated kitchen table. "Did Ben get in touch with you?" asked Charlotte. "When I spoke to Nathan, he said he was trying to get through."

Jess nodded. "Yeah, I spoke to him about an hour and a half ago. They were halfway home and stopping off for something to eat at a motorway service station. He said he thought they'd be back between nine and ten." She listened to the rain battering against the kitchen window. "Although it might be a bit later if this weather doesn't ease off."

Charlotte called through to the living room. "Alright with everyone if we eat in about half an hour? Yes? Good." She rinsed her mug under the tap and flicked the kettle on again. "Right, I'm just popping to the bathroom. Back in a sec."

Jess took her wine through to the living room. "Have you found anything you fancy, Olivia?" she said, squeezing onto the couch next to Ava.

"I think I like this." Olivia held up a diamond teardrop necklace. "Charlotte said she was going to wear it on her wedding day, but she ended up wearing her Dad's crucifix instead."

"Oh, yeah, that's right," said Jess, nodding. "I'd forgotten about that. Gosh, that was an emotional day. I was surprised any of us had any tears left by the end of it."

"It was a wonderful ceremony, wasn't it?" said Ava. "I don't think I've ever been to such an uplifting wedding."

Charlotte reappeared in the doorway, her face as white as a sheet. "I'm sorry to be a party pooper, but..."

Jess was out of her chair in a second. "What's up?"

"I think I need to get to hospital." Charlotte bent forward with the force of a contraction. "Owwwww!"

Everyone else got to their feet and began to rush around like headless chickens.

"You'll have to drive her!" said Ava, throwing Charlotte's car keys at Olivia.

"*What*? No I won't, I can't drive!" said Olivia, throwing them back. "*You'll* have to drive."

"What do you mean, you can't drive?" said Ava, with a look of astonishment. "You're an Executive Chef, for goodness' sake!"

"Surprisingly, being able to drive isn't one of the criteria for producing five-star cuisine," retorted Olivia, giving Charlotte a sideways look of sheer panic.

"But I'm used to an automatic, so I can't drive a car with a manual gearbox," said Ava. "If I get my pedals mixed up, I could kill us all."

"Well, what are we going to *do*?" said Betty, wringing her hands and looking concerned in Charlotte's furry, pineapple-print onesie.

"We all need to calm down, that's what we're going to do," said Harriett, authoritatively, in a pair of Winnie the Pooh pyjamas. "And I don't know why you two are arguing about who's going to drive, because Jess has her car here. You *did* drive here, didn't you?"

Jess shook herself and nodded. "Sorry, I wasn't thinking. Yes, I drove here. My car's outside. Thank goodness I've only had a sip of wine."

"Okay," said Harriett, taking charge. "Charlotte, you go with Jess, Ava, and Olivia, and Betty and I will keep an eye on the girls and the dogs. And I'll go and get your case from upstairs. Is it still in your bedroom? Right, action stations, everyone, Operation Baby Costello is underway!"

———————

Despite Molly's protests, Charlotte wanted her to stay at home.

"I think it's best you stay here until Daddy gets back, sweetheart. He'll bring you with him when he gets here, okay?"

"Mummy, I don't like it when you're hurting," Molly wailed, clinging onto Charlotte's cardigan. "It makes me scared."

"You don't have to be scared. It's not very bad pain," Charlotte fibbed as she tried to reassure Molly through gritted teeth. "It's just the pain the baby gives me because it wants to come out so badly and meet us all. Look, I have to go now, but I'll see you very soon, alright?"

She let out a huge breath as she shuffled her way into the front seat of the car. Jess reached out and squeezed her hand. "I'll get you to the hospital as quick as I can, okay?"

They set off, with Ava and Olivia jabbering away in the back, giving Charlotte words of encouragement as they made their way to the hospital.

"Yes, Jess is taking me now," said Charlotte to Nathan. "Harriett and Betty are looking after Molly, Erin and Esme, and Ava and Olivia are cheering for me in the back seat. I know, I wish you were here, too, but I'll see you at the hospital as soon as you can get there. What? Hang on. How long do you think it'll take, Jess?"

"With any luck, about ten minutes," said Jess. "There are hardly any cars on the road."

"About ten minutes," Charlotte reported back to Nathan. "Look, I've got to go, I've got another contraction coming. And don't forget to stop off to pick up Molly, will you? Yes, love you too. I'll see you soon."

You'll be able to wait ten minutes, or so, won't you?" Jess looked anxiously at Charlotte who was bracing herself against the dashboard.

"I should think so." Charlotte groaned.

"How long did he say he was going to be?" asked Ava.

"Another hour, at least," said Charlotte. "It'd be nice if he got here in time for the birth, but I have a feeling the baby's going to beat him to it."

They drove on, the wipers squeaking as they flailed against the windscreen at full speed, trying to keep it clear from the deluge of rain that was falling from the saturated sky.

"Oh no... I don't believe it," said Jess. "*Damn it*!" The car came to a stop.

"What's happened?" said Ava, her voice rising. "Have we broken down?"

"No, we haven't broken down." Jess pointed. "Look."

The headlights picked out the fallen tree ahead of them, its thick trunk straddling both kerbs and its branches strewn across the pavements.

"No wonder there's no one else coming this way," said Jess. "It's probably been on the traffic news."

"It's the tree Betty and Harriett told us about, but I completely forgot about it," said Ava. "They said the coach driver was told he'd have to take the long way round to avoid it."

Charlotte looked pleadingly at Jess. "How long d'you think the long way round will take?"

Jess glanced at Ava in the back seat and tried to keep her voice calm. "Well, it would usually take about forty-five minutes, but in this weather, it might take a bit longer."

"How much longer?" asked Charlotte, panting.

Jess shrugged. "I honestly don't know. About an hour and a half, maybe." She grabbed Charlotte's hand when she saw the look of panic cross her face. "Look, try to keep calm. Maybe we should call an ambulance."

"I'll do it," said Olivia, dialling 999 and glad to be of use.

Don't worry, Charlotte, everything's going to be fine." Jess looked across to Ava again. "Isn't it Ava?"

"Of course it is." Ava frowned at Jess as Charlotte let out a worrying groan.

"No, actually, that *doesn't* help!" said Olivia, stabbing angrily at the screen of her phone to end the call. "The ambulance can't get here. It can't even come the other way down the high street, because there are trees blocking it for half a mile. And the operator said the long way round is taking even longer at the moment, because all the usual traffic is going that way, as well as the motorway traffic, which has been diverted. She said an ambulance could take anything up to two hours to reach us, and that's with its blue light flashing. God knows how long it'll take you to get there if you turn around and go that route, Jess—about three hours, by the sound of it."

"Oh, my godfathers!" said Ava, flapping a street atlas in front of her face. "What are we going to *do*?"

"Well, you helped when Molly was born," said Jess. "Can't you do the same again?"

Ava's eyes widened. "That was inside, in daylight, with lots of room, Jess, not in the pitch of night in the back seat of a car in the middle of a rainstorm."

A huge clap of thunder sounded right above them.

"Make that a thunderstorm."

"Look!" said Charlotte, firmly. "I don't care how, but I have *got* to get to the hospital. If you have to go the long way round, then please just do it, Jess. Please try."

"I could get you there quicker, Charlotte," said Olivia, quietly.

Three heads turned in unison.

"And how exactly to you intend to do that?" said Ava.

Olivia chewed on her lip. "I'll carry her."

"*Carry* her?" chorused Jess and Ava.

"Don't be so ridiculous!" said Jess. "In case you hadn't noticed, the rain is like stair-rods, it's blowing a gale and the puddles are two foot deep."

"Have either of you got any better ideas?" Olivia said, with a glare. "This way is the quickest route to the hospital, but the car can't make it. If you turn around and go the other way, you have no idea how much traffic you'll get caught in. If I take her on foot, we'll get there in half an hour, max. She's going to get soaked, but I'll get her there as fast as I can." She leaned forward. "What do you think, Charlotte?"

Charlotte forced a smile. "Well, as much as I think it's a wonderful idea, it might have escaped your attention that I'm nine months pregnant and I weigh a ton."

Olivia chuckled. "Is that all you're worrying about?" She sat up straight and flexed a bicep. "Look at me, Charlotte. I can carry a side of beef on these shoulders and I've got arms like ham hocks… and it's about time I used them for doing good, rather than for pushing people around. I'm strong, I don't fold under pressure, I'll be careful, and I can do it."

"But what about your hair? It'll get ruined."

Olivia rolled her eyes. "I don't give a stuff about my hair, Charlotte. I just need you to trust me."

Charlotte looked at her for a while. "If you really think you can, then I trust you."

Olivia nodded and sprang into action. "Right, we can use this blanket for starters," she said, pulling it off Ava's knees. "And, Jess, do you have anything else in the boot we can use to cover her up with?"

———————

When Charlotte was bundled up in two blankets, a plastic poncho, and a baseball cap from the back of Jess's car, Olivia lifted her so easily into her arms, it was as though she was made of cotton wool.

"Are you comfortable?"

"Not really," said Charlotte, "but I'm no less comfortable than I was in the car. Look, Olivia, before we set off, are you absolutely sure you can carry me all the way there?"

"I promise you, I won't stop until we get there—unless you need me to—and I won't let you fall. Just put your arms around my neck and hold on tight, okay?"

"Come on then," said Ava. "

"You're not coming, too, are you?" said Olivia.

"Well, someone's got to bring the suitcase," said Ava, her arms pumping up and down as she splashed along in a pair of Charlotte's wellington boots. "I knew all that speed-walking would come in useful one day."

"And if you think *I'm* missing out on this, you've got to be joking," said Jess, locking the car and turning up the collar on her jacket. She linked arms with Ava, and took the suitcase from her hand. "Everyone ready? Then let's go."

———————

True to her word, twenty-seven minutes later, Olivia strode into the foyer of the *St. Eves' General Hospital*, her heavy boots squelching underfoot.

"Please don't tell me you *carried* this woman here?" said the woman behind the desk as Charlotte was settled into a wheelchair, and Olivia, Jess and Ava dripped water all over the floor."

Beaming with pride, and with her teeth chattering, Ava patted Olivia on the back. "*She* did. For almost thirty minutes. We had to stop five times, on account of Charlotte's contractions—which are around five minutes apart, by the way—but Olivia carried her all the way."

Jess nodded. "If we'd had to wait for an ambulance, or go the route that wasn't blocked, we'd probably still be hours away, and Charlotte would be having her baby in the back of my car."

Charlotte hung up the phone and handed it to Jess. "I've told Nathan I'm here and he's going to bring you all some dry clothes." She looked at the woman on the desk. "I don't suppose you could give them a towel, or something, till my husband gets here, could you, please?"

The woman smiled. "Leave it to me."

Charlotte nodded, then held out a hand to Olivia. "I don't know how to thank you for this."

Blushing, Olivia took Charlotte's hand and looked away. "No thanks necessary. I'm just glad you're alright."

Charlotte started to speak but a contraction took the breath from her words as she was wheeled away.

———

Molly cradled the baby in her arms, tears rolling down her cheeks.

"Why are you crying?" said Charlotte.

"Because he's so perfect," said Molly, staring at the baby's crumpled face. "Look at his tiny fingers and fingernails. And his tiny feet and tiny toes. He's like a perfect little dolly. And he's my brother and I'll get to see him every day. I love him so much, Mummy."

"Well, that's good," said Charlotte. "I'm glad you like him. It would have been a bit of a problem if you didn't, because we can't send him back, you see."

Molly giggled and cried at the same time. "Can we have another one?"

Charlotte held up a hand. "No more babies, sweetheart. This is *definitely* the last one. I'm a bit too old for any more."

Molly nodded and kissed the baby on the forehead. "What are we going to call him?"

Charlotte looked at Nathan, who'd arrived home, then walked all the way to the hospital with Molly, and a bag containing dry clothes for everyone.

"Well, Daddy and I were thinking…"

———————

As Ava and Jess cooed and ooohed and aaahed over the baby, passing him from one to the other, Olivia looked on awkwardly from the end of the bed.

"I'm not very good with kids," she said. "Never have been, really. I don't think they really like me."

A hand slipped into hers. "You were good with me, Oliver," said Molly. "And *I* like you."

Olivia chuckled. "Yes, but you're different. You're not like other kids. You're just… I don't know, but you're different. I think I scare lots of children, but I don't scare you, do I?"

Molly shook her head. "Nope." She looked at Charlotte and Nathan for her cue and returned Nathan's discreet wink with a very obvious one. "Oliver?"

"Yes."

"We've got a surprise for you."

"Oh?" Olivia said, warily. "What surprise?"

"You know my baby brother?"

"Er, yes."

"Well, d'you know what his name is?"

"No. I didn't know you'd decided."

"Yep, we have."

Olivia shrugged. "I've no idea."

Molly grinned. "Well, we've named him after a really, really good friend... who we all like very much, and think is brilliant," she added, for good measure.

"Oh, right," said Olivia. "And who's that then?"

"Can't you guess?"

Olivia sighed. "No, Molly, I really can't."

Molly squeezed Olivia's big hand with her small one. "*You*, silly. We called him Oliver."

CHAPTER 24

Gordon Buckingham shuffled to the kitchen to throw the leftovers of his TV dinner for one into the waste bin.

He hunched over the sink, his hands clutching the counter, and blinked back the tears.

Since Izzy's arrest, he'd been searching for the positives in his situation, and the bright side he always looked for, but he hadn't been able to find either.

It didn't help that Lara wasn't there to talk to, and he had no idea when she was coming back. He didn't blame her for going back to the cruise ship with Joseph, but he missed her terribly.

Surprisingly, though, the past few months had brought him an unexpected friend in Olivia. She'd arranged for a company who specialised in mobility aids to call round and fit him out with whatever he needed to make his life more comfortable, and she visited him as often as she could.

But, as hard as he tried not to be, he was sad.

It was early, just before eight, and the May sky was still blue as the onset of summer marched on.

His carer had left half an hour before, and he wasn't expecting company, so was surprised to hear a knock on the door.

He wiped his bleary eyes and shuffled down the hall, making sure the chain was securely in place before he opened the door.

It took him a while to focus. He took off his glasses and blinked.

"Hello, Gordon."

The woman on the doorstep had aged twenty-five years but, to him, her face was as beautiful as it had been on the day he'd last seen it.

"Melanie?"

"I'm so sorry to turn up like this, out of the blue." She wiped the palms of her hands on her skirt. "Would you like me to leave?"

Gordon stared at her for a while. "I can't take any more upset at the moment."

She nodded. "I'm sure you can't, and it's not my intention to upset you. Can I come in, please?"

He stared at her again, then stepped aside. "You know where everything is."

Melanie made her way into the kitchen and perched on the edge of a chair. A smile spread across her face. "I don't believe it, you've still got my Princess Diana mug!"

Gordon blushed. "Hmpf, well, you know I don't like to throw things away. It's a perfectly good mug, after all. I didn't keep it for sentimental reasons, if that's what you're thinking." He grimaced as he settled himself in his usual chair, his fingers clenched around its arms. "What do you want, Melanie? I'm tired."

She turned her chair so it was facing his. Her dark hair, streaked with copper highlights and swathes of grey, was cut to her chin, and she tucked a lock of it behind her right ear. "I suppose I might as well just come out and say it." She chanced a smile. "I'm sorry I left. I know it sounds feeble, but I am. I've regretted it every single day since then."

Gordon fixed her with a glare. "You obviously didn't regret it enough to come back, though, did you?"

Melanie nodded. "But I did. I did come back. I came back twice. I spoke to Lara the first time."

Gordon's brow creased. "What d'you mean, you came back twice? Why didn't I see you, then?"

"Because the first time, you had a doctor with you and Lara wouldn't let me in. In fact, not only would she not let me in, she told me that if I ever showed my face around here again, or tried to get in touch with you, I'd be sorry. Honestly, she was vicious."

Gordon stared, his mouth hanging open.

"Anyway, I hoped the passing of time might have made her less antagonistic, so I came back again a few years later."

Gordon shook his head. "She never told me."

"That's because she wasn't here, and neither were you. She'd taken you to a physio appointment. I had the dubious pleasure of speaking to Izzy, instead." Melanie shuddered. "I told her I wanted to see you and she said you'd been through enough, and that she and her mother were making sure nothing ever upset you again. Then she told me I had ten seconds to make myself scarce before she stuck a knife in me."

Her gaze dropped to her hands folded in her lap before she raised her eyes to meet Gordon's. "I promise what I'm telling you is true. I know I did wrong by walking out, but I was young, and scared, and I didn't know how to cope with the situation. I should have stayed with you—in sickness and in health—just like I promised I would. Remember?"

She slid off the chair and knelt down next to Gordon. "I'm so sorry I hurt you. I swear I never meant to, but I did, and I can't take that back." She took his hands in hers. "But I can try to make up for it… if you'll have me."

Gordon flopped back in the seat. "Are you saying you want to come back? After all this time?"

"I would have come back years ago if I could have. I'm only brave enough now because I know Lara and Izzy are out of the way. I love you, Gordon… I've never stopped." Melanie held up her hand with the wedding ring she still wore, and brought his hands to her lips. "I hoped, as you never got in touch to ask for a divorce, that you might still feel the same way I do. I know it'll take a long time, but do you think you'll ever be able to forgive me for leaving you?"

His eyes shone with tears as he took her hands and pulled her into a hug. "Do I think I'll be able to forgive you?" His chest heaved with a sob. "Oh, Melanie, my love, of course I forgive you." He pulled away from her and ignored the tears that fell onto his cheeks. He cupped her face in his hands and smiled.

"Forgiveness is the only way, you know… forgiveness is the only way."

CHAPTER 25

On an autumn day – the best kind, when the sky is blue, the air still holds its warmth, and nature's colours are vivid and warm – a steady stream of guests arrived at All Saints church to celebrate the wedding of Olivia Elizabeth Floyd-Martin and Roy Ashwin Tanner.

In Olivia's living room, Charlotte stood back and brushed a tear from her eye.

"You look incredible, Olivia. Absolutely gorgeous. Who'd have thought there was such a beautiful woman hiding under all those chef's whites, combat trousers, and tee-shirts?"

Olivia looked at her reflection in the mirror. "Roy isn't going to believe it when he sees me. I mean… just look at me. For the first time in my life, no one could ever mistake me for a man."

"His eyes are going to pop out of his head," said Charlotte.

As if to remind Charlotte that she was still the same old Olivia, despite being dressed in her full wedding regalia, she turned and clutched her in a massive bear hug that almost crushed her ribs. "You know I didn't want a lot of fuss with pageboys and bridesmaids, but thank you for agreeing to be my Matron of Honour. And thank you for everything else. I don't know what I would have done without you these past few months. You've been so good to me."

Charlotte shook her head. "Don't be daft, I haven't done anything no one else would have done. And, anyway, look at what *you* did for *me*!"

"That's because I care about you, and I knew you had to get help."

"But that's what friends do, isn't it?" said Charlotte. "They look out for one another."

Olivia shrugged. "I 'spose, but as I've never really had any friends, I'm not used to it."

Charlotte gulped. She was as surprised as Olivia that they'd become so close. And the once-surly chef's sudden show of affection had left her unexpectedly emotional. "Well, you've got one now. And Roy, of course... and don't forget Ava—she's been very supportive, too."

Olivia nodded. "Yes, she has. I'll be sure to thank her. You know, I wish there were more people I could have invited. The church is going to look so empty on my side. Not that it matters, I suppose, but it would have been nice if there'd been a few more than just my mum, dad, a few ancient aunts and uncles and you, Nathan, Ava, Harriett and Betty."

Charlotte settled the back of Olivia's veil. "That's the last thing you want to be worrying about today, of all days. It doesn't matter a jot how many people are on either side of the church. What matters most is that you and Roy will be there for each other, with the people you love. It doesn't matter if *nobody* else turns up." She noticed the look of panic on Olivia's face. "Not that that's going to happen," she said, quickly.

The door flew open and Olivia's parents burst in.

"Sorry we're late. We realised ten minutes ago that your dad had pig poo on the bottom of his shoe," said Penelope, brushing frantically at the clump of dog hairs she was attempting to remove from her skirt. "We had to pull over to get rid of the damn-awful smell."

"Heavens above!" Grantley came to a grinding halt.

"What? What is it?" said Penelope, grabbing his arm. "Your hip hasn't popped out again, has it?"

Grantley pointed a shaky finger. "Look at her, Penny, just look at our girl."

Having never seen Olivia in a dress, let alone one as beautiful as her wedding gown, he was stunned beyond belief. He took a timid step towards his daughter, as if it was the first time they'd ever met. "I can't believe it. Olivia, my darling, you look beautiful. There's just no other word for it." He shook his head. "Not that you haven't always been beautiful to me, of course, but you've never looked so radiant." He clapped his hands together. "I can't wait to see Roy's face when he sets eyes on you."

Olivia threw her arms around him, not caring that her tears might ruin her makeup.

"Me neither, Dad."

———————

The first bars of the wedding march announced the arrival of Olivia and Grantley. The church doors swung open and they began their slow walk up the aisle.

Gripped with sudden anxiety, Olivia raised her eyes from the floor to Roy's side of the church. As she'd expected, it was filled, almost to the back pew, with his family and friends. Her heart fell a little as she turned her head to the other side of the church, and did a double-take.

There wasn't a seat, or a space to be had.

Smiling and waving at her from every pew were customers from *The President* she'd known for years, all of whom had come along to wish her well on her wedding day, and her kitchen staff, who'd seen a transformation in Olivia they never thought possible, were there in force. Since Olivia had found contentment, the hotel kitchens had been much better places to work.

Gordon and his gentle-faced wife, Melanie, sat halfway down the church. His hair was neatly trimmed, and his face had filled out, and it cheered Olivia to think he must be eating regular, home cooked meals. But better than anything, he looked happy—like he didn't have a care in the world.

And as Olivia made her way up the aisle to where Roy was waiting with tears dripping from his chin, neither did she.

EPILOGUE

Olivia's kitchen table was full.

Roy and Olivia had invited Charlotte, Nathan, Molly and Oliver, along with Ava, Derek, Harriett, Leo, Harry, Betty, Pippin and Panda, to join them for a post-honeymoon lunch.

"Have you seen the postcard we got from Gordon and Melanie?" said Roy, passing it across the table to Charlotte.

"Are they enjoying themselves?" said Ava.

"They say they're having a fantastic time, and Gordon's surgery to repair the nerve damage to his nose is scheduled for next week. Apparently, if they can fix that—which should hopefully give him back his sense of smell—then his sense of taste may come back on its own. If not, they'll try something else. The surgeons are hopeful, in any case."

"And what about his knee?" said Nathan, as he rocked Oliver to sleep.

"He's already had that done," said Roy, "and Melanie's having a job keeping up with him, apparently. He's racing around like the bionic man."

"Amen to that," said Betty, raising her glass to Olivia, who was multi-tasking in the kitchen, moving between basting a rib of beef, chopping vegetables, and stirring a sauce.

"When are you going back to work?" asked Derek. "The guests at the hotel must be missing you."

"Well, I'm going back next week," said Olivia, "but only until the spring."

"What do you mean, only till the spring?" said Charlotte.

"I mean, that's when I'll be leaving the hotel."

"*Leaving*?" said everyone at once.

Olivia nodded. "Roy and I have talked about it a lot, and I've discussed it with Simon and my sous-chef. They weren't very happy about it, but it's what I want. It's been agreed that I'll stay on at the hotel for six months to work with each member of the kitchen teams individually, and that'll be it. After that, *The President* will have a new Executive Chef.

"I never thought I'd want to leave, but I want to give my marriage a proper chance, and I can't do that if I only ever see Roy for a few hours here and there because I don't get home till midnight. The thought of leaving the hotel makes me feel so weird, but excited, too. I can't wait." She sent Roy a smile across the kitchen.

"They're going to miss you," said Leo. "You're like a piece of the furniture. It'll take them a long time to get used to not having you around."

"What are you going to do with yourself all day?" said Harry. "I've never had you down as a lady of leisure."

"Well, amongst other things, I'm thinking about writing my autobiography. I hadn't even given it a thought, but I was talking to Dirk Boulder in the restaurant the other day, and he said he thought I had an interesting story to tell. He's right, too, I have. I've done things you wouldn't believe, led a life that many could only wish for, had opportunities that most people wait a lifetime for, and met people that others only dream of meeting. Plus, with everything that's happened recently, and all the inaccurate stuff that's been reported in some of the papers, I'd like the opportunity to tell my side of the story."

"Who on earth is Dirk Boulder?" said Betty, chomping on a handful of peanuts.

"Isn't he the chap who bought a place in St. Eves last year?" said Harriett. "He's the lead singer of that heavy metal band, isn't he? What's it called?"

"Nails Down a Chalkboard," said Olivia. "Yes, he's still settling in, but he told me he's in the middle of writing his own autobiography, and he's finding it very therapeutic. He's had a lot of problems with drugs and all sorts, but he's clean now. He was telling me that he doesn't even have to type—he got this piece of kit that records everything he says and transcribes it onto his computer. Anyway, hearing what Dirk had to say made me think I'd quite like to write *my* story."

"And she's going to donate all the royalties to charity, aren't you, Liv?" said Roy.

Olivia blushed. "You didn't have to tell them that."

"Why not? I'm proud of you, and I want everyone to know you're doing good things. Not everyone who makes mistakes tries to put them right, you know." Roy strolled into the kitchen to fetch another bottle of wine and looked over his shoulder at his guests. "*And* she's going to teach me how to cook!"

"And what are you going to do for Olivia?" asked Harriett.

"I'm going to look after her, and teach her how to have fun," said Roy, creeping up behind his wife and sneaking his arms around her waist. "She's never had anyone to do either, but I plan to change that. And I'm going to help out with fixing the library roof—they put out a call for volunteers, so that'll keep me busy for a while. And when that's finished, I'm taking a course in dog grooming, so I can get a job and do my bit. I'm not going to be a kept man."

"Dog grooming?" said Ava. "Well, that's a career change, if ever I heard one. You've gone from being a medical supplies salesman, to working in a care home kitchen, to dog grooming."

"Actually, I've wanted to do it for years," said Roy, "but I rarely did anything *I* wanted to do in my last marriage because I usually ended up doing what Becky wanted. Anyway, we've got lots of plans, haven't we love?"

"You could take up Ju-Jitsu with Harriett and Leo," said Ava. "They're looking for new members to join the club. Isn't that what you said? Why are you staring at me like that?"

"*Finally!*" said Harriett, raising her glass. "You got the name right."

"I knew it'd get through that thick skull of hers sooner or later," said Leo, with a chuckle, as he dodged the serviette that came flying his way.

"I doubt joining a Ju-Jitsu club is the sort of thing Roy was referring to when he said he and Olivia have lots of plans," said Harry.

Olivia laughed. "Not really, but I'll have to do something because sitting at home all day writing would drive me round the bend. Something that allows me to keep cooking—but not so much that it takes up all my time—would suit me perfectly. I'd love a little place like yours, Charlotte, but there's no way I'd open one in St. Eves. It would be too much like competition and I don't want to get into that."

As the chatter flowed, a thought entered Charlotte's mind for a fleeting moment, before she dismissed it and joined in with the conversation.

———————

"We're so lucky, aren't we?" said Charlotte, that evening, gazing at Molly who'd fallen asleep in the armchair next to Oliver's cot.

"Yes, we are." Nathan put his arm around her and moved a little closer on the couch. "You've been a bit quiet since we got back from Olivia's. Is everything okay?"

Charlotte nodded. "Yes. Actually, no."

Nathan turned to face her. "What's up?"

"I don't know… it'll probably pass."

"Come on, tell me."

"I missed out on so much with Molly," said Charlotte. "I know we were really fortunate that we had Ava and Laura to look after her while I was working, but I missed out on so many things because I wasn't with her. I don't want to miss out on *anything* with Oliver."

"So… what are you saying?"

She looked up at Nathan, her eyes filled with tears. "I want to sell the café."

Nathan's eyebrows almost disappeared into his hairline. "*What?*"

"As soon as Oliver was born, I knew it was what I wanted. I want to be at home for him and Molly as much as I can. I can't expect Laura to cover for me at the café until they're grown-up, can I? She's only standing in because she thought I'd be back at work in a few months, not years. It's Jess I feel terrible about. She's worked with me since the beginning. What if she can't get another job?" Charlotte blew her nose and blinked back the tears.

"Well, if this is what you want, you don't look very happy about it," said Nathan, pulling her to him. "Are you absolutely *sure?*"

She nodded and wiped her eyes. "I wouldn't make a decision like this lightly, Nathan. You know how much that café means to me, but Molly and Oliver mean more. I should never have gone back to work so soon after Molly was born, but she seemed so happy with Ava and Laura, I let it go. But I don't want to let it go this time. Selling the café will break my heart, but not being there for the kids will be worse." She burst into tears and buried her face in Nathan's shirt.

"I haven't said anything about it before, because I couldn't bring myself to put the café up for sale. I don't want strangers trudging through it—people who don't know how special it is and who might not look after it. But when Olivia said she'd like to have a place of her own, it suddenly seemed like the obvious solution. She'd appreciate it, and maybe she could even keep Jess on?"

"Look, why don't you sleep on it?" said Nathan. "You don't want to rush into a decision like this."

"It won't make any difference," said Charlotte. "And I'm not rushing into it. I've been thinking about it for ages and I've made up my mind. I'm going to ask Olivia if she wants to buy the café and, if she does, I'm selling."

———————————

Early one spring Saturday morning, Charlotte slid the key into the lock of her little café one last time.

Usually, a smile curled her lips when she stepped through the doors but, today, her heart was heavy.

Hoisting herself onto a stool at the maple and limestone bar, she ran her hand over the old wood, cool under her fingers. She looked around, her eyes taking in every detail of the place she'd owned and loved for so many years.

This place—in which lifelong friendships had been forged, and lifelong memories made—had helped to heal her following the loss of her parents. It had brought her comfort, friendship, happiness and love, and saying goodbye to it was breaking her heart.

She wiped a tear from her cheek and laughed as memories flooded her thoughts. The best of times with the best of friends.

"Room for another at the bar?"

Charlotte turned to see Jess poking her head around the door.

"For you, always," she said, holding out her arms to draw her friend to her in a hug.

"I'm going to miss you so much," said Jess, with a gulp. "I know we'll still see each other all the time, but not working together is going to be so weird. It's always been me and you."

"I know, but you can come and visit any time. And if you don't, Molly will come looking for you." Charlotte grinned and pulled a fresh tissue from her pocket. "I'm so glad Olivia wanted you to stay on, and that Laura can still do the odd shift if she wants to. D'you still feel okay about working with her?"

"Surprisingly, I do. She was a nightmare at school, and even worse afterwards, but she's changed so much for the better since Roy came along. I think we're going to be just fine. She's not you, though."

Charlotte waved a hand. "Don't start me off again, please—although I didn't think I had any more tears left after yesterday. Honestly, it was amazing. I couldn't have wished for a better last day at work."

"I was concerned the customers would be a bit anti-Olivia when they first heard about her taking over," said Jess, "but they've all been fine about it. I think they can all see how different she is now. And *The President* is okay about it, too, because this place won't be any competition to them."

"Mummy! *Mummy*, where *are* you?"

Molly's voice echoed along the footpath at the side of the café, her footsteps getting closer before she appeared in the doorway. "*There* you are! Hi, Jess. Are you coming for breakfast with us?" She skipped towards Charlotte and peered at her with a frown. "Hmm, Daddy was right. He said you'd be crying."

Charlotte put her arms around her and held her close. As she dried her eyes again, Nathan appeared outside with Oliver in his pushchair, and blew her a kiss. Molly ran out to them, bending to give her brother a kiss. He puffed out bubbles from between his rosebud lips and giggled.

"Hurry up, Mummy! Oliver's here!" called Molly.

Olivia looked around the door with a grin. "Now that there's someone who actually *is* called Oliver, I think it's about time Molly learned how to say Olivia, or it's going to get confusing. Is it okay to come in?"

"Of course it is. This place is almost yours now. I was just saying goodbye before I hand the keys over. I know it probably sounds silly to you that I'd want to, but I couldn't leave if I hadn't."

Olivia sat down next to her. "I'll look after it well, you know. I know what a special place this is."

Charlotte nodded, not trusting herself to speak.

"I'll wait outside so you can finish your goodbyes in peace," said Olivia.

Jess slid off the stool. "I'll come with you."

Charlotte cast her eyes around the café once more, and locked the doors for the final time.

She looked at Oliver, gurgling with delight at a dance Molly was performing for him, and at Nathan, laughing at them both. She laughed too. They were her future, and she couldn't wait to start the new chapter in her life with them.

She would never forget her past, though. And she knew it wouldn't have been nearly as happy as it had been without the café. She turned, one last time, and laid a hand on its cool stone wall.

"Mummy, come *on*!" called Molly.

"Goodbye old friend," she whispered. "Thank you for everything."

The End

If you'd like to receive notifications of my new releases, please join my Readers' Group at https://sherribryan.com

Details of my other books are on page 340 but, if you'd like a taster of book one in The Bliss Bay Village Mystery Series, here's the first chapter.

Bodies, Baddies and a Crabby Tabby

Chapter 1
In the village of Bliss Bay, there was trouble afoot.

Murder, to be precise.

At the Laugh Till You Cry Comedy Club, Detective Sergeant Harvey Decker pulled on a forensic suit and rocked back and forth on the balls of his size-eleven feet.

"It wouldn't surprise me to learn there's a whole list of people who held a grudge against Andy. I heard he had trouble with a few customers over the years, not to mention all the villagers who were against him when he bought this place."

The wind howled and gusted as horizontal rain lashed the windowpanes. Far away, thunder rumbled above the grey clouds as the crime scene photographer snapped his last shot. For the Scene of Crime Officers, who moved in to hunt for any forensic evidence left behind by the killer, it was just another day at the office.

"Well, someone obviously isn't very fond of him, or he wouldn't be slumped over a table with a foot-long pole sticking out of his chest." Detective Inspector Sam Cambridge blew out a measured sigh. He took a step forward from his vantage point and looked at the deceased through narrowed lids. "It looks like a stake someone would use to support a sapling or shrub. Or something beans would grow up, maybe. Definitely something you'd use in a garden, I'd say."

"I'm impressed, boss." Harvey grinned. "I didn't know you knew so much about the great outdoors."

Sam shot his sergeant an incredulous glance, his eyebrows arching over a steely-blue glare. "If you think someone's garden qualifies as the great outdoors, lad, you need to get out in the world a bit more," he said, with a shake of his head. "And, for your information, I happen to enjoy a bit of gardening when I get the time. Not that I often *get* the time, mind you."

Harvey leaned closer to the body and peered at what appeared to be particles of bright yellow powder on its cheek. "What do you suppose that is?"

"No idea," said Sam, "but no doubt we'll find out when Forensics have finished doing what they need to." He scratched his jaw, shaded by stubble because he hadn't had time to shave before leaving the house, his gaze coming to rest on the recently deceased.

Five years previously, ex-prison officer, Andy Cochran had caused uproar in the village when he'd bought the derelict Bliss Bay fire station and turned it into a live comedy venue.

Situated on the outskirts of the village, it was far enough away from any residential area not to be a nuisance to anyone, but many of the villagers had vehemently opposed it nevertheless.

Had one of them taken a grudge too far?

Sam stared out of the window at the rain bouncing off the pavements and adjusted the hood of the ill-fitting forensic suit that hung off his wiry frame.

The word 'murder' didn't belong in the same sentence as 'Bliss Bay'.

Village crime was usually of a petty nature. Village crime didn't usually upset the balance of the community, or give the residents undue cause for concern.

Andy, however, was the victim of a crime that would most certainly cause undue concern amongst the locals once word got out.

From the first day of opening, he'd quickly gained a reputation for having little patience with customers who didn't follow his rules—*No Spitting, No Throwing Glasses, No Fighting, No Arguing With the Staff*—and had taken great pleasure in forcibly ejecting anyone who thought they were above them. As far as Andy was concerned, his club was no place for troublemakers.

It was fair to say that, over the years, he'd most likely acquired more than a handful of enemies from careers past, and most recent.

"Who found him?" Sam called across to Fred Denby, the village police constable who'd been the first to attend the scene, and was standing guard at the entrance to the club.

"Mary Tang, boss. She cleans in the morning and works behind the bar three evenings a week. She had a terrible shock when she came in at five-past seven this morning."

"Yes, I can imagine. Did she say anything that might help us find out who did this?"

The constable scratched the end of his bulbous nose with his pen and flicked back in his notebook. "Well, I don't know how useful it'll be, but she mentioned that his gold earring was missing. It had a microphone hanging off it, apparently."

"A microphone?"

PC Denby cleared his throat. "She said, "I saw Andy at around ten-past twelve, just before he closed up. I was the last person to leave the club. When I got here this morning and saw him, I screamed the place down. When I got closer, I could see it was too late to help him so I called the police right away. While I was waiting, I noticed that he wasn't wearing his earring—it was a gold hoop with a microphone charm hanging off it. We all clubbed together and bought it for his birthday. It was perfect for him because we used to call him Mr Mike—he'd get on the mike and warm up the crowd before the comedians came on to do their turns, you see. He always wore it. That's why I noticed it was missing." PC Denby snapped his notebook shut. "That's all, boss. She was too upset to say much more."

"Was the door open when she arrived?"

"No, it was closed, but not locked. Apart from Mary, Andy had the only other set of keys and they're still attached to his belt."

Sam Cambridge looked over to the body again. "Get statements from all the staff and find out from someone if Andy Cochran had a partner, or any family, we need to break the news to. I've got a feeling this is going to be a very long day."

OTHER BOOKS BY SHERRI BRYAN

The Charlotte Denver Cozy Mystery Series
Tapas Carrot Cake and a Corpse - Book 1
Fudge Cake, Felony and a Funeral – Book 2
Spare Ribs, Secrets and a Scandal – Book 3
Pumpkins, Peril and a Paella – Book 4
Hamburgers, Homicide and a Honeymoon – Book 5
Crab Cakes, Killers and a Kaftan – Book 6
Mince Pies, Mistletoe and Murder – Book 7
Doughnuts, Diamonds and Dead Men – Book 8
Bread, Dead and Wed – Book 9
Book 10 – To be announced

The Bliss Bay Village Mystery Series
Six book series
Bodies, Baddies and a Crabby Tabby – Book 1
Secrets, Lies and Puppy Dog Eyes – Book 2
Malice, Remorse and a Rocking Horse – Book 3
Dormice, Schemers and Misdemeanours - Book 4
Book 5 – To be announced
Book 6 – To be announced

A SELECTION OF RECIPES FROM THIS BOOK

Chocolate Crunch

Makes eight portions

Ingredients

210g/7oz plain flour
30g/1oz cocoa powder
150g/5oz butter or margarine
150g/5oz sugar
1 egg

Method

1. Preheat oven to gas mark 7, 220°C, or 200°C fan oven and line a 10" x 10" x 2" tin with baking paper.
2. Melt the butter or margarine and the sugar in a saucepan over a low heat.
3. Mix the dry ingredients together in a bowl, then add the wet ingredients to them and mix thoroughly.
4. Press the mixture into the prepared tin and bake for 15 to 20 minutes, until a skewer or knife comes out clean.
5. Mark into sections with a knife while still warm.
6. Allow to cool and dust with icing sugar.

Lemon Biscuits
Makes 16 biscuits

Ingredients

2 level cups/8oz/225g plain flour
Half a teaspoon of salt
Half a cup/113g/4oz unsalted butter, at room
temperature
1 cup/8oz/225g sugar
1 egg
Half a teaspoon of baking soda (Bicarbonate of soda)
1 tablespoon finely grated lemon zest
6 tablespoons lemon juice

Method

1. Preheat oven to 180°C/350°F, and line two
   baking sheets with baking paper.
2. Whisk together the flour, salt, baking soda and
   zest.
3. In another bowl, mix butter and sugar until
   fluffy.
4. Add the egg and lemon juice and mix together
   well.
5. Tip the flour mix into the wet ingredients and
   mix until everything is combined.
6. Drop walnut-sized blobs of the batter onto the
   prepared sheets and press down the top with a
   wet spoon. (The biscuits will spread as they
   cook, so don't be tempted to put too many on

the trays, or you'll end up with one enormous biscuit).

7. Bake for 15 to 20 minutes until the edges are golden.

8. Allow to cool before eating.

Sweet Potato Gnocchi with Tomato and Spinach Sauce
Makes six portions

Ingredients for the sauce

Four tablespoons of olive oil
2 lbs/1 kilogram ripe tomatoes, chopped
1 medium onion, peeled and chopped
1 clove garlic, crushed
1 level teaspoon dried oregano, or 2 teaspoons fresh oregano leaves
Half a teaspoon of dried thyme, or 1 level teaspoon of fresh leaves,
1 small dried chilli (if you don't like the heat, you can leave this out)
1 bag baby spinach leaves
1 cup of cream
Salt and pepper to taste

Ingredients for the gnocchi

1lb/500g of sweet potato
1 cup/250g/8oz full fat ricotta cheese, drained of all excess liquid
½ cup/60g/2oz freshly grated Parmesan cheese
1½ teaspoons of salt
½ teaspoon pepper
1¼ cups/160g/6oz plain flour, plus extra for dusting

To serve

Freshly grated Parmesan cheese

Method

To make the tomato sauce

1. Heat the olive oil over a gentle heat in a large pan.
2. Add the chopped tomatoes to the pan with the chopped onion, crushed garlic, salt, pepper and chilli, if using.
3. Add the herbs and cook over a gentle heat until the tomatoes are soft enough to blend.
4. Allow the sauce to cool for a few minutes before blending in a blender, or blitzing with a hand blender until smooth. **Note: Take care, because the sauce will still be very hot.**
5. Return the blended sauce to the pan and add the spinach leaves. Cook until they are just wilted.
6. Add the cream to the sauce, heat through, and check for seasoning. Cover and set aside until your gnocchi is ready.

To make the gnocchi

1. Prick the sweet potatoes with a fork all over. You can either bake them in the oven, or the microwave but, either way, they need to be completely soft. This should take around an

hour in a regular oven, or between seven and ten minutes on full power in a microwave oven, depending on how powerful your microwave is.

2. When the potatoes are soft, allow them to cook a little, then scoop out the flesh into a bowl and discard the skins.

3. Add the parmesan and ricotta cheeses to the bowl with the sweet potato, together with the salt and pepper, and stir until everything is smooth.

4. Add the flour a little at a time, kneading gently after each addition. **Note: It is very important that you don't over-knead it at this stage, or the final gnocchi will be tough and chewy, instead of light and melt-in-the mouth.**

5. When all the flour has been incorporated, transfer the dough onto a floured board, or kitchen counter, and form it into a rectangle. Cut slices from the dough and roll them into long, thin sausage shapes.

6. To shape your gnocchi, cut each sausage of dough into approximately one inch pieces. Make sure each piece is coated with flour and place on a plate or tray. **Note: After the gnocchi has been cut into one inch pieces, it can be frozen or refrigerated for use at a later date.**

7. Bring a large pot of salted water to boil, turn down the heat to a simmer, and add the gnocchi, cooking until they rise to the top. Leave them for a few seconds to bob about on the surface,

then remove them from the pan with a slotted spoon and place on a plate until all the gnocchi is cooked.

8. Add the cooked gnocchi to the hot tomato, spinach and cream sauce, and toss until every piece is coated in sauce.

9. Serve in large bowls with plenty of parmesan to scatter on top, and bread to mop up the sauce.

Raisin Bread
Makes two loaves

Ingredients

1 x 7 g/¼ oz packet of dry yeast (2¼ teaspoons)
¼ cup/60 ml/2 fl oz warm water (about 110°F/43°C)
1½ cups/190 g/6½ oz raisins (you can use sultanas, cranberries, or other dried fruit, if you prefer)
¼ cup/2oz/57g butter, softened
¼ cup/2oz/52g sugar (I have only tried this with white sugar, so can't vouch for results with brown).
1½ teaspoons salt
½ cup/125ml/4 fl oz warm milk
3¾ cups/450g/1 lb plain (all-purpose) flour
2 large eggs, beaten

Method

1. Preheat the oven to 375°F/190°C and grease two 8" x 4" loaf tins.
2. Add the yeast to the warm water and mix until dissolved. Set aside.
3. Put the raisins, butter, sugar, salt, and warm milk into a large bowl, and stir until the sugar has dissolved. Let the mixture stand and cool till it's just lukewarm.
4. Stir 1½ cups of the flour into the raisin mixture and beat well until smooth.
5. Now add the yeast mixture and the eggs to the raisin mixture and mix everything together well.

Add just enough of the remaining flour to make a soft, stiff dough.

6. Turn out the dough onto a lightly floured surface and knead it until it feels smooth and elastic. This should take around 15 minutes.
7. Rub the surface of a large bowl lightly with oiled kitchen paper and place the dough in it.
8. Roll the dough in the bowl to ensure the whole surface is covered in oil.
9. Cover the bowl with a clean tea towel and let it stand in a warm place, free of draughts, until it's doubled in size, which should take between 1 and 1½ hours.
10. Give the dough a punch and split it into two equal portions. Cover the dough again with a tea towel, and let it rest for 10 minutes.
11. Shape the dough into two loaves and place them in the prepared tins.
12. Cover the tins with a tea towel and leave the loaves to rise for between ¾hour and 1 hour, or until the dough has almost doubled in size.
13. Bake for 25 minutes. If it looks like the bread is browning too much, cover the loaves with foil for the last ten minutes of baking.
14. Turn the loaves onto racks and allow to cool.

Please note: I followed the cups measurements for the Lemon Biscuits and Raisin Bread when I made them, but I have attempted to convert them to ounces and grams for anyone who might like to try them using imperial or metric. Whilst these should

give similar results, I cannot vouch for them
personally.

A MESSAGE FROM SHERRI

Hello, and thank you for the taking the time to read this book, the ninth in the Charlotte Denver mystery series.

The fictional setting of the town of St. Eves was inspired by many happy holidays spent in the beautiful English counties of Cornwall and Devon, and by Spain, the country I now call home.

I've loved writing every book in the series, and I hope you've enjoyed them, too. Whilst I've tried to be accurate throughout, at times—for dramatic purposes—my imagination may have called for actual facts and procedures to be slightly 'skewed' from time to time.

If you've enjoyed the book, I'd love to hear from you. Your feedback is so important—constructive criticism included!

Also, if you'd like to, I'd appreciate it very much if you'd please consider leaving me a review. No pressure at all, of course, but thanks if you do. Feedback from readers is so important to indie writers, and your opinion could help other readers to decide whether or not to take a chance on a book.

As with all my books, this one has been proofread, edited, and then proofread again—more times than I can recall—but there may still be the odd mistake within its pages. If you should come across one, I'd be grateful if you could let me know so I can put it right.

You can contact me by email at sherri@sherribryan.com, on Twitter at @sbryanwrites

or on Facebook at
https://www.facebook.com/sherribryanauthor. Even if
you'd just like to drop me a line to say hello, please do!
I'd love for you to get in touch!

If you'd like to receive notifications for
forthcoming book releases, along with details of
discounts and other book-related news from time to
time, please visit my website at https://sherribryan.com,
or my Facebook page, where you can join my Readers'
Group. Please don't worry, I promise I won't flood
your inbox with messages and, as I respect your
privacy, I won't share your name or email address with
anyone, either.

Thank you again for your support,
With warm regards, as always,
Sherri.

ABOUT SHERRI BRYAN

Sherri lives in Spain.

If she's not tapping away on her keyboard, you'll either find her with her nose in a book, creating something experimental in the kitchen, walking the dog, or dreaming up new story ideas.

ALL RIGHTS RESERVED

No part of this publication may be reproduced, distributed, or transmitted in any form, or by any means, including photocopying, recording, or other electronic or mechanical methods, without the prior written permission of the copyright owner, and publisher, of this piece of work, except in the case of brief quotations embodied in critical reviews

This is a work of fiction. All names, characters, businesses, organizations, places, events and incidents are either the products of the author's imagination, or are used in an entirely fictitious manner.

Any other resemblance to organizations, actual events or actual persons, living or dead, is purely coincidental.

Published by Sherri Bryan
Copyright ©2018

Printed in Great Britain
by Amazon

54458792R00203